Missing the Signs

A Columbia Gems Baseball Romance

MJ Compton

Comptonplations Publishing

NOTE TO READERS

This book was previously published as **Summer Fling.**

Major League Baseball, like most other sports, periodically updates its rules. Some practices in Triple A baseball have changed since I first wrote this story. Any errors are my own.

WARNING

This book contains sexually explicit scenes and adult language and may be considered offensive to some readers. This book is for sale to adults ONLY, as defined by the laws of the country in which you made your purchase. Please store your files wisely, where they cannot be accessed by under-aged readers.

Chapter One

I never thought the indiscretions of my youth would return to bite me in the butt by walking through the door of the Susie Buddha Café in Syracuse's trendy Armory Square district, but they did. Or rather, one did. Winslow Winthrop Winston the Whatever, commonly known as Win.

I don't know if I lost my ability to breathe because I was terrified he'd recognize and expose me or because he was just so darned good-looking. Probably the result of both. Win had always had a paralyzing effect on me.

Chuck somebody or other, one of the Syracuse Saltboilers baseball team board members, accompanied Win. They headed straight for our table.

There was no escape. Life as I knew it was about to end.

"James!" Chuck greeted my father.

Dad stood, shook Chuck's hand, and then turned to Win. "Welcome to Syracuse and the Saltboilers, Winston."

Win's gaze, however, fixed on me. "Carrie? Carrie Thorpe?"

I held my breath. It had been seven years. Surely I'd changed enough that Win couldn't be certain of my identity. "Caroline Maplethorpe," I corrected in a tight voice.

That might have been the end of it except for my father's ego. People don't usually ignore him. He liked to think of himself as the George Steinbrenner of Triple-A Baseball, even though he owned only a few shares of the Saltboilers. And Win had ignored him.

"Do you know Caroline?" Dad asked.

I blinked and waited to see what Win would say.

Chuck interrupted. "Win, this is James Maplethorpe, one of the Saltboilers' shareholders."

Win's gaze jerked away from me and focused on Dad. "Nice to meet you, sir," he said as he gripped Dad's hand.

"Why don't you join us?" Dad invited. "Then you can tell me how you know my daughter." He looked around the table, as if searching for an empty seat or two.

Of course, there weren't any. Dad had called us all together for this dinner meeting at the minuscule Susie Buddha Café, and there was barely room for the ten of us at the table.

I briefly thought about vacating my chair. I already didn't want to be at a family dinner. Win's appearance put the cherry on my resentment.

"We don't want to intrude," Chuck said.

Win nodded at me, and the two of them continued to a tiny table crammed into a remote corner of the café.

"How do you know Win Winston?" my father asked me once the other men were out of earshot.

I picked up my glass of water and sipped. I couldn't tell him the truth, especially not with the entire family and its satellites sitting there. Waiting. "What makes you think I know him? He didn't even get my name right."

I glanced at Chandler Goodeve, my date for the evening. He seemed unperturbed. He was one of the Blandroids, the men our father had chosen for my sisters and me. Beige hair, beige eyes, beige skin, well-bred, and boring. Even their names were banal: Brandon Cummings, Andrew Armstrong, and Chandler Goodeve. The Blandroids.

I wondered what it would take to provoke a reaction from Chandler. Setting him on fire? A knee in the privates?

My answer seemed to satisfy my father. At least he dropped the subject. We were supposed to be having dinner to plan a tribute to my mother during the Syracuse Saltboilers baseball game on Mother's Day. The Saltboilers always staged their Breast Cancer Awareness Day promotion on Mother's Day. Dad decided the Kathryn Maplethorpe Foundation should participate. Dear old Dad would do anything to make himself look good to the community. Never mind the truth. As long as the result reflected positively on James Maplethorpe, he was content.

My old resentment against him preened for a moment. Then I reminded myself I'd outgrown my rebellious teenage furor, and I was a civilized woman now. I might never forgive Dad for what he'd done, but he was still my father. And I loved him.

Besides, I had bigger things to worry about. Like Win Winston showing up in Syracuse.

My head throbbed. My appetite fled. I forced myself to ignore the twosome at the corner table. For all of Syracuse's size—one of New York State's "Big Five"—it's an incredibly small town. Six degrees of Kevin Bacon could take lessons. If Win was pitching for the Saltboilers…

"What's wrong?" my sister Victoria whispered in my ear when the server whisked away our salad plates. Across the table, my younger sister, Alexandra, watched me with solemn eyes.

I shook my head and made sure I smiled. "I don't know why Dad has to make a big production."

"To assuage his guilty conscience," Victoria assured me.

She and I were close, but even she didn't know everything about me, especially about the summer I'd met Win. That was my secret. My shame.

I glanced around the table, wondering what these people would think if they knew the truth about me. My father would blow a gasket. Polly, my stepmother, would be shocked. Her mother, Marsha Lee, would smirk and gloat. Victoria would be appalled. Alexandra would be curious. Polly's brother, Marc, would want the prurient details, and the Blandroids would probably not react at all. They were expected to merely marry James Maplethorpe's daughters and be appropriate husbands, as long as they used my father's definition of "appropriate."

Winslow Winthrop Winston the Whatever—and yeah, "whatever" really was part of his name—had it in his power to expose all my secrets and destroy the life I'd so carefully pulled back together after that summer. The summer I went crazy. It had been seven years, but there is no statute of limitations on shame.

I barely touched my pumpkin chili. I usually loved the hearty vegetarian fare at Susie Buddha's, but tonight I couldn't force it down.

My father droned on about his plans for the tribute to my mother. Some of the players would use pink bats. Dad was donating money for pink baseball caps for the first five thousand women. There would be booths on the promenade distributing literature and selling merchandise, such as Second Base Club T-shirts. He wanted the Kathryn Maplethorpe Foundation to do something specifically in my mother's name and solicited ideas from us.

So why include Polly and her family? It had to have been awfully awkward for Polly to listen to Dad ramble on about Mom.

Why include the Blandroids? They'd never met Mom.

I very nearly suggested that we include Win but caught myself in time. He'd have a lot more to contribute than the Blandroids because he'd dealt with the mess that was me after she'd died. But then, he didn't know that. He didn't know anything. Not even my name.

I needed to get out of there.

I stood. "I'm sorry, but I'm not feeling well." It wasn't exactly a lie.

Dad didn't even pretend to be concerned. Victoria promised to have my uneaten food boxed and would bring it to the office in the morning. Chandler decided it was his duty to escort me home.

I couldn't help but glance at the corner table as Chandler helped me with my coat. Win's dark gaze fastened on me.

I hadn't fooled him at all.

Cold April air slapped my cheeks as I stepped out of the café. Chandler gripped my elbow.

"This isn't necessary," I said as I punched in the security code to my apartment. I lived over the café. Walking me home was ridiculous.

"Don't be silly," Chandler said. "My mother raised me better than that."

The door opened, and Win stepped out. He nodded rather curtly at us and then took off down the street. A few stubborn snowflakes danced in the chilly night. Apparently, the weather hadn't heard opening day of baseball season was less than twenty-four hours away.

I opened my door and flipped on the stairwell light. Chandler followed me up the steep, narrow stairs to my second-floor apartment. I unlocked the door at the top of the landing. "Thank you," I said. My mother had raised me right too.

He leaned in for a kiss, but I averted my face. "I might be contagious," I muttered.

In reality, I didn't like kissing him, although he kept trying. He wouldn't take no for an answer. My father's blessing seemed to be enough for Chandler.

"Thank you," I repeated. "Good night." I slipped into my apartment and closed the door before Chandler could follow me inside. I leaned against the door in the dark and finally let myself collapse. I'd been so tense since seeing Win that my muscles ached.

I inhaled and exhaled deeply, concentrating on my breathing. My father's foolishness had already infused the evening with devastating emotion. Add Win to the mix, and it was a wonder I wasn't a screeching, drooling maniac.

I snapped on a light, greeted my terrarium, hung my coat in the entry closet, and made my way to my bedroom.

Ten minutes later, I wore a flannel nightgown and velvet robe. A heavy afghan acted as armor against drafts in the window seat where I curled to watch the night. The scent of chamomile tea wafted from the mug I cupped in my chilled hands, the fragrance battling with the vanilla candles I lit throughout the room.

This was my life now. Calm. Orderly. Mundane. I had this great Armory Square apartment, I was on speaking terms with my family again, and I had a job I enjoyed. It was enough.

The intercom buzzed, but I ignored it. Drunks stumbling out of the multitude of bars often amused themselves by annoying the residents. Chandler would have either returned to the café or gone home, and my family always called before they visited me.

A lone figure lurched into view, shoulders hunched against the cold. Snow swirled around him. He stood under the streetlight, looking up at me.

Win.

Our gazes met. I swallowed hard. Just like that, he knew where I lived, and that was not a good thing. He stared at me for what seemed like forever, then ambled away.

My intercom belched again. I uncurled from my perch and stumbled to the speaker. "Yes?"

"Carrie Thorpe."

I still heard that voice in my dreams. I was going to have to speak to Win eventually. Might as well get it over with.

I buzzed him in. Then I opened the door and watched him lumber up the dimly lit stairs.

He was larger than life, filling my doorway with his height and bulk, bringing the cold and the scent of winter with him.

I didn't offer to take his coat. "What do you want?"

His dark eyes glittered in the flickering candlelight. Flakes of snow melted in his black curls. "Carrie Thorpe."

"There's no such person," I said.

"No wonder I couldn't find you." His deep voice rumbled through me. "I looked, you know. For years. On every form of social media I heard of. But no Carrie Thorpe ever popped up."

"She doesn't exist," I repeated, not believing him.

"Caroline Maplethorpe slumming it in Cortland." His tone was bitter.

"Caroline Maplethorpe trying not to trade in on her father's name," I retorted, stung by his accusation. The truth was far less dramatic.

Win still had the power to annihilate me, but I'd never let him know how vulnerable he made me. Survival. That was my priority.

"You've done well for yourself," I said. I'd followed his career to the majors, his injury two seasons ago, and the subsequent surgery that led him to a rehab stint in Syracuse.

"If you mean better than Flash, then yeah."

Flash. Jordan "Flash" Gordon. He'd introduced Win to me, in a manner of speaking.

"I got called up for three games, and you disappeared," Win said. "I went a little crazy."

"It was time for me to leave. College was starting. The timing had nothing to do with your getting called up."

That was the truth. Part of it anyway.

He stared at me. Through me. He'd always been able to peer into the crevices of my soul.

"What do you want?" My voice shook.

The intensity of his gaze never wavered. "I don't know."

That was new. Seven years ago, Win Winston had always known what he wanted.

"I thought I wanted you, but now you're telling me you don't exist."

There were many things I could have said. I could have asked if he'd never had a meaningful relationship with another woman, but that would imply he'd found our relationship meaningful. While it was certainly memorable, I doubted it had much meaning for him.

Didn't he understand the rules? What we'd had that long-ago summer was a fling. He was a young, good-looking, up-and-coming pitcher, and I was a young, out-of-control, self-destructive girl on the run from emotions I couldn't handle. I would have done anything to be able to feel.

I did everything I could in order to feel something. Anything.

"Why are you here?" I asked.

"I'm pitching for the Saltboilers until I'm ready for the majors again."

"I meant, why did you follow me out of the restaurant?"

"Why are you surprised I did?" he countered. "Although I guess that should tell me something."

We stared at each other for several silent moments.

"You sent your boyfriend home," Win finally said. His voice was husky, and his gaze flicked to my left hand. "A husband wouldn't have left, so I know you're not married. You should have known I'd be knocking on your door."

I struggled for cool. A third party had never stopped him—or me—in the past. "I think you'd better leave."

Was it the muted light, or did his expression darken? I couldn't tell.

"I meant what I said to you that summer," he said.

The problem was that he'd said a lot of things. We both had. I hadn't meant much of what I'd said, and based on the facts, I'd assumed he hadn't either. Besides, the *spoken* words hadn't defined the rest of my life.

I wasn't prepared for his hand to hover over my cheek. Heat from his palm drew my face like night-vision goggles to prey. His thumb flicked a strand of hair off my brow. When his lips brushed mine, a shock of familiarity, of yearning, bolted through me.

"You're right," he said, his voice a harsh rasp in the quiet of the room. "I'd better leave while I still can."

"You should have stayed last night," Victoria told me the next morning.

We worked together at the Kathryn Maplethorpe Foundation, the not-for-profit my father had started in our mother's name, five years after her death, which focused on breast-cancer awareness and research.

Victoria dropped her designer bag into the bottom drawer of her desk. "Dad suggested that you, me, and Lexi sing the National Anthem while he throws out the first pitch."

I booted up my computer, staring at the screen, not my sister. "I hope you talked him out of it."

"Polly did. She wants to sing. Singing was her talent on the pageant circuit."

Ah, yes. Miss Perennial Runner-Up. I tolerated Polly. We all did. It wasn't her fault our father was an idiot.

"Then Marsha Lee volunteered."

That pulled my attention from my computer screen. "To sing or be the first bitch?"

Victoria laughed. Polly's mother was the same age our mom would have been had breast cancer not stolen her from us. Marsha Lee Matthews was an awful woman. Loud. Brash. Snooty. Alexandra claimed she dressed like a 1970s kitchen and called her *Grandmama* to annoy her.

"Sing. Marc shot that down. You really should have stayed. It was quite amusing."

I didn't reply. Being amused hadn't been high on my list of priorities last night.

"So what's the story with that Win guy?" Victoria tried for nonchalance, but she failed. I wondered if her curiosity was genuine or if our father had put her up to digging into my business. "He's kind of cute."

I shrugged, then opened my e-mail and pretended fascination with the spam in my in-box. "I suppose."

"So how do you know him?" Victoria pressed. "And why did he call you Carrie Thorpe?"

"We met a couple of years ago, and for really boring clerical reasons, people thought that was my name." I wasn't lying. Exactly.

"Okay, I guess I can understand that. But that Win guy seemed kind of intense for being merely someone you met a couple of years ago." She wasn't going to drop the subject until she was satisfied.

"What if I told you we had a torrid affair, and he has a really big...bat?"

Victoria's green eyes widened ever so slightly. "I'm listening."

"What if I told you we were camp counselors together?"

She smiled. "I'd say you're a liar."

"What if I told you it was none of your business?"

The smile faded. "I'd say I'm your older sister, and I love you, so if it was something that hurt you, then it is very much my business."

"What if I told you it was all of the above?"

"I'd call you a liar about the camp thing."

Everyone else in my family believed I'd worked at a church camp on one of the Finger Lakes the summer I'd turned eighteen. My crazy summer. Victoria was the only one who'd sensed I lied. But even she didn't know the truth. Today she acted as if she were awaiting a confession of some sort.

"Does it really matter how I met him?" I sounded as weary as I felt. Nightmares plagued my sleep after Win left my apartment. After he'd kissed me.

What kind of cruel trick was it that he'd reappeared in my life at the same moment my father was reopening the wounds of my mother's death? My mind would always connect her dying to Win.

"So, any ideas about how the foundation can participate at the ballpark?" I asked. Victoria wasn't the only one who could change the subject. "Are the Blandroids involved?"

Victoria smiled. "No one mentioned anything. Every time the word 'breast' was mentioned, Brandon blanched."

Brandon Cummings was her Blandroid. Victoria was actually engaged to him. She sported a cluster of diamonds on her ring finger, but they hadn't set a date. No hurry there. Probably waiting until after polo season or something.

I don't know where my father found these men. Maybe the Internet.

"Is this Win person going to make going to games awkward for you?" Victoria asked.

The family sat in Dad's luxury box at Saltboiler Stadium, but I preferred being in the stands. My half brother, Matthew, liked sitting with me. It had taken me a long time to warm up to Matthew, but now we were close. Sometimes Polly acted as if I were going to sacrifice him to a foul ball or something, but I usually just bought him a lot of unhealthy food and let him gorge himself.

As I said before, I was on speaking terms with my family again, and it was no more Matthew's fault than it was Polly's that my father was an idiot.

"He'll either be in the dugout or on the mound. He won't even know I'm in the stadium," I said.

Victoria's smile turned sly. "So it might be a problem. Sounds like more than just someone you met at church camp."

She already knew too much.

"I honestly don't remember," I lied. There was no way I'd ever be able to forget. The repercussions of careless youth had scarred me. Literally.

Victoria crossed her arms. "I don't believe you." She'd always had a great natural bull-crap detector. Neither Alexandra nor I had been able to get away with anything as children, and after Mom died, Victoria took her role of eldest sister far too seriously.

I shrugged as if her belief didn't matter to me. "Don't we have a gala to plan?"

Chapter Two

The sun lied by shining brightly on opening day at the stadium, almost mocking the league for scheduling a baseball game in early April. It was cold enough to snow. The mouthwatering aromas of hot dogs on the grill and popcorn in a helmet welcomed the fans home after their winter absence.

Because of the cold wind, Polly insisted Matthew stay in Dad's luxury box, so I sat alone behind the visitor's dugout along first-base line.

Chandler rarely attended games, appearing only when my father so commanded. Chandler looked like a lacrosse fan, and I had a vague, uneasy impression that he thought he could turn me into one too, if he could ever force a ring on my finger. Or maybe he liked boxing.

Sometimes I almost felt sorry for his beige little soul.

The stadium was crowded despite the weather. It had been a long, snowy off-season. Opening day was a more enjoyable barometer of impending warmer weather than fragrant flowers or twittering birds.

I have always loved baseball. Especially in the minor leagues. There was something soul satisfying about being at a ballpark and forgetting the hassles of the day while watching a game. I have never liked football or hockey. I watched college basketball—it's practically a law in Syracuse—but it was tiring. There was no space or time to breathe the way there was in baseball. Baseball was spiritual, like yoga.

I didn't need anyone to sit with me. In fact, I preferred sitting by myself. I had season tickets independent of Dad. Two seats. The only person I ever let sit with me was Matthew, because six-year-old boys ought to be up close and personal at a ball game.

I'd never paid attention to stats or who was pitching or any of that sort of pregame stuff, so learning that Win would be the starting pitcher was...disconcerting. Okay, maybe I should have checked beforehand, but in the end, it wouldn't have made any difference. I was *not* going to let Win Winston drive me away from my baseball. Besides, he'd never see me in the stands. I sat behind the visiting-team dugout. The only time he'd be looking in my direction would be to check the runner on first.

I loved watching Win on the mound. He was throwing strikes, upward of ninety miles per hour, and his teammates had his back. He retired the first three batters.

That's when Marc joined me, plopping into my spare seat. He handed me a cup of beer.

Marc is Polly's younger brother, which would make him my step-uncle. He's my age. He's irritating but not nearly as obnoxious as his mother is.

"Why aren't you up in the box?" I asked him. I was annoyed he'd just assumed I would welcome him, even if he had bought me a drink. I took a sip. Moonsinger. My brand. Marc was such a suck-up. He could have given lessons to a vacuum cleaner.

"Your father sent me down to tell you he's having a get-together tonight. Informal, at his house."

I checked my cell phone. I hadn't missed any calls.

"He said to tell you the only excuse for skipping tonight is death. Yours." Marc grinned. He was good-looking in a Blandroid sort of way, a little less beige, a touch more golden.

"Command performance," I muttered.

"More or less."

I sighed and turned my gaze to home plate. "What time?"

"Seven." He leaned back in his seat, prepared to stay and watch the bottom of the first inning with me.

"Why?"

Marc shrugged. "James Maplethorpe wants."

That sounded right.

"Fine. I'll be there." I sipped my beer.

"So what's going on with you and Win Winston?" he asked.

Not this again. My father had to be the source of all these questions, although why he thought I'd talk to Marc was a mystery not worth solving.

I made a noise expressing my impatience. "Uncle Marc, even if there was something going on, which there isn't, it would be none of your business." I made sure my tone oozed sarcasm.

Marc hated it when I called him uncle.

"Should I warn Win to watch out for your wicked tongue?"

My cheeks heated. *Win already knows everything there is to know about my wicked tongue*, I wanted to shriek.

But I didn't. I rolled my eyes and watched the game.

If Marc had picked up the undercurrents between Win and me at dinner last night, then those currents must have been pretty strong. Marc was self-absorbed, and nothing less than a baseball bat upside the head usually got his attention.

"You can tell my father I'll be at his house," I said. "And in case you missed it, that was a hint for you to go back to the box."

"If there's nothing going on between you and Winston, why is he watching you?"

Beer sloshed over my hands as I jerked my gaze from first base to the dugout. Win leaned against the railing at the far end. I didn't need to see his number to recognize him. Yeah, he'd bulked up since our Cortland days, but he still carried himself the same way.

"He's watching the pitcher," I said. It could have been true. I wanted it to be true.

Marc stood. "You keep telling yourself that, Caroline, but here's a bit of advice from your Uncle Marc: a man doesn't look at a woman the way Winston looks at you unless there's something going on."

Marc left.

The manager pulled Win in the middle of the fifth inning. It was probably because he'd reached his pitch limit. Everyone in the stands applauded as he walked off the diamond. Except me.

I could never applaud Win walking away.

The Saltboilers won three to zip, and Win got the win.

At six forty-five p.m., I locked my apartment door and headed down the stairs. I planned to take a bus to my father's house in the Sedgwick Farms area of Syracuse. City buses didn't actually run in my father's neighborhood, but they traveled up and down James Street on a regular basis. Dad and Polly's house was only a few blocks off James.

When I opened the downstairs door, Chandler was there, poised to ring my doorbell.

"Were you watching for me?" he asked.

"I'm on my way out," I said, pulling the door shut.

"Right. I'm here to drive you."

I cursed under my breath. I didn't want one of my father's flunkies chauffeuring me. Oh well. At least I could always catch a bus home if Dad's soiree got too irritating.

I said nothing as Chandler and I walked four blocks to his luxury SUV. I owned a car, a little lavender punch buggy, but I mostly kept it parked in an overpriced garage around the corner from my apartment. I lived and worked downtown. I took the bus to the stadium and to Dad's house. The only regular use I had for a car was for grocery shopping because there aren't many grocery stores in the city and none downtown.

Besides, my use of public transportation irritated my father, who publicly blustered about urban revitalization but who was secretly a snob.

"Did you enjoy the game?" Chandler asked me—all politeness—as he pulled away from the curb.

"It was cold," I replied.

He made some sort of sound to indicate he'd heard me.

Why did my father insist on throwing us together? Chandler was probably as bored as I was, and if he wasn't, he should have been.

My father didn't live in the house in which I'd grown up. Mom had gotten that in the divorce. After her death, Dad wanted to buy it back from my sisters and me, but we sided with Polly. She and Dad needed their own house. If Polly had her way, they'd have moved from the city proper to one of the wealthier suburbs on a nearby lake. But Dad embraced the convenience of urban life. His new house was in the same neighborhood as the house where he'd lived with my mother.

It was too cold to hold an event on the patio. The only warning I had about what was to come was the number of manly vehicles parked at the curb around my father's house. This wasn't a family get-together. There were guests. Lots of them, judging by the clogged street.

"Any idea what's going on?" I asked Chandler, who located a parking spot five houses away from Dad's house.

"I think your father invited some of the baseball team to celebrate the start of the season and to announce the deal on the new stadium." He sounded distracted.

I unbuckled my seat belt and waited for him to do the open-the-car-door thing. "New stadium?"

The topic had been a battleground for years. The only thing on which everyone agreed was the current ballpark—built during the Korean Conflict—desperately needed replacing. Most people also agreed the team needed to leave the south side, but contentious debate continued as to whether to build downtown or near the delirious-to-develop waterfront area.

"The county exec, mayor, and team management signed the deal today. Congratulations. The downtown contingent won."

"That's good." I'd be able to walk to games.

"It's quite a coup for your father."

All my instincts went on high alert. "Why?"

"Maplethorpe Enterprises is building it."

There had to be more to the story. My father's company built a lot of things. Why should the stadium merit any more fanfare than a hospital expansion or the latest trend in retail design? Why throw a party? I mean, the timing of the announcement was good—opening day and all that—but something felt off to me. Maybe it was Chandler's nonchalance.

Then I saw a television satellite truck, shrink-wrapped in a multicolored logo, creeping up the hill toward my father's house.

No question: something else was going on.

I didn't want any part of it. Chances were good that Win was at the party, and after what he'd said to me about slumming in Cortland, I didn't want to give him more ammunition. Not that I cared what he thought. Much.

I refastened my seat belt. "Take me home." I spoke quietly. As much as I wanted to scream, Maplethorpes do not raise their voices.

"What's your problem?" Chandler's voice actually had an inflection. I was impressed. "You like baseball."

"You don't. I'm not in the mood to smile at a lot of strangers, and I don't want to be part of a news conference." Especially if Win Winston was inside. And he probably would be. "Let's blow off this shindig and grab a bite to eat at Yakker's or something."

Chandler opened his door but paused to look at me before he climbed out of the SUV. "That's the first time you've ever suggested we do something together."

No doubt he was right. I wasn't interested in a relationship with him. Or anyone. My indifference wasn't personal.

He seemed to consider the idea. Then he shook his head. "Your father wouldn't appreciate that kind of rudeness."

As expected, he walked around the front of his vehicle to open my door. I briefly thought about walking to James Street and catching a bus home, but he gripped my elbow as if he could read my mind. It wouldn't look good to my father if Chandler showed up without me.

I should have relocated to a different city after college, one where Dad couldn't try to manage me.

I saw Win as soon as I walked in the door. I was tempted to flirt with Chandler, but using him like that wasn't right, especially given what he'd just said to me.

I ignored Win and dragged Chandler in search of my father. I needed to prove that we had put in an appearance.

"Caroline! Caroline!" Matthew rocketed toward me like a line drive.

I scooped him up. "Hey, buddy. I missed you at the game today."

He squirmed and made a face. It was scary how much he looked like my father. "Mom said I had to stay in the box because it was too cold to sit with you."

"Moms are usually right about stuff like that," I said, even though I thought Polly coddled him a bit too much.

"See what I got?" He shoved an autographed ball at my face. "I'm getting all the Saltboilers to sign it tonight."

"That's an excellent plan," I told him as I set him back on the floor.

"I know," he said. Then he spotted someone whose signature he still needed and took off like a base stealer toward the new third baseman.

"There you are." My father approached me. "Glad you could make it. You too, Chandler."

"Do I really need to be here?" I asked Dad in a low voice.

"Of course." His voice boomed like a cannon. I was the fodder. "The Maplethorpe family supports community baseball, and we have a big announcement to make tonight."

I winced as I looked around for my sisters and their Blandroids, but there was no sign of them. "Where are Victoria and Alexandra?"

"Victoria had a previous engagement with Brandon—something about their wedding. Alexandra should be here with Andrew soon."

At least I'd have someone other than Matthew with whom to speak.

"What would you like to drink?" Chandler asked me.

"Moonsinger, if there is any," I replied. After two years of escorting me to my father's events, Chandler should have remembered my preferred drink. I remembered his preference: single-malt scotch, just like my father.

Chandler excused himself, and I turned to mingle. Dad had different ideas. He latched on to my arm with one hand while he summoned Win with the other. "Let's talk to Win."

Win sauntered over, lean-hipped, dark-eyed. The shadow of his beard more resembled midnight than five o'clock. Wisps of curly black hair peeped from his open collar. "Mr. Maplethorpe," he said. He nodded at me.

Dad was not subtle. "So you two know each other?"

Win looked at me. He raised a bottle of Moonsinger to his mouth.

I looked at Win as if trying to remember where we might have met. "Church camp?"

Win nearly choked on his drink.

That shut Dad up.

"I don't think so," Win said once he got his breath back. He didn't pick up on my hint. "I've never been to church camp in my life."

Dad stared at me.

Chandler arrived with my drink. For the first time in my life, I was glad to see him. I tasted my beer and wished he would rescue me, but Chandler was oblivious to my tension. As usual.

I shrugged. "My mistake."

"Weren't you an intern for the Cortland Crowns?" Win asked.

It was my turn to choke.

"What?" Dad narrowed his wintry gray eyes at me.

The Cortland Crowns were a Class A Short Season team in the next county. Not too far from the church camp where I'd allegedly worked during my crazy summer. And actually, where Win and I had met.

"Caroline?" I knew that tone. Except Dad kept forgetting I was an adult now. Maybe that tone worked on Matthew, but I'd long ago outgrown the quaking-in-the-shoes routine.

I shrugged and sipped my beer. The noise from the party faded. Even my father seemed to dissolve until only Win and me were left in the hallway between the family room and the entry.

The phenomenon lasted a second or two.

Then Chandler reached into his pocket and pulled out his *super phone*—he always had the latest gadget—and scowled at the screen. "I have to leave," he said. He didn't sound apologetic. "Work emergency."

I wasn't even sure what Chandler did for a living except that he was some sort of junior executive for my father, who thought very highly of him.

"Will you be able to find a ride home?" Chandler asked me after he and Dad exchanged jargon.

"Can you drop me off?" I asked. I was ready to leave.

He shook his head. "I'm going in the opposite direction."

Oh well. I still had bus fare in my bag. I would finish my drink, then melt into the twilight before Dad's announcement.

Chandler bussed my cheek, shook my father's hand, and nodded at Win, who should have used the opportunity to excuse himself but didn't.

"Caroline!" Matthew skidded into my leg.

"Matthew!" I squatted so I was at his level.

He held up his ball and started reciting all the autographs he'd managed to collect so far.

"That's really awesome," I said. "Have you gotten Win Winston's yet?" I glanced at Win from the corner of my eye.

He was watching Matthew and me with a completely blank expression.

"Is he here?" Matthew's big gray eyes grew round. "Doesn't he really play for the Gems?"

"He sure does," Dad said. "But he's standing right here. Matthew, this is Win Winston. Win, my son Matthew."

Win seemed frozen for a moment. Then he slapped on his talking-to-a-fan smile and squatted to take Matthew's ball.

The room swirled around me. Win, me, and a six-year-old boy huddled together. Something in my ears roared. My face hurt from forcing my smile.

"Excuse me." I stood and fled to the powder room tucked under the stairs. I locked the door and leaned against it and tried to pull myself together. A lilac-scented candle burning in the cramped space nearly suffocated me. I dashed cold water on my face. My hands trembled slightly.

I needed to escape this party. I could sneak out the back door. No one would miss me—no one I wanted to see or talk to anyway. I felt like my father had set this whole thing up to trap me. Me and Win. Dad needed to control every aspect of my life, and mostly I let him because it was easier to go with the flow than swim upstream. But Win belonged to a time in my life when no one had control of it, not even me. He had to stay there.

I was going to have to talk to Win in private. I didn't want to explain myself to him—the Caroline of seven years ago—but he was going to blow my life to smithereens if he didn't show some circumspection. We needed to come to some kind of truce, some kind of understanding to keep the past in the past.

But not here, not tonight. Someplace neutral. Switzerland was too far away. There had to be a more realistic opportunity.

I opened the lavatory door and came face-to-face with my sister Alexandra.

"What's wrong with you?" she asked. "You look like a spiderweb."

Alexandra was an English major and working on the Great American Novel, so she tended to speak in obscure imagery.

"Where's Andrew?" I asked, looking around for her Blandroid.

"Work emergency." She sounded happy.

Andrew also worked for my father, so he was probably with Chandler, dealing with gobbledygook.

"What's going on with you?" she asked again as we walked toward the kitchen. "Dad's on the warpath. You know. About you and that pitcher guy."

"Nothing is going on. We haven't seen each other in years."

Alexandra's gaze slipped past me and focused on something, someone behind me. "Marc." Quiet delight filled her voice.

My sister and my step-uncle?

Actually, the relationship made a lot of sense. And Marc could be amusing. When he wasn't sticking his nose in my business.

"Lexi Lou," he said. "Caroline, your father's looking for you."

Someone clamped my elbow. Tightly. "So am I," a too-familiar voice rumbled. "Are you ready to leave?" Win asked.

"Yes." I handed my beer to Alexandra. "Tell Dad I had an emergency, and I'm sorry I had to miss his big announcement."

Win seemed surprised I didn't kick up a fuss about leaving with him. We managed to escape by the front door without running into anyone else from my family. He practically dragged me to a black SUV with Ohio plates. I climbed in willingly when he held the door for me.

Okay, his vehicle wasn't the neutral territory I wanted, but it was better than staying at Dad and Polly's soiree. What needed discussion was for Win's ears only. "We need to talk," I said.

"We certainly do." He sounded grim. "Where to?"

We were stopped at the sign at the foot of the hill. I sneaked a look at Win's face. His mouth was tight. A muscle in his jaw bulged.

Then I noticed his knuckles on the steering wheel were white.

He didn't have any right to be that upset with me. It wasn't as if I'd come barging into his real life and started his family wondering what he'd been doing when he'd first been drafted into pro baseball.

"Where are we going?" Win asked again in a growl.

I nearly answered, *You're driving*, but that wasn't exactly the message I wanted to give him. I didn't want him at my apartment, and I sure as heck wasn't going to set foot in wherever he was currently living.

The only private place to which I had access was my office. My space at the Kathryn Maplethorpe Foundation was the perfect spot for our conversation.

We didn't speak again until we reached the foundation offices on the eighth floor of the Rockwell Building. Once there, I let the reception area speak for me. A large portrait of my mother dominated the space.

Mom was beautiful in the picture, with her soft blonde curls and laughing green eyes. Luminous pearls circled her throat and shimmered like candlelight in her earlobes. Victoria and Alexandra both took after her, while I favored my dark-haired, gray-eyed father.

"Kathryn Maplethorpe," Win said. "A relative?"

"My mother."

We stood in the middle of the lobby, and I let him read the plaque under Mom's portrait.

He was quick. He noticed the year she'd died right away. "I'm sorry," he said. His obsidian gaze fixed on me. "Okay," he said. "I get it. Your mother died, and I was the beneficiary of your grief. But that doesn't give you the right to keep my son from me."

Chapter Three

I couldn't breathe. I thought my heart stopped for a second. "What?"

Fury etched new character lines on Win's face. "My son." He practically spat the words.

I gulped in air. "What are you talking about?"

"Matthew."

"Matthew?" The name came out as a squeak. "My brother?"

"Your—our son. You can't fool me."

"Hold on," I said. Oxygen flowed into my bloodstream again. "Back up. Why on earth do you think Matthew is yours?"

He started ticking off points on his fingers. "He looks exactly like you. He's the right age. He's a baseball fan like me. You turned white as first base in a no-hitter when the three of us were kneeling together in the hall."

I inhaled deeply. "Whoa. Matthew looks like me because we both look like my father. Matthew is Polly and Dad's kid. I'm sure if you ask nicely, Polly might show you the video of his birth. And Matthew likes baseball because our father likes baseball." My voice shook, just like my insides.

His glare didn't soften. "I seem to recall one time—"

"Yeah. So?" I knew the exact incident about which he spoke. I summoned every ounce of bravado I could. "Why do you think that happened? My sister called me and told me Polly was pregnant, and I freaked."

"Freaked? As I recall, you jumped my bones. Not that I'm complaining. But we didn't use protection, which means you could have gotten pregnant. And how could Polly be pregnant if your mother had just died?"

I inhaled another deep, shaky, centering breath. "Because my father divorced my mother two weeks before she was diagnosed with breast cancer. Then he married Polly."

He was silent for a moment and then uttered, "Oh shit."

My internal trembling slowed to a stutter. "I was crazy that summer. That's what I'm trying to tell you. That girl was an aberration."

He arched one black, devil's eyebrow. "Are you saying that what happened that summer with you, me, and Flash was just acting out your anger at your father and mother? Because that's not the way I remember things. But then, I'm remembering Carrie Thorpe, not Caroline Maplethorpe."

"Carrie Thorpe doesn't exist. She never existed."

"Oh, that's where you're wrong." Win's voice was soft and edged with something else, something I couldn't identify.

"She existed here." He tapped his temple. "She still haunts my dreams. She's the standard by which I judge every other woman."

I didn't say anything. I knew what it was like to have dreams shatter with just a breath.

"I remember the first time I saw you. The first time I touched you, fucked you, kissed you. I remember every detail of every time we were together."

I felt the blood drain from my face. Each of his alleged memories was like a blow to my body, and I wasn't prepared to absorb such raw truths. I sank to the gray leather sofa and stared up at him.

I remembered most of what he remembered. Not the first time he'd seen me, though. He'd been hiding in a closet, watching while his roommate—Flash—banged my brains out.

Win joined me on the leather cushions, his hard thighs pressing mine. He braced his arms on either side of me, caging me in place. Heat pulsed off his body, welcome in the chill of the office. My breasts tingled.

"Classy place, but after seeing your father's house, I expected classy. Do you wear pearls and designer shoes when you come here to work every day, Miss Maplethorpe?" His question came out in a harsh whisper. His pinkie finger outlined the ridge of my collarbone through my sweater. My nipples tightened, something he could probably see if he'd bothered to look. But he wouldn't look. Not when he could paralyze me by gazing into my eyes.

"I don't like being one of your secrets, Carrie." His yeasty, beery breath wafted over my face.

"What do you want?" Amazingly, my voice didn't tremble.

He ran his finger up the side of my neck to my jaw. Shivers skittered along every nerve ending in my body.

"I want you. I want to know if the reality of you meshes with my memories."

His finger found its way to the corner of my mouth. He lightly traced the outline of my lips. "I want to know if Caroline Maplethorpe fucks in her pearls and high heels."

"Caroline Maplethorpe doesn't fuck."

"Maybe that's her problem."

I should have slapped his face, but I couldn't move. My eyes crossed as he leaned closer. Our body temperatures collided and then merged.

I freed my hand from his spell. The tips of my fingers skimmed the dark scruff of beard on his cheek and then his jaw.

He flinched as if I'd grabbed his privates. The shock of touching him filled me. "Be more specific." My throat was so tight I was amazed I could manage a whisper.

"Get rid of the boyfriend. Be with me while I'm here."

He could leave tomorrow if the Gems decided he'd rehabbed his elbow sufficiently.

"Chandler and I aren't exclusive."

Anger flared in the depths of his coal-black eyes. "I told you after Flash left. If I had seen you first, I never would have shared you, and I have no intention of ever sharing you again."

His mouth came down on mine. Not the soft caressing of lips that had happened in my apartment last night but hard, bruising, demanding. He tasted like the fulfillment of all my shameful fantasies.

I kissed him back. My arms went around him, clutching him to me as if he were once again the lifeline to my sanity.

We somehow ended up sprawled across the sofa. Win was on top of me. His erection pressed into my belly. His tongue teased mine. Everything I thought I'd gotten out of my system came roaring back. I was wanton, crazed, and needy. Pathetically needy.

I kissed him with all the pent-up longing of seven years' denial. Maybe he was right. Maybe Carrie Thorpe was my alter ego. The woman without inhibitions who paid no attention to the strictures of polite society.

"Caroline?"

I hadn't heard the door open, and although I heard my sister say my name, it didn't penetrate the passion Win wove around me.

"Caroline!"

Win stopped kissing me. Stopped pressing me into the leather cushions.

I blinked and realized Victoria and Brandon were staring down at us.

Win sat up. He scrubbed his cheek with his palm.

"What's going on?" Victoria asked. "Do you have regular trysts here after hours?" She seemed truly appalled that she'd found Win and me tangled on the sofa.

I sat up and brushed my hair off my forehead. "What are you doing here?"

"I need to pick up a file on the Mother's Day Gala."

"Win, have you met my sister Victoria?" I tried to sound natural, but my body was in shock from gorging after a famine of biblical proportions.

Win stood and offered his hand to Victoria. Brandon stepped between them. "You're that baseball player," he said. "The pitcher."

"Win Winston," Win said. "I play for the Columbia Gems."

"Where is Chandler?" Brandon asked me, but his glare fixed on Win like rifle sights. As if he wanted to call Win out for a duel over my honor or something.

"He had to leave Dad's soiree early. Work emergency, I believe he said." I smiled insincerely at Brandon. "Win offered to drive me home."

"I realize you girls are putting in a lot of hours lately, but this isn't where you live." Brandon had a knack for stating the obvious, a talent he was cultivating for his political career.

"Politically incorrect to call us girls, Bran. Vic, call off your watchdog."

Victoria narrowed her eyes at me.

I met her gaze without flinching. Neither Win nor I had bothered to remove our coats. Victoria and Brandon had interrupted a kiss. That was all. So, it wasn't an innocent kiss, but it wasn't anyone's business who I kissed or where I kissed him.

"Look," Win said. "This is my fault. I asked about your mother, so Carrie brought me here to see her portrait. Then one thing led to another. Ready to go, Carrie?"

"You'll lock up?" I asked Victoria.

She nodded.

Win said nothing but followed me out of the office and onto the elevator.

"What was that about?" he asked once the doors slid closed. The scowl on his face could have blistered wet paint.

"Victoria considers herself my surrogate mother."

"You were an adult when your mother died. You didn't need a surrogate." His scowl deepened. "Tell me you weren't jailbait that summer."

"I was old enough. You're safe."

"Now what?" he asked as we exited the elevator into the dim hush of the building lobby. He didn't physically touch me, but his gaze did things to me that shouldn't be legal without written, notarized consent.

A gust of wind blew around the corner as we stepped out of the lobby. Winter in central New York was barely over. After the heat of Win's embrace, the air was excruciatingly frigid.

Those moments on the sofa had catapulted me back to when we were young and hungry for each other. Not that I wanted to relive those months. I struggled never to remember the things I'd done because of my anger at my father. I'd blamed him for Mom's death. I'd believed he'd abandoned her when he learned of her cancer. My craziness that summer wasn't a lie, nor was it a convenient excuse.

"Take me home."

"Have you eaten?" Win asked.

I shook my head.

"Let me buy you a burger."

Susie Buddha herself greeted us at the door. "Hi, Caroline. Hi, tall, dark, and handsome stranger. Dinner for two?"

Susie Buddha was short and thin. She looked like she could have been a waif supermodel or had an eating disorder. She was the best cook I knew. I often teased her that she needed to bulk up to improve her image.

"I like him better than your Blandroid," she told me. Susie Buddha had coined the term.

"What's a Blandroid?" Win asked.

"Caroline's usual taste in men." She led us to the same remote table at which Win and Chuck had sat the previous evening.

"Caroline won't be seeing him anymore," Win told her.

"Good. Your aura is much more complementary to hers than his is." She then rattled off the menu for the evening.

"If I recall correctly, you eat healthy," I said in response to Win's grimace at the choices. He never used to be a fussy eater. "Susie Buddha's food is organic. Very healthy."

His gaze was bright as he watched me. "I take good care of my body, and I'll be very happy to show you whenever you want."

"I'd take him upstairs right now," Susie Buddha said.

Win ordered the soup-and-lentil-burger special for both of us.

"I looked for you in almost every city I went," Win said after Susie Buddha returned to her kitchen. "I even checked phone books and called every Thorpe listed and asked to speak to Carrie."

"Phone books are so nineties," I murmured. I tried to inject my words with nonchalance, but he'd stunned me. He'd had my phone number. I'd kept the same one just for him. All he'd needed to do was call me. His lie hurt me all over again.

But I wasn't going to berate him for something he hadn't done seven years ago.

"I felt pretty stupid when I walked in here and learned your real name."

"I never expected to see you again," I admitted.

"I used to wonder about that time when you jumped me, and we didn't use any protection."

My stomach knotted. *Liar!* I wanted to scream, but my mother taught me not to create a scene in a public place. I knew the truth. I could be gracious. "No wonder you were so quick to think Matthew was yours."

His mouth settled into a grim line again. "What if I want DNA tests?"

"You don't believe me? Fine. It's your money." I plucked a hair from my scalp and flicked it at him. "Just remember, Matthew and I have the same father."

Keeping Win focused on Matthew was safe.

Win stared at me for a few minutes. I glared back.

"Look," he said. "I see a lot of guys getting a lot of girls pregnant and paying out a lot of money for abortions and child support. It doesn't matter to them as long as they don't have to deal with it. I've never been one of those guys."

Interesting opinion he had of himself. Susie Buddha came out with my spring-pea soup. I crumbled two of her homemade oat crackers into the brilliant green liquid.

Awkward silence. I dipped my spoon into my soup. Tasted. Added a grind of pepper.

"So," I finally said. "What have you been up to besides playing ball, getting injured, undergoing Tommy John surgery to reconstruct your elbow?" Safe, shallow conversation. I knew he hadn't gotten married.

"You forgot looking for you." His tone was wry.

"Come on," I said, trying to inject a little jocularity into our evening. Win used to be fun. Intense but fun. "You can't make me believe you haven't had a girlfriend or dozen since you left me."

He shrugged. "I haven't been celibate."

I had. But he didn't need to know that. And I noticed he didn't ask. He'd sort of met Chandler and jumped to conclusions based on the Carrie Thorpe he'd known. I could probably tell him a zillion times that my nymphomania of that summer belonged only to those two and a half months, and he'd never believe me.

Regret slashed through me. I hated the girl I'd been when I was eighteen.

"Are you going to see that guy again?" Win asked after a few more moments of awkward silence.

"You're asking me for exclusivity while you're here, but what happens when Columbia calls you up? You go on your merry way just like you did before. Where does that leave me?"

I remembered too well where it had left me the last time. I let my spoon rest on the lip of the soup bowl. He ignored his. "You were the one who left."

"Wait a minute. You were called up. I carried on with my life. Now you're asking me to put my life and relationships on hold to accommodate you? Pretty selfish, if you ask me. Besides, I'm not the same person I was seven years ago," I said. "Haven't you changed? Matured?"

"I hope I have." His eyes narrowed. "But we'd have changed anyway. And I don't want to lie to your father."

"I don't want you talking to him."

"He's a shareholder of the team I play for," Win said, not that I needed reminding. "Talking might happen."

"If you tell him what happened between us seven years ago, he might shoot you. He's old-fashioned like that."

"I'm not going to lie to him," Win repeated. He sounded reasonable.

So why did it feel like blackmail?

My throat closed. I shoved my bowl of soup away. "Thanks for dinner." I stood and made my way through the maze of empty tables.

Win made no move to stop me. Didn't utter a sound. He probably didn't want a scene any more than I did.

I punched in the security code for my apartment and let myself into the stairwell. My private little nest, my sanctuary awaited me.

My phone rang. I checked the caller ID. Alexandra. Plus I'd missed a call.

"Hi," I answered, plopping onto my sofa. I pulled an afghan off the back and draped it over my lap. Old buildings are charming, but sometimes the heating leaves a lot to be desired.

"Dad is furious," Alexandra said. "You shouldn't have sneaked out with your pitcher."

"He's not my pitcher," I said. "And we didn't sneak out."

"Well, you didn't say good-bye to him or Polly, so as far as Dad's concerned, you sneaked out, thereby missing his big announcement."

I should have known she wouldn't give Dad my message. When it came to being self-absorbed, Alexandra made me look like a self-sacrificing saint. "And what was his big announcement? Maplethorpe Enterprises is building the new sports complex downtown?"

"Very good! But you forgot about the naming rights," she said.

"What?"

"Yup. Dad took our inheritance and bought naming rights to the new complex. The Maplethorpe Lion's Den or something."

I laughed. Alexandra might be oblivious to anyone but herself, but she did have a sense of humor. The inheritance bit was a running joke with us.

"And Dad vented a little about you and your pitcher."

"He's not my pitcher. We knew each other a long time ago. That's all."

I must have snarled, because she said, "Hey, don't bite off my head. I think he's hot, and you should go for him."

I sighed and then apologized. "Thanks for the warning."

"You'd do the same for me," Alexandra replied. For a moment, I thought she sounded hopeful, which was odd.

Then I remembered Marc.

We chatted a few minutes about nothing. When we finished, I checked the missed call, and sure enough, my father's number popped up.

I listened to his message. His tone was testy. "*Caroline, I am not pleased with your behavior this evening. Call me.*"

Call him? Not likely. "Well, guess what?" I asked my terrarium. "I wasn't pleased with his behavior this evening either."

Being with Win again had made me feel fragile. A feeling I didn't like and one my father would certainly exploit.

And that led me straight back to Win. I couldn't believe how close we'd come to making a giant mistake. If Victoria hadn't interrupted when she had, who knew how far out of control things would have gone?

It was embarrassing to know I had as little willpower now as I'd had when I was eighteen. Humiliating.

If only my family would stop making such a big deal out of the fact that Win and I might have known each other a long time ago, we could all get on with our lives.

If only Win had kept his mouth shut instead of calling me by name in the restaurant last night.

If only he hadn't wrecked his elbow a year ago, undergone Tommy John reconstructive surgery, and then come to Syracuse on his rehab journey through the minors.

I couldn't live my life on *if only*. Otherwise, I could think: if only Chandler Goodeve were the man of my dreams, life would be perfect.

But Chandler Goodeve was a blip on my radar because my father had put him there, and the man of my dreams, well, unfortunately he looked an awful lot like Win Winston.

Chapter Four

"You didn't return my call," my father growled in my ear when I answered my office phone the next morning.

I braced myself to deal with him. I loved my father, but part of me still resented how he'd treated my mother and sisters. Me? I'd struggled to accept—with grace and compassion—the choices he'd made about his life. And most of the time I succeeded.

This wasn't one of those times. "I wasn't feeling well."

"Don't think you can dance around my questions about Win Winston."

My scalp tingled as my blood pressure spiked. I forced myself to inhale deeply, drawing air into the very bottoms of my lungs. "I'm not dancing around your questions. Any relationship I may or may not have with any man of my choosing is none of your business."

Victoria leaned against the doorjamb, openly eavesdropping. Her eyebrows shot up her forehead. People didn't talk back to James Maplethorpe without consequences.

I listened to my father bluster for several moments, yawned through his litany of what an ungrateful daughter I was, and so on and so on. I hadn't slept well. Whether in my bed or merely my memories, Win had a way of keeping me awake.

Eventually I had enough of my father and interrupted him. "Dad, I love you, but that doesn't give you the right to pry into my personal affairs." I tried to emulate my mother's gentle, calming tones, but my voice cracked.

"You wouldn't have your cushy job if I hadn't started the foundation."

"You wouldn't have started the foundation if you hadn't felt so guilty about ditching Mom to marry Polly."

Oops. Did that sentiment actually emerge from my mouth?

Victoria gasped. Dad went silent.

I'd just said what I'd vowed never to say since Mom died. To my father, that was. I'd been frank with my sisters but had never even hinted at my feelings to Dad. I must have been in shock or something.

"Do you want me to resign?" I kept at him, hoping his silence meant vulnerability. My throat threatened to seal shut, but I forced my words past the compressing walls. "I mean, if working for the foundation means you get to have a say in every aspect of my life, then I don't want to work here."

Victoria's eyes kept growing wider and wider. I waited for the rest of her face to collapse into the sinkholes of her eye sockets.

"That wasn't a nice thing to say to me," Dad eventually said.

"No," I agreed. "It wasn't. But it wasn't a nice time in my life or my sisters' lives—or Mom's life. There are consequences for every action. And seven years ago, I was very angry at you. Right now, I'm very angry at you. Sometimes the truth is ugly. I don't have a hidden agenda, Dad. I'm telling you clearly: butt out."

He harrumphed a bit, regaining his bearings after I'd blindsided him.

I, however, felt a whole lot better. I'd let him know I wasn't a child he could bully.

"Bye, Dad," I said, interrupting him. I hung up the phone, not understanding why my hand trembled.

"Oh. My. God," Victoria said. "He'll cut you out of the will."

"There won't be anything left after he names the new sports complex." I opened the pink-ribbon file folder in front of me, signaling Victoria that I didn't want to dissect my conversation with Dad.

She ignored the sign. "What's happening with you?"

The words on the page in front of me dissolved into gibberish. She'd asked a good question, one for which I had no answer.

"It's him. That pitcher person I caught you with last night."

"You didn't *catch* me with anyone last night. You interrupted a kiss."

"If we'd been five minutes later, I'd have interrupted a lot more than a kiss," she said.

I supposed I owed Victoria some sort of explanation. My mind flitted over a dozen rationalizations, all of which would be true, and somewhat relevant, and none of which I felt like voicing.

Still, I needed to tell her something.

"I met him the summer Mom died. I was trying to...justify some of my behavior to him."

"That doesn't sound like you. What happened that you felt you needed to justify anything?"

I swallowed hard. This was the tricky part. Not that anyone ever listened to me. "When Matthew was showing me his autographed baseball, Win jumped to an erroneous conclusion."

I held myself very, very still.

Victoria wasn't a stupid woman. "I see," she said after a long pause. "What did you tell him?"

"The truth." I looked her square in the eyes. Didn't blink. "Matthew is Dad's son with Polly. Win muttered something about DNA tests, so I gave him a hair from my head and reminded him that Matthew and I have the same father."

"That's not what I meant," Victoria said. Her tone was tight. Her gaze attempted to penetrate my defenses.

I pretended I didn't understand her. After all, she didn't know anything, and any suspicions she had couldn't possibly be related to reality.

Damn Win for showing up and reopening the past.

I picked up the folder again and opened it. Stared at the blurs on the papers inside it.

"You can't hide forever," Victoria said.

I wanted to dare her to prove it, to make a bet with me, give her statement some guts. Instead, I kept my mouth shut about personal garbage. I was functioning, and that was all that mattered. "Can we go over the stuff for the gala? I want to try to get to the game this afternoon."

"Win's not pitching."

"I know that," I said with exaggerated patience. "Win has nothing to do with my desire to go to the game. You know I try to get to all the home games." Duh! That's why I bought season tickets instead of depending on Dad, who hadn't been dependable about tickets since Matthew's birth.

She plopped down in the chair in front of my desk. "Are you going to invite Win to escort you to the gala?"

The weekend-long gala included a fund-raising dinner with members of the baseball team putting themselves on the block for a bachelor auction, part of the Saltboilers' ongoing support of breast-cancer awareness and research. "I'll probably go with Chandler, just like I always do."

Boring, bland Chandler. Safe Chandler.

"Don't use Chandler to make Win jealous."

That she thought I would even consider doing something like that hurt. If nothing else, from the time my crazy summer ended to the present, I'd tried to be meticulously scrupulous in my dealings with other people, especially and particularly my sisters. They were all I had left of my mother.

"I don't play those kinds of games."

"I know, but I'd hate to see you start doing it now."

"How many reservations for the dinner do we have?" I asked.

She consulted her folder as the personal surrendered to the professional, just the way office time should be.

The afternoon was even colder than the previous day had been. Salt-boiler Stadium wasn't nearly as crowded, thanks to the weather and the two o'clock start time. Many fans took opening day off from work. Few bothered with the other day games. I preferred the smaller crowd.

I huddled in a blanket and watched Win sign autographs outside the home-team dugout. His breath hovered over his head like a cartoon dialogue balloon, and I wondered how the players would cope with the cold. Most of them were natives of more southern climes.

I loved watching new players every year. Part of the charm of the minor leagues was not knowing who would be on the team on any game day. Players were called up, sent down, and traded like their cards. I once saw a player start a game and leave after a few innings because his contract had been sold to a team in Japan.

And pitchers, like Win, were the most tenuous and valuable of all.

Oh, I didn't want to think about Winslow Winthrop Winston the What-ever. It was bad enough I'd dreamed about him—about the weeks after Flash's injury, which left Win and me alone, changing us from a *ménage* to a couple, and twisted me from crazy to scared.

And yet those few weeks between Flash's departure and the start of my freshman year of college were among the happiest of my life. Maybe that's why I'd been so frightened. I hadn't deserved to be happy. Didn't know what to do with that pocket of bliss.

But I hadn't been content or calm, not the way I was now. I'd been jittery, wired, zinging with adrenaline and rebellion. Win had taken advantage of that wildness.

Well, I'd paid my dues. I'd moved on. I didn't need or want Win Winston stirring up those memories. Yet it seemed all he had to do was look at me, and I zoomed back to eighteen.

I pulled my fleece closer and hunched against the wind as the Saltboil-ers' rookie pitcher walked the first two batters. I focused on him, a young phenom from San Diego. Maybe I'd get to see one of his purported hun-dred-mile-an-hour fastballs.

The autograph seekers were gone, and Win had disappeared into the darkness of the dugout.

I spotted him—purely by accident—at the bottom of the inning. He wasn't on the bench with the rest of the starting pitchers. Nope. He leaned against the railing at the edge of the dugout.

I wasn't at the stadium to stare at my youthful mistakes.

The aromas from the concessions filled my senses, making my mouth water and my stomach growl. At the next break in the action, I went to the grill on the third-base side of the concourse for a hot dog. I took my time returning to my seat, where I forced myself to focus on the pitcher, the batter, the catcher—even the third baseman—so I wouldn't stare at Win as I nibbled my lunch.

I let the game absorb me, forgetting Win for three outs. But at the end of each half inning, reality jolted me as I couldn't keep my gaze from drifting his way.

The bottom of the fourth inning gave me something else to look at: scoreboard greetings. But those were as sparse as the crowd. Two birthdays. One anniversary. One school group. That was it.

"Excuse me."

I ripped my gaze from the scoreboard to the intern hovering next to me. I'd been a ballpark intern once, so the kid had my sympathy.

Then I saw the flowers.

"Are you Caroline Maplethorpe?" The young man consulted the card attached to the bouquet of sunny-faced daisies. His voice cracked. "Also known as Carrie Thorpe? Section 105, row one, seat one?"

I nodded.

"These were delivered for you." He thrust the bouquet at me and practically ran his escape up the steps.

A floral delivery at the ballpark?

My gloved fingers fumbled with the envelope bearing my name, but I already knew who'd sent them.

It bothered me that Win remembered daisies were my favorite flower. Girls remember those sorts of details, not big macho jocks. I'd filled my cheap room with bouquets I'd picked in the wild back then. An inexpensive way to personalize the drab space. These daisies had to be a coincidence. No man would remember something like daisies for seven years.

One afternoon shortly after Flash had left, Win and I looked for fresh daisies and had to settle for black-eyed Susans. It had been a rare afternoon off for Win, and he'd chosen to spend it with me. I'd gotten my period that morning. While I'd been pushing my sexual boundaries that summer, there were some things I wouldn't do. Win hadn't seemed to mind. Had held my hand. Kissed me. Picked wildflowers for me.

No. He couldn't possibly share that tender memory with me, because it wouldn't have meant the same thing to him. He was a *guy*. Guys don't get sentimental.

I glanced toward the dugout. Win hadn't moved from his spot on the railing. I held up the bouquet and nodded in his direction, acknowledging receipt.

He nodded back.

I didn't want to think about how he'd managed to find out my seat number or how he'd managed to have flowers delivered during a game.

But those things were easier than thinking about why he'd done it. *Why* scared me.

I wasn't surprised when Win called me at work the next morning.

"You shouldn't eat hot dogs at the stadium. It gives the players ideas."

"Then they shouldn't sell them," I replied.

"*You* shouldn't eat hot dogs." His voice was husky. "Nobody cares about the fat guy in general admission. Do you have lunch plans?"

This close to the gala, lunch was a hope, not a given. "Yes."

"Well, I would have called you for dinner last night, but I don't have your number."

Thank goodness. "Thanks, but—"

"Then dinner tonight after the game. I'll pick you up."

That was a worse idea. "I don't think we should—"

"It's a date, Carrie. That thing people do when they're attracted to each other and want to get to know each other better."

I picked up a paper clip and started twisting it. "We know each other well enough."

"We have seven lost years to catch up on," Win said. "I've missed you every day of those years."

When he put it like that, I felt churlish for refusing. This was *Win*, not some stranger I'd met online. But my survival instincts had matured since we'd first known each other. "Win, I have a different life now. Different goals." Not that I'd had any goal that summer other than survive the betrayals of my parents.

Win didn't answer right away.

The now-mutilated paper clip in my fingers snapped as I waited.

"Look," he said after releasing a heavy sigh. "We never finished our conversation the other night. I thought I'd give you time to cool off. Don't you want privacy for our discussion?"

He had me there. I'd walked out on him. And we did need to talk. Privately. He still hadn't heard me about circumspection, although it might be too late for that now. "Maybe I can rearrange my lunch plans and meet you somewhere."

"I thought we could eat here at my place. I'll pick you up."

"There?" Only sheer willpower kept my voice from squeaking. "As in your apartment? No. Forget it."

"It's just lunch. I promise."

Apparently I didn't sound as cool as I thought I had. His tone was gentle, as if I were a frightened animal he was trying to calm. And that gave him power over me. Power I wasn't going to let him keep. I knew he needed to be at the ballpark by two, and nothing distracted Win Winston from baseball. Ever.

I swallowed my trepidation. "I'll meet you there."

Turned out he lived in a residential hotel a couple of blocks from my Armory Square apartment—walking distance from my office. His brief tenure in Syracuse warranted nothing more permanent.

I knocked on the door of his suite. My legs wobbled. I tried to convince myself I wasn't falling into the same old destructive patterns. Destructive wasn't my style. My crazy summer had been an aberration.

Win answered his door almost immediately.

My anxiety must have been apparent.

"Hey." He put his forefinger under my chin and adjusted my head so that I was looking at his face instead of his feet. "Food and talk only. I promise." He stepped aside so I could enter.

I don't know why he thought I'd believe his promises.

This hotel was a vast improvement over the seedy motor court in which he'd lived in Cortland. I reminded myself seven years had passed and we weren't teenagers anymore. That we were successful adults. I no longer lived in a seedy motor court either.

The detail that got to me was the vase of daisies sitting in the middle of the table. Guys don't buy flowers for their temporary bachelor pads. I stared at the white-and-yellow blossoms as Win puttered in the kitchenette.

A moment later, he handed me a tall glass of iced tea, complete with lemon garnish like a wedge of sunshine on the rim. "Pull up a chair and sit down. You still drink iced tea, right?"

He was creeping me out, like he'd become a time-traveling stalker. He hadn't seen me in almost a decade, but he remembered the minutia of me. Unlike Chandler, who'd been in my life for the past two years.

I nodded but didn't drink.

"I didn't slip you a date rape drug."

"I didn't think you did." My voice was finally working. Some of the inner quaking had abated. "I never thought that about you or Flash."

"There's no one in my closet."

I tightened my fingers on the sweating glass of tea to keep from opening the door and checking. "Don't you have to go to the stadium to warm up and stuff?"

"I'd rather eat lunch with you than grab takeout on my way to work."

Right. The routines were starting to come back to me. The foods he ate and the order in which he consumed them. Lean proteins. Water. Some complex carbs before a game, but always lean proteins and fresh produce. No pink-slimed fast-food burgers for Win Winston. "I'm not hungry," I said. "The only reason I'm here is to talk."

He pulled out a chair at the table and waited for me to sit. "Talk while I eat," he said.

He was being reasonable, so I sat.

He sat across from me, his long legs folded. Even so, his knees brushed mine. He raised his glass of water as if to make a toast. "To us."

I put my glass on the table. "There is no us."

"Why don't you want your family to know that you and I were lovers?" he asked as he helped himself to a wrap from a platter in the center of the table. The faint tang of garlic hovered nearby.

"Looking for more blackmail material?" I asked.

"I'm not blackmailing you." He sounded testy. "I want to know why you're ashamed of me."

His words prickled and shocked me. "Are you kidding? I'm not ashamed of you. I'm not proud of some of the things we did, but I'm not ashamed of you." And that was true.

"Then why do you act like I'm something you need to scrape off the bottom of your shoe?"

"I thought I explained this to you the other night."

"Well, I must have missed something, because I don't remember you saying much of anything except you went a little crazy the summer your mother died."

"That wasn't *me* that summer."

"You know what? I'm not that guy you were with that summer either. I was in a strange place, fresh out of high school, and dealing with some of my own...challenges."

"You're still talking about sex." My stomach gurgled, and I eyed a wrap. I could see the edges of turkey, cheese, and lettuce.

Win must have heard my hunger, and pushed the platter of wraps toward me. "I'm not talking about with Flash. I'm talking about you and me. We never gave what we had a fair chance. We were good together."

We had been good together...sexually speaking.

"There was a lot of hurting going on in my family that summer. That's why I lied to them about working at a church camp. It's taken us a long time to put the past behind us. What would be the point in telling anyone what we...explored?"

He choked on his water. "I wasn't talking about what happened with Flash. I'm talking about you and me. Flash was just...the catalyst that brought us together. We never needed him."

My body started reacting to his version of our past. I certainly hadn't needed Flash. Not after Win joined our little equation. But Win was right. We hadn't ever really ended our involvement. Not formally. He'd been called up to Double A, and I had my freshman year of college awaiting me.

"I'm involved with someone." A weak excuse.

He didn't accept my reason any more that afternoon than he had the first time I'd used it on him. "If you're involved with that guy, I'll eat my ball and glove," he said.

What was I doing there? I must have completely lost my mind when I'd accepted his lunch invitation.

"I can't get involved with you," I said. "Not again."

He would rip my world apart in more ways than anyone could fathom.

"We never gave ourselves a chance. That's all I'm asking, Carrie. A chance."

That name. The abbreviated version of my given name. The only people who'd ever called me that were the people with whom I'd worked that summer with the Crowns.

I stood. "I'm sorry, Win." There were things I couldn't tell him. Things about that summer that had irrevocably changed my life. "I can't go back. I won't go back."

He pushed away from the table. "I don't want to go back either. I want to move forward with you. I'm not asking you to give up your life, your job, your freedom, your home—anything. I don't know how long I'm going to be stuck here and—"

"Stuck here?" At last. Something on which to hang my anger that wouldn't bare my soul. "You want to just pass time with me? That's what you call giving us a chance?"

"That came out wrong," he said.

I was having none of it.

"It's taken me years to get to this point. Where I'm content. Where I can have a relationship with my father, his wife, and new family. I'm not going to throw away my stability to cater to your ego."

"Stability? Or rut?" he snapped back.

"This was a mistake," I muttered. I grabbed my purse from his sofa and headed for the door.

My real mistake was turning my back on him.

He caught me around the waist and twisted me until I faced him. I wasn't prepared for his mouth to come down on mine. He tasted faintly of the garlic and basil, but mostly, he tasted of Win. Addictive Win.

"Tell me that isn't worth giving another chance," he muttered a moment later after he'd completely destroyed all my defenses.

"We gave it a chance seven years ago, and it didn't work," I whispered.

"We were too young to give it enough of a chance." His hands slid down my back. He cupped my butt and pulled me closer to him. "But I'm still attracted to you. And I think it's mutual."

"I need to get back to the office," I said, my voice all shaky again. "And you need to get to the ballpark."

"We'll continue this conversation after the game tonight."

One of the things I'd always liked about Win was his inability to compromise when it came to his game. His ability to focus. Pitchers need to focus. I just didn't want him focusing on me.

I shook my head. "I have other plans."

"You're a season-ticket holder. Games are your plans."

"Not every night," I lied. Well, not exactly lied. There were a few home games I didn't attend. But not many. Tonight would be one.

"So it's war?"

Not jumping into his bed again equaled a declaration of war?

"Why does it have to be sex or war? Why can't we continue with indifference?"

"Because we have unfinished business."

"We're finished." My voice felt tight and brittle. "We finished seven years ago when you went your way, and I went mine."

"Then let's start again. Fresh and new." Maybe it was my imagination, but I thought I heard hope in his tone.

I shook my head and left.

Chapter Five

"You lied about working at the church camp." Dad's tone was disapproving, as though lying about church-related activities was somehow worse than lying about going to the grocery store or something.

He'd called as soon as I returned from lunch.

I nearly hung up on him. I shouldn't have answered it when I saw his number pop up, but then I thought it might be Matthew wanting to sit with me at the game I wasn't attending.

"I checked with the Crowns. You were an intern there when Winston said you were."

"What's your point?" There was no sense denying anything.

"Why did you lie about it?" Dad asked.

"I needed to not be part of your family," I replied. Tears welled in my eyes, but I blinked them away. I hadn't cried about his betrayal seven years ago and refused to indulge now. "What is the point of reopening all these wounds?"

"You lied about your age. I could have Winston arrested for statutory rape."

"No, you can't," I said, feeling weary. "Age of consent is seventeen. Besides, you have no right to sit judgment on me when you were sleeping with a girl who's only a year older than Victoria."

"I'm your father."

"So? You're still a dirty old man, and I'm a slut. Can we just move past the past?" I was sick and tired of the angst brought into my life by Win Winston.

Why couldn't he have stayed healthy? Stayed in the majors, stayed out of my life? I'd been doing fine. Just fine.

"I'm having a meeting in my box tonight before the game. People from some of the other breast-cancer organizations will be there. I expect you and Victoria there at five o'clock."

He hung up before I could respond.

"Damn it!" I wanted to throw the phone against the wall.

Victoria appeared my door, tall, slender, and graceful. Always the good daughter. She'd not only inherited our mother's looks but also her sweet, even temperament. "I take it Dad told you about tonight's meeting."

"I hadn't planned to go to the game tonight." I racked my brain for an acceptable excuse to blow off the meeting.

"Liar."

Maybe Victoria's temperament wasn't so sweet.

"How was lunch with Win?"

"He's declared war because I won't sleep with him. Except I think Dad just disarmed him."

Victoria arched one slender eyebrow.

"Dad checked employment records at the church camp and at the Crowns. Busted. I don't see what the big deal is." I straightened a pile of papers on my desk. "It's just a control thing."

"Win or Dad?"

"What?" I couldn't believe she'd asked me such a silly question. Then I realized I couldn't answer it because they were both trying to control me.

Brazening it out with Dad felt good, but I didn't quite trust Win to be discreet about...everything.

It didn't matter to me if Dad knew we'd been lovers. It was the other stuff—the before-and-after stuff—that had me worried. And Win could blow the before stuff up in my face. And the after? Well, that was my secret, my motivation for everything that had come after I left Cortland. Victoria had hinted once or twice that she knew something—had guessed something—but she didn't know everything. That was my privilege.

I went to the meeting. There were all kinds of people in Dad's luxury box, people involved in the breast-cancer-awareness world, but few of them knew much about baseball beyond the pink bats and cleats used by some of the players. Others were affronted by the concept of the Second Base Club T-shirts and other merchandise. I was all for using anything to draw attention to the disease that had stolen my mother. After the official portion of the get-together, I could have stayed in the box and watched the game. But Polly arrived with Matthew, who wanted to go down and harass the visiting team. I tried to convince Victoria to take him to my seats, but she pleaded prior evening plans with Brandon and left. Dad was still doing his magnanimous-host thing. Polly didn't want the wind to muss her hair. Matthew knew just how to play me.

I bought him a hot dog, then wandered around the concourse.

"We missed the first pitch." Matthew tugged on my hand.

"There will be plenty more," I assured him.

"But I like to see the first batter." Matthew's tone bordered on whining, which was odd because he wasn't a whiny kid.

"We can watch from right here," I said.

Saltboiler Stadium had been built so the diamond could be viewed while one purchased food. Just about the only places from which one could not watch the game were the souvenir shop and the bathrooms. I hoped the new stadium would be as accommodating.

Matthew was having none of it. "I want to sit."

"Let's go back to Dad's box."

"Win won't pay me unless you're in your seat."

Everything inside me froze. Fortunately, my voice still worked. "What?"

"Win won't pay me if you're not in your seat," Matthew repeated.

Okay, my ears were working fine too.

"When did Win offer to pay you?"

"He called for Dad this afternoon, and I answered the phone, so he talked to me instead."

I distinctly recalled telling Win not to talk to my father.

The food I'd eaten in the box rose into my throat. I swallowed hard as I squatted next to Matthew.

"What did Win say to you?"

Matthew wasn't looking at me but everywhere else. "Only that he likes to see you sitting in the stands but that you weren't going to the game tonight, so I told him you were going to a meeting in the box, and he said he'd give me twenty dollars if I could get you to sit in your seat for the game. Oh, and not to tell you about it."

His little-boy energy stilled. Large gray eyes went perfectly round as his gaze met mine. "Uh-oh."

Yeah, uh-oh.

I briefly considered offering Matthew twenty bucks to let me take him home, but that wasn't the right thing to do. I wasn't going to undermine Polly's efforts to raise a good kid.

"Here's the deal, buddy," I said. "What Win did was wrong."

"Are you going to tell Mom?" He sounded worried.

That was good. I knew Polly and Dad didn't abuse the kid. My father was a decent father. He was great when I was a kid, and the two of us came to the ballpark together.

"You didn't do anything wrong. Mr. Winston shouldn't have tried to bribe you."

Matthew's eyes grew wider. "Will the coach fine him?"

I suppressed a smile. "No, it wasn't that kind of mistake."

Matthew's scowl grew fierce. He looked like a miniature of my father. "Is he trying to hurt you? Because if he is, I'll fix it. Brothers are supposed to take care of their sisters."

It took all my willpower not to laugh.

"I think he wants to kiss me," I confided in a near whisper.

Matthew's scowl turned into a mask of horror and disgust. "Yuck."

"Yeah," I agreed. "Yuck. How about I call your mom and see if it's okay if you and I go to a movie or something?"

Matthew shook his head. "I wanna see the game, and I want Win's money. He should have to pay for doing something wrong. And when he pays me, I'll tell him he can't kiss you, or I'll kick him in the nuts."

It was really a good thing I wasn't eating or drinking anything. "Matthew James Maplethorpe!" I put everything I had into sounding appalled.

"It really, really hurts bad," he said.

"You shouldn't say things like that in public or to girls," I explained. "It's not nice."

I considered asking him to let me watch, but that was definitely not the right thing to say, at least not then. Maybe in twenty or so years, Matthew and I could look back on the day and laugh.

Why would Win be calling my father? My stomach clenched anew at the thought.

"Let's sit down," Matthew said. "Win's not pitching, so what difference does it make?"

I'd told Victoria I wouldn't let Win drive me from my games. Here was my chance to prove it.

Matthew and I made our way to my seats, where we had to have an usher eject a couple of interlopers. I ignored the home-team dugout, but Matthew waved.

Baseball failed to work its usual magic on me that evening.

I briefly considered telling Dad and letting him handle it. After all, Win was virtually a stranger to Matthew, and what he'd done was way out of line. But I didn't want Win and Dad speaking. Win never should have called my father's house. He was trespassing where he didn't belong: my life.

My phone rang at the end of the fourth inning. Most people knew better than to call me during a baseball game. I didn't recognize the number. "Hello?"

"Meet me for dinner after the game."

"How did you get my number?" I couldn't believe Win was calling me. To say phone calls from the dugout were frowned upon would be an understatement. He'd probably be fined.

"That Matthew is a great kid."

I glared at Matthew, who was busy watching Salty the Mascot's antics. "Do you always take advantage of the innocent?"

His voice lowered and grew husky. "Oh, I wouldn't say you were an innocent."

"How much did you offer Matthew for my phone number?"

"Gotta go," he said and then disconnected.

I programmed his number into my phone. He wouldn't catch me unawares again.

It was time for another heart-to-heart with my kid brother.

"Did you give my telephone number to Win Winston?"

"Yeah."

"How much money did he promise to pay you for that?"

"What? Oh, nothing. I mean, it's an honor for somebody as famous as Win Winston to want your phone number."

"I told you. He wants to kiss me."

"Yeah, but he didn't tell me that when he asked me if I knew your number."

Great. Just freaking terrific.

I inhaled deeply. "Has Dad or your mom ever talked to you about giving out family information?"

He glanced at me through his lashes, shook his head, and focused on the pitcher.

"Did you give Mr. Winston Victoria or Alexandra's numbers?"

"He only asked for yours. I think it's cool Win Winston likes my sister. And it's kind of cool that he wants to kiss you. You should let him. Yes!" Matthew jumped to his feet and pumped his tiny fist in the air as the pitcher struck out the third straight batter.

My cell phone rang again.

"Meet me for dinner after the game."

"Where?"

I think my ready acquiescence surprised him. He was going to be even more surprised when I cut him a new one for his antics with my brother.

"I'll get back to you." He disconnected.

"If Win wants to kiss you, let him," Matthew said. "He *likes* you."

I considered my options. Matthew needed to learn not to give out private info, but I didn't want to bring my father into it. "Okay, Matthew, listen up. I won't tell Dad or your mom what you did, but I think you need to understand that giving out my phone number was wrong. So after tonight's game, you can't sit here at least for a month."

"Why?" He sounded genuinely upset.

"Because you did a naughty thing. It's bad enough you're taking money from Mr. Winston, but giving him my cell phone number—well, Dad would discipline you even worse than I am for doing that."

Matthew begged through the top of the sixth inning, but I was firm.

I was ready when my cell rang at the bottom of the sixth. I didn't even get a chance to speak.

"An hour after the game. Yakker's."

Yakker's was a sports bar a couple of miles from the stadium. Several former Saltboilers owned it. The place was always packed with athletes, media types, and fans of simple tavern food.

Fortunately, I'd driven to the game because of Dad's meeting.

My lavender punch bug was easy to park. The sidewalk was jammed with smokers clustered around the entrances like ants on honey. I pushed my way through the toxic fog into the noise.

I was early. I found an empty stool at the bar and ordered a glass of cranberry juice with a squeeze of lime. I didn't watch the door. I didn't study the crowd. Instead, I watched the end of a baseball game on the television mounted over the bar.

Win was late. I decided to give him ten more minutes. I had to go to work the next morning. I couldn't be hanging out in bars all night.

Finally, I drained my glass, hitched my bag onto my shoulder, and slid off my stool. I hadn't realized how stuffy the bar was until the cool spring air slapped my face like a reality check.

I was halfway up the block to my parking spot when someone grabbed my arm. My heart leaped into my throat, forcing a scream toward my mouth, but my assailant spoke before more than a squeak emerged.

"Sorry I'm late."

I recognized the tall, dark form standing next to me. "You nearly gave me a heart attack." I yanked my arm out of his grasp.

He cupped my elbow and turned me around so I was heading back to the bar. "I'm starving," he said. "Let me buy you a burger."

Ballplayers tended to eat light before a game and have their main meal after playing. The players can pay to have the clubhouse cater. But Win wasn't a long-termer, and he could afford better.

By the time we made our way inside the bar, several of his teammates were ensconced in the back room. They called for Win to join them.

I felt him tense. "It's okay," I said. "I won't embarrass you in front of your teammates for what you did to Matthew."

He looked down at me—he was over a foot taller than I was—and said, "Is that why you agreed to come out with me? So you can yell at me again?"

"I'm pretty upset with you."

"You wouldn't be upset if you didn't care," he said. "Sitting with a crowd isn't what I had in mind. Guess we'll have to have that private chat another time." He steered me toward the table with his teammates.

I blew that one.

I wasn't the only woman at the table.

The others, however, were blonde. Brightly so, with salon tans, whitened teeth, and gold gleaming in their earlobes and around their necks. I'd seen them—or others just like them—hanging around the visitor's dugout before. Garishly dressed in tight jeans and skimpy tops suited more for the dance floor than the bleachers. Groupies. *Blonderoids.*

"Everyone, this is Carrie," Win said as he pulled out a chair for me.

Carrie. Not Caroline. And that was okay. I felt a little dowdy in my Salt-boilers sweatshirt and sneakers. It was almost like our Cortland days.

When the waitress showed up, Win ordered a grilled chicken sandwich and a Moonsinger while I stuck with my cranberry and lime.

I was the only person at the table without an alcoholic beverage. Lots of beer and pale white wine. I didn't participate in the conversation either. The guys rehashed the game, and the girls chattered about... Whatever it was, it was so inane that I can't recall.

This was not the life I wanted. I finished my drink, thanked Win, and pushed away from the table.

"Hey!" His white napkin fluttered from his lap to the floor as he stood to snatch at my arm again.

"I need to go. It's almost midnight," I said. I didn't even know what I was doing there. It seemed like every time Win snapped his fingers, I obeyed like a trained seal or something. If I didn't want him in my life, why was I letting him call the shots?

"Hold on." He took out his wallet and dropped a twenty on the table to cover our share of the bill. Once again, he cupped my elbow and steered me through the crowd.

I couldn't shake him off without creating a scene. *Maplethorpes do not create scenes.*

He opened the door, and we stepped into the cool night and a cloud of nicotine. We didn't speak as we walked up the quiet side street on which I'd parked my car. He, it turned out, was parked behind me.

"This is your car?" He sounded incredulous.

I nodded.

"I never would have picked you as a Love Bug girl."

"That's because you don't know me," I replied. "Look, I'm upset that you pulled Matthew into your game playing. I'm tempted to tell my father."

He took both of my hands and laced his fingers through mine. "You won't tattle to Daddy," he said in a hushed voice. He stepped nearer, closing in on me until my back was against the driver's door of my car. "You know, it's not like I want you to do the things Flash wanted you to do."

He stood so close that heat from his body warmed me. A small dog yipped in the distance. The streetlight flickered, sending shadows dancing across Win's face. "I don't want another man—or woman—in our bed. We don't need anyone to make magic, sweetheart. You don't need anyone else with me, the way you had to supplement Flash."

Heat filled my face, and I was glad for the darkness.

"But I want to make love to you again. I've dreamed of making love to you again." He bent a bit and rubbed his nose against mine. His breath was hot and smelled faintly of beer. "You never gave us a chance, Carrie. You cheated me."

I tried to free my hands from his, but he was a pitcher. His fingers were strong.

Before I could give him a reality check, he covered my mouth with his.

Every time he kissed me, I lost all perspective, all common sense. All I could think about was kissing Win Winston forever.

I turned my face from his. "I told my father that we were lovers."

The words sounded strangled. The tightness in my throat probably had something to do with that. "And I told him it was none of his business."

"Good." Win freed his right hand from mine and cupped my cheek. His palm was calloused. His thumb caressed under my eye. "No more secrets. Except Flash. We won't tell anyone about Flash."

Flash was only one of my secrets.

I changed the subject. "Why did you call my father today?"

"I was returning his call."

Oh. Dad had been busy. Shouldn't he have been breaking ground for his new stadium instead of digging into my past?

"Do you always return phone calls?" I wanted to catch Win in a lie.

"Yeah, I do. If I know who it is."

Apparently a guy saying, *I'll call you*, wasn't the same thing. Guys did things like that so often it was a stereotype. I, however, was an adult now.

I wasn't going to hold an unanswered message against him. Even if he'd returned my call, the outcome would have been the same.

"I have to go," I said.

"I'll call you tomorrow," he replied.

"No," I said, struggling to keep my tone as flat and neutral and disinterested as possible. "You're temporary. You were temporary seven years ago, and nothing has changed."

He tensed. "I get that you think you used me to get back at your father for divorcing your mother and marrying a younger woman. That you think you used me to act out your anger at your mother's death. But you've got it all wrong, sweetheart. You used *Flash* for those things. I was your knight in shining armor." He stepped back. "Call me when you get home so I know you made it okay." I turned, my hands shaking as I unlocked the car door.

Win checked my backseat. He waited. He stood in the shadows under the street lamp and watched me drive away.

I know because I was watching him in my rearview mirror.

Chapter Six

I didn't call Win. I'd been getting home without him just fine for seven years.

The Saltboilers were in Rochester the next night. I half expected to hear from Win even though I'd told him not to call. I listened to the game on the radio while I puttered around my apartment.

Chandler called. He wanted to make plans for the next evening. Something at one of the art galleries in Armory Square, but I wasn't feeling particularly artsy or accommodating.

I nearly missed the postgame report and the preview of the next game between the Rollers and the Saltboilers with Win Winston and Silvio somebody-or-other on the mound.

I snapped off the radio. I didn't want to hear all the conjecture about Win's rehab and estimates of when the Gems would recall him.

The next morning, I checked my calendar. Rochester was a mere ninety minutes west on I-90. I frequently drove there for meetings.

I closed my calendar. I didn't need to watch Win pitch.

According to the Rollers' website, I could buy tickets online, or I could call the box office.

But I had a day packed with meetings. I had a desk piled with work. A briefcase heavy with projects. A Mother's Day Gala dinner and bachelor auction that needed my attention.

Win wouldn't know if I was in the stands or not.

I called the box office at Millwheel Park and scored a seat next to the visitor's dugout.

At four o'clock, I told Victoria I had a meeting and left for the day. Playing hooky was marvelously freeing.

Once at the stadium, I went straight to my seat. Millwheel Park isn't at all like Saltboiler Stadium, and I noted all the differences. Maybe I could give my father some tips for his new ballpark.

Win looked good as he warmed up with his catcher. Most of his pitches were over ninety miles per hour. They wouldn't play him many innings. His rehab from the surgery had taken nearly a year with slow, specific progress. He was on schedule.

His start was shaky, but once he found his rhythm, he was vintage Win Winston.

At end of the first inning, as the Saltboilers were leaving the field, Win's head shot up. His eyes scanned the stands until his gaze fixed on me. I must have purchased my seat too close to the visitor's dugout.

I waited for Win to smile. It was a good thing I wasn't holding my breath. Time seemed to suspend itself. I found myself struggling against the depths of those devil-dark eyes.

It had been that way from the beginning. From the moment Flash had invited him to leave the closet where he'd been watching and join us.

The memory sharpened as if I were viewing the past through a crystal ball. *The heat of his gaze, the wedge of silky dark curls on his magnificent bare chest, his erection tenting the front of his black bikini briefs, and his intensity and focus. How he'd emerged from the closet. Those obsidian eyes fixed on me. Him kneeling on the bed. Reaching for my breasts. Caressing, stroking...*

I swallowed hard, flushing away the memory. Win ducked into the dugout, and the stadium announcer hyped the between-inning fan-participation stunt currently in action on the field.

Flashbacks like that weren't good for my health.

At the end of each inning, Win stared at me as he left the field.

I stayed through the bottom of the sixth, which is when Win was pulled from the game. The Saltboilers were ahead 4–2.

My phone chirped when I was halfway to my car. I let the call go to voice mail. Once I was safely locked in my bug, I retrieved the message and heard Win tell me the name of the team's hotel.

I listened to the end of the game on the radio as I drove home.

I didn't hear from Win again while the team was in Rochester.

I went out with Chandler that Friday. He'd procured tickets to a traveling Broadway musical. We conversed during intermission and critiqued the show while we indulged in a post-performance glass of wine in a tiny club a few blocks from my apartment. I even let him kiss me at the door.

Scranton, another city within easy driving distance, was next on the Saltboilers' schedule. I kept telling myself I'd survived many seasons of baseball without watching my team play on the road. But like the clichéd moth drawn to the flame that would kill it or the male praying mantis approaching the female in order to procreate, then have his head ripped off, I could no more avoid Scranton the night Win was slated to pitch than any other creature drawn to its death.

So I phoned the Scranton ticket office, purchased a seat along the first-base line, told my sister I had a meeting, turned off my cell phone, and left work early to go to a baseball game.

This time, I disguised myself in the team's big-league parent logo, hoping to blend in with the home crowd.

Which I managed to do until the bottom of the first. Win started to walk off the field after retiring the first three batters, then paused and scanned the crowd. I was four rows behind the dugout, hunkered down in my seat with my head tilted so that the visor of my cap hid my face.

Nope. It was as if after allegedly losing me for seven years, he'd developed an internal GPS as far as I was concerned. He nodded in my direction.

I tried not to let the acknowledgment please me.

"Ooh, he's hot," one of the perky blondes sitting near me said.

I'd noticed the two women earlier. Their revealing clothes and thin gold chains layered around their too-tan-for-late-April necks made them hard to miss. Weren't they cold?

"He looked right at me," the second woman said.

Jealousy flared. Didn't the Blonderoids know Win had been looking for me?

"He's the one everyone is here to see," Blonderoid One said.

I vowed to ignore them, along with the nasty hooks of possessiveness piercing my heart. Focus on the game, I reminded myself.

Fortunately, the Blonderoids moved down a few seats. Closer to the end of the dugout where they'd better be able to attract the attention of a horny ballplayer.

At the bottom of each inning, Win's gaze found me as he left the mound. I knew I wasn't interfering with his concentration. Since he'd spotted me, he'd struck out almost every batter and given up only one hit.

I stayed until the middle of the seventh when the Saltboilers announced a new pitcher.

I kept my phone turned off as I headed for my car. I didn't want to know where the team was staying. Didn't want to know if Win expected me. Didn't want to think about Blonderoids getting lucky with him.

I turned on my cell phone when I got home. I'd missed calls from Victoria and Dad. Win had texted me the name of a chain hotel.

I was such a coward, but being with Win seven years ago had nearly killed me. I had the hospital bills and scars to prove it too. I couldn't risk it again. Right. That's why I'd gone to Scranton and to Rochester. Because I wanted nothing more to do with Win.

The phone rang in my hand as I sat in my living room ruminating. I checked the number before answering.

"Hi, Victoria," I said.

"Where have you been?" she practically shrieked into my ear. "I've been trying to touch base with you since five o'clock."

"I had a meeting. Then I went out to dinner with an old friend." Not exactly a lie.

"There wasn't anything scheduled on your calendar," she retorted. "We've got problems. Dad caught Alexandra and Marc together. In bed."

Crap. Didn't I have enough issues without being dragged into yet another Maplethorpe family drama? Alexandra was an adult. So was Marc. And Marc was too sly to do anything to jeopardize his meal ticket.

Besides, it was none of my business. Or Victoria's or Dad's business. Just because Dad had decided Andrew was right for Alexandra didn't mean it was true. Like me and Chandler.

I remembered Chandler's kiss and resisted wiping my mouth.

If I had to be on any side in this, it was Alexandra's side.

"You make it sound like she's jailbait, and it's incest. They're both of age, and they're related only by marriage."

"Caroline!"

"Lexi's sex life is none of our business. If she and Marc want to bonk each other's brains out, more power to them."

"What about Andrew?"

"Obviously Lexi doesn't love Andrew any more than I love Chandler."

I admired Alexandra's guts, and I wished I had the courage to say to hell with everything and indulge in Win again.

My brain went numb, if such a thing is possible. From where had that thought come—the one about me and Win and sex? From the warmth gathering in my lower torso, I guessed my body was ahead of my mind on that topic.

"You don't love Chandler?" Victoria sounded surprised.

"Not all of us can be so lucky as to fall for the Blandroid Dad brought home for us." I succumbed to reflex and scrubbed my mouth with the back of my hand, even though it had been a couple of days since Chandler's kiss.

"Did you know about this? About Alexandra and Marc?"

"I sensed something at Dad's opening-day soiree," I admitted. "She was happy about Andrew's work emergency and way too happy to see Marc."

"Why didn't you say something?"

"It's her business, not mine. Does she tell you that you shouldn't marry Brandon because he's a yawning bore?"

Victoria said nothing.

I'm not one of those telepathic souls who can tell shocked from stunned silence on the other end of a phone connection. Or maybe Vic was pissed. If I were her, I would be.

"Not everyone needs their *kicks*," Victoria finally responded.

"Wild oats are healthy. Whole grains and all that," I said. "Cut the kid some slack. We can't all keep our white stockings clean like you."

I didn't know why I was being mean. I knew I'd regret it in a bit—Victoria is a good person. I was just so tired of living as if we were all conjoined like Siamese twins.

"White stockings?"

"You know. Like good little girls wore back in the Victorian age, with their black Mary Janes and their starched pinafores. Because that's the way Dad treats us. He found us suitable men and expects us to obediently marry them. That worked really well for him, huh? Marrying Kathryn the Appropriate?"

I stunned myself with that bout of verbal diarrhea. Guess my resentment hadn't dissipated at all. It had merely burrowed beneath my shame.

"Not that I'm bitter," I joked, but that fell flat too. Especially since I was still bitter and hadn't even known it. Any second I was going to burst into tears. Large, loud, inconsolable sobs.

Maybe if I'd been able to cry seven years ago, I would have worked at the church camp instead of for the Crowns.

I needed to smooth over things with Victoria. "My meeting didn't go so well, my dinner was inedible, and I am really not in a tolerant mood. Leave Lexi and Marc alone. They'll sort themselves out."

"You think I'm making a mistake by marrying Brandon?"

What the—

"That's what you're saying. You're saying that I'm only marrying Brandon to suck up to Dad."

"Um, Vic? This isn't about you. Is it?"

"Why am I always the one who has to toe the line?"

"You don't want to marry Brandon Cummings?" Maybe Mom was in heaven watching out for us and answering my prayers. "If you're having second thoughts, now is the time to do something about it."

"Who said anything about second thoughts?" She sounded as if she were crying. "It's just that Dad expects so much from me. I didn't become an accountant so I could front Dad's charity. I expected to be working in the corporate office, not the nonprofit division."

Her attitude shocked me. I loved and missed my mother so intensely I couldn't imagine *not* working for the foundation. Of course, I wouldn't want to do Victoria's job. Too much responsibility. I was the one who took afternoons off to go to ball games.

"I'm sorry you're not happy," I said. "But you're the only one who can change that. If that means not doing what Dad expects, then that's what you have to do. I think that's what Alexandra is doing. Her life, her terms."

And probably what I should be doing.

"As if I'd take advice from you." Victoria's tone was stilted.

"I'm not the one complaining about my life."

There was silence again. My phone signaled another incoming call.

"I have to go. Can we talk in the morning?"

"Sure."

I thought I heard a sniffle again. "Good night, Vic. Love you," I said.

"Love you too." But she sounded reluctant.

My phone beeped a message. I was glad the call had rolled into voice mail, because the incoming call was from Win. And I needed to rethink Win before I spoke to him again.

Chapter Seven

T he Saltboilers came home five days later. Five days of dodging my family. And working with my sister didn't make that an easy thing. Fortunately, we were busy getting ready for the gala.

Alexandra buried herself in finals and writing her novel. I figured her involvement with Marc was just research. I envied her nerve. I'd never had that kind of courage, not even in Cortland. Cortland had been craziness.

I had more important things to mull than my sisters' love lives. Things like Winslow Winthrop Winston the Whatever. And Chandler.

Chandler was a nice enough person, but there was no attraction between us. Yet it seemed since Win's arrival, Chandler wanted a bigger piece of my time. Syracuse's cultural season and baseball season overlap in April, and Chandler suddenly seemed to have tickets for everything: opera, symphony, theater. None of these activities tempted me. Nor did I invite Chandler to share baseball with me.

Baseball was for Win.

Win awakened emotions in me that I thought were so dormant as to be dead.

Why not? I thought. I knew how to protect myself these days. My motivations were completely different than they'd been seven years earlier. I was no longer a raw nerve.

If my baby sister had the courage to reach for what she wanted, why couldn't I? What was Dad going to do? Write me out of the will? That had probably happened when Matthew was born.

I knew the score with Win: he was temporary.

The day I stopped lying to myself about Win was the same day he was scheduled to pitch the first game of the next home stand. After rebuffing his last couple of attempts to see me, I knew the next move had to be mine.

The evening was warm. Very springlike. Leaves were starting to be visible on the trees between the stadium fence and Onondaga Creek. Puffy white clouds littered the sky like crumpled batting gloves.

I headed to the ballpark early, driving myself and fighting increased traffic. Every time Win was scheduled to pitch, the size of the crowd swelled, which disgusted me. I was a fan of the game, not the celebrity.

I bought a hot dog, then went to the third-base stands to watch the pitchers throw. The bull pens at Saltboiler Stadium were in the open, so fans could see what was going on.

Win saw me right away and seemed surprised. I hadn't returned his phone message or his text, and he hadn't tried to contact me again.

I stayed until it was time for the National Anthem, at which point I went to my seat.

Marc was waiting for me with a beer.

"Hello, persona non grata," I greeted him as I took the proffered cup from him. I plopped into my seat and wished him away.

"I take it you've heard." He sounded glum.

"Oh yeah." I sipped my beer. Moonsinger. Marc was good.

"I've been banished from the box."

Oh crap. I did not want Marc loitering in my extra seat lest Win see him and mistake him for a Blandroid.

"Didn't you buy a ticket to get in?" I asked, hoping he'd take the hint. Where was a baseball bat flying into the stands when one was needed?

"Yeah, but it's for general admission, and it's standing room only up there because Win Winston is pitching."

Not my problem. I had the second seat for my comfort and my convenience, not for freeloaders.

"If it's any consolation, I told Victoria that whatever is going on between you and Alexandra is no one's business but yours."

His mouth thinned, and a knot in his jaw throbbed. He jerked his head in acknowledgment. Then he sprawled as if he planned to stay.

Not good. Why did this have to happen the night I finally decided to give Win a chance? I didn't want the aggravation of company. "Marc, you can't stay here."

"C'mon, Caroline." Now he sounded wheedling, petulant. Even Matthew had better manners.

Then Win came onto the mound and started his warm-up. I sat up, blocking out everything except that long, lean body in motion.

The first batter stepped to the plate.

Usually by this point, the ushers had rid the aisle next to me of autograph seekers, but Marc was still there.

Win struck out the first batter, and I started clapping.

"So it's like that," Marc murmured.

I sank back in my seat. "Marc, either haul your butt out of my seat, or I will find an usher to haul it for you."

I didn't want someone spying on my every reaction to Win's game.

"What is going on with you and the pitcher?"

"I'm trying to watch him pitch. Leave."

Win hit the next batter on his second throw. The rest of the inning didn't go much smoother, but Win managed to get out of it with no damage to the scoreboard.

I ached as though I'd been pitching right along with him.

And Marc was still next to me.

I stood, stretched, and looked for an usher. "Last warning."

Marc laughed.

So I sauntered up the steps to where an usher lazed against the railing, chatting with a fan. I glanced back at my seats. The sun glinted off Marc's fair hair. I interrupted the conversation, explained my dilemma to the usher, who looked annoyed at being asked to do his job, and watched with nasty satisfaction as the usher asked to see Marc's ticket.

I ignored the laser glare Marc aimed at me as he left the section. Everyone thought I was a pushover because I never shoved back when they nudged me. No more.

I finally had space to breathe and privacy to watch Win with all the emotions inside me unleashed. The way I'd watched him pitch for the Crowns all those years ago.

He wasn't having a good game.

They pulled him in the fourth inning. Too many pitches. Plus they didn't want him batting. At this level of baseball, the pitchers batted if neither affiliate's parent team used a designated hitter. If at least one team was DH-friendly, the teams could opt to use one. I was surprised they'd started Win against Indianapolis. Someone in rehab from Tommy John surgery didn't need to be swinging a bat.

I stayed until the end. After Win left the game, I watched him hanging on the railing of the dugout, intent on the action. A loss would be a bitter blow.

I texted him at the end of the game. *Going home. Grilling chicken. Hungry?*

I'd picked up a couple of boneless breasts to toss on the countertop grill so he could get his protein meal after the game.

He texted back a terse, *OK.*

Every inch of me tingled.

Unfortunately, I ran into my father in the parking lot. He was alone. Too late for Matthew on a school night, and Marc had been banished.

"Caroline," he barked. "What were you doing with Marc? I suppose you're taking your sister's side in this nonsense."

I rolled my eyes, but it was dark and the gesture was lost on my father. "Frankly, Dad, I haven't given it a thought except when someone else brings it up. I do have a life of my own, you know."

"Mooning over Winston? I saw you at the game in Scranton. You were right there, big as life in your team jacket, on TV."

TV? The game had been televised in Syracuse?

"I don't know who you were trying to fool in that getup, but Scranton fans don't cheer for Gems—or Saltboilers—pitchers. He's going back to Columbia soon. Back on the road until October."

As if I this was news to me. "If I don't have a problem, why should you?"

"I don't want to see you hurt." That's what fathers were supposed to say, so he said it.

I didn't believe him.

"Is that why you're pushing Chandler at me? I would think you'd be excited that I was seeing a baseball player."

"Baseball players don't make good husbands."

"I appreciate your concern, but I'm not looking for a husband." I sighed and turned to find my car in the general lot.

"Just how well do you know Winston?"

"I don't," I admitted. "I met him in Cortland, and I used him as a boy toy. Every horrible thing you're thinking is true."

His thoughts would be G-rated compared to the reality.

The bus rumbled by, belching diesel fumes. I sighed again and wished I hadn't driven to the stadium that evening. I could have simply hopped on the bus and escaped instead of standing there defending the indefensible.

"I love you, Dad," I said as much to remind myself as to defuse him. "But that doesn't give you the right to censor my relationships. Have a nice evening."

I barely made it through my door before my intercom buzzed. Win, I thought. Gooey warmth oozed through me.

"Yes?" I practically chirped into the speaker.

"Caroline?" Warbling female voice. Sniffling.

Alexandra.

"Oh crap!" I said to my terrarium, but I buzzed open the door so she could come up. "What's wrong, honey?" I asked when she stumbled into my living room.

Red rimmed her green eyes and tinted her nose. Black mascara smeared her cheeks.

"Dad's cutting off my living allowance. He's punishing me just because he doesn't want me in love with Marc." Her words ran together. "Did you know I'm in love with Marc? Andrew is so boring, and Marc is really not boring, and sexy and smart—"

"And your step-uncle and Dad's brother-in-law," I interrupted. "How much have you had to drink, Lexi Lou?"

"I'm over twenty-one." She sniffled again and dropped onto my sofa.

I could have gotten ripped off the fumes. Oh boy. No way could I let her drive home.

Why tonight?

"I know how old you are," I said. "I want to know how much you've had to drink, but I guess it doesn't matter. You're drunk."

"I'm drunk," she agreed. "I'm staying with you tonight."

This was one of the major drawbacks living in Armory Square. It was too easy for inebriated friends and family to decide my place was their crash site.

"I love Marc," Alexandra repeated. "You gave me the courage to be in love with him. You inspired me."

"I'm flattered, but I haven't gotten drunk in years," I told her. I didn't think I'd ever been drunk the way she was that night. "Don't blame me for your current condition."

"Lovelorn?" Alexandra hiccuped. "Bereft?"

"Drunk," I said.

She shrugged as if it were of no consequence. In her mind, it probably wasn't. It would never occur to her that the apartment was my private property. That I might have other plans. That I had a personal life.

She only wanted to wallow in her creative misery.

Lovelorn indeed. What did she know about it, really?

Love was *hard*. More difficult than any other emotion, more difficult than anything else a person had to do in a lifetime.

I'd loved Win once upon a time. Maybe. For a couple of weeks.

The realization sucker punched me. Especially the part where I admitted I might have residual feelings for him. It wasn't all about sex. Since he'd emerged from the smelly closet in the drab motor-court room in Cortland, there'd been a connection to him.

I still craved him. I desperately needed what he offered. Not sex but sanctuary. All this time, I hadn't realized it was also love.

Except he'd abandoned me when I'd really needed him. Maybe the yawning emptiness wouldn't have been so vast if I'd been able to share my agony with him. Being with him now made it so easy to forget that devastation. Tonight, I wanted to forget it.

"Shall I call Marc to come and get you?" I offered.

Alexandra burst into tears. God save us all from unhappy drunks. "He thinks we should *cool* it until Daddy gets used to the idea. How can I cool it when he makes me so hot? Marc, I mean. Not Daddy."

"Too much information," I said.

"You'd think Daddy would understand, what with him and Polly."

"I have a date." I handed her a box of tissues.

"You're seeing Chandler when you've got a hunky pitcher after you?"

"The hunky pitcher is going back to the majors soon, but no, Win is coming here for dinner tonight."

"And I ruined it!" Alexandra wailed. She pulled a fistful of tissues from the box and buried her face in them. "I'll just go into your bedroom and pass out. You guys can use the sofa."

"Thanks." My sarcasm went over her head.

"I love you, Caroline," Alexandra said.

"I love you too. Do you need help getting to the bedroom?"

She shook her head and then lunged to her feet, teetering on too-high heels before stumbling toward my room.

I'd just finished slicing a cucumber into a bowl of greens when the intercom sounded again.

Win. Finally. I met him at the top of the stairs with a kiss.

"Well," he said a moment later as he took off his jacket. "I don't know what that was about, but I like it."

He followed me into the kitchen and helped himself to a bottle of water from my refrigerator. He sat at the table and watched me putter.

"Remember how you used to make tomato soup and grilled cheese sandwiches for our lunch?"

I'd forgotten, but his words brought back a rush of memories. Toasted cheese sandwiches and tomato soup were about all I could cook back then.

"Things haven't improved much," I said as I served the chicken. I mean, grilled chicken and bagged salad would never land me on the Cooking Network.

He dished salad into his bowl. "So who was the guy sitting with you during the first couple of innings?"

"Marc. My stepmother's brother. You probably met him at Dad's opening-day party."

"Why was he sitting with you?"

I had to tell him the truth. "There's a little bit of a family to-do going on. My younger sister and Marc have gotten...involved. Intimately. My father caught them in what I gather was a compromising situation."

"Naked and in bed?"

"That's what I heard thirdhand. So Dad won't let Marc sit in his box anymore. Marc thought he could mooch a better seat off me. He's the type of guy who loathes the unwashed masses in general admission."

"Sounds like an asshole," Win said. He cut into his chicken breast.

"He's really not, and he's probably better for Alexandra than Andrew—her Blandroid. He told Lexi they should cool it for a while. She's not taking it well." The chicken tasted just right. I was pleased.

"So how upset is your sister?"

"She showed up here tonight."

He stopped chewing.

"Drunk."

He laid his knife and fork across his plate.

"She's passed out in my bed."

Win's dark gaze never left me.

"That's not what I'd planned for the evening when I invited you over," I said and then laughed shakily, trying to disguise my discomfort. Then I added in a voice so soft I barely heard myself, "I'm sorry. I couldn't let her drive home. I'm as disappointed as I hope you are."

"Do you need to stay here with her?"

I shook my head. Yeah, it was late, and yeah, I had to be at work in the morning, but if Win and I were going to...reconnect, then I needed to adjust my schedule. His needs, in this instant, took precedence over mine.

He exhaled heavily as if he'd been holding his breath. His focused on his meal. When he finished eating, he pushed away from the table and carried his plate and silverware to the sink.

"You don't have to do that," I said as he rinsed his dishes and then put them in the dishwasher.

"I want to get us out of here," he muttered. "I want to get you alone."

He cleared my place while I shoved the leftovers in the fridge.

I took one last peek at Alexandra before turning off all the lights except the bedside lamp and a night-light in the bathroom.

Win waited by the door for me with my jacket in his hand.

"Where to?" he asked as I locked the door. "My place?"

I led the way down the stairs. "No." I had a real problem with going to his place. "Let's find a hotel. I'll pay."

"What's wrong with my place?"

"Too many closets," I said.

He didn't argue. "Then you choose the hotel, and I'll pay."

He drove toward the spot on Seventh North Street where I-81 and I-90 cross. A mushroom bed of hotels and motels.

"Pick," he grumbled.

If I selected the venue, then he couldn't be blamed for anyone hiding in a closet. I settled on an inn that wasn't part of a national chain, and that had a decent restaurant in it.

As soon as Win keyed us into our room, he pressed me against the wall and kissed me.

Our mouths fused as he struggled with my jacket, and I returned the courtesy. We left them on the floor where they dropped.

Win finally just scooped me up as if I were no more than a dust bunny who'd escaped housekeeping's vacuum, and carried me to the bed. All pretense of finesse disappeared.

He fumbled with the zipper on my jeans, and I did the same to his. He managed to get one leg off me and then yanked down his own jeans.

"Protection," I croaked. I'd purchased a box of condoms earlier in the day. They were in my purse. But Win wasn't without his own and, cursing all the while, freed a condom from his wallet and quickly rolled it on.

Then I was on my back, legs spread. He plunged and entered me.

The shock of him filled me. His mouth came down on mine again. I couldn't breathe. I'd been faithful to Win, and I wasn't quite ready for the reality of him. But he didn't seem to notice. He thrust so hard the bed squawked in protest. All I could do was grasp his shoulders and hang on for the ride.

After a moment, Win tensed and shuddered. I could feel his penis twitch deep inside me.

Win collapsed, his breath hot against my neck and air rasping in and out of his lungs as if he'd just run ten miles in under a minute.

I tried not to cry. I should have known better than to expect my memories to live up to reality.

Eventually Win's breathing slowed. He raised himself on his elbows and looked down at me. "Sorry. I've been crazy since I came to Syracuse and saw you sitting in that restaurant." He slowly withdrew his softening penis. "I'll be right back." He planted a kiss on my forehead.

I didn't know what to do while he was in the bathroom. Did I get dressed, or did I remove the rest of my clothing? I would have known what to do with the old Win.

I heard the toilet flush.

This dithering was ridiculous. I'd come to a hotel with Win to be naked and in bed. Why was I acting like an adolescent caught doing something forbidden?

I finished removing my clothes, leaving everything in a heap beside the bed, then crawled under the covers.

"Hey there," Win said, emerging from the bathroom. He'd shed his clothes too. "I didn't dream you."

I stared. He was magnificent. There is no other way to describe his long, lean body. His shoulders were broader now than they'd been seven years ago, and more dark, silky hair covered his chest. His upper body was fuller. His thighs were bigger too. Pitchers run a lot to keep their leg muscles in shape. His penis, though, looked the same. Still thick, still long, still jutting almost purple from a nest of crinkled hair.

"Sorry about that," he said, sinking onto the bed next to me. "I've been waiting so long I went a little crazy." His pinkie finger wandered down the slope of my breast.

My nipples puckered as if to say, *Hello? Attention please!*

"I think I've improved over the years, not regressed to adolescence. And now I'm going to prove it to you." The skin around the corners of his dark eyes folded into squint laugh lines. "Better than old times. I promise."

I loved that he realized I hadn't climaxed, and felt bad about it. I was more than ready for make-up time. More than ready to head back to those few short weeks between Flash's departure and Win being called up to Double A. The best weeks of my entire life.

"You have the prettiest breasts I have ever seen," he said. "They're even prettier than I remember them."

His tanned hands, shadowed by the dark hair on their backs, contrasted against the paleness of my skin. He cupped my breasts, pressing the nipples between his thumbs and forefingers.

Little stabs of pleasure shot straight to my groin.

"You still like that," he said.

"How do you remember?" I whispered.

"I remember everything about you." He lowered his mouth, gently brushed his lips to mine.

I didn't believe him. My heart couldn't afford to put any credence in words that so easily fell from his mouth. Besides, guys don't remember things like that.

His mouth forged a trail along my jaw and down the side of my neck as his hands continued to tease my breasts.

This is what I remembered. The breathless anticipation of Win's hands and mouth on me. The way he knew exactly how to touch just when I needed to be touched. Sometimes it had felt as if we'd shared one body. That's how connected we'd been. He knew what felt right to me because it felt right to him.

When his tongue traced the contours of my left nipple, I arched toward the source of so much pleasure. I barely noticed his calloused palm gliding down my belly. When one finger burrowed deep and found my clitoris, I sighed with contentment. It had been so long since anyone besides me had bothered to see if it still functioned.

I was close, so close. I tensed when Win's mouth left my breast and kissed a trail down my torso, pausing ever so briefly to rim my navel.

His hands cupped my bottom, and he lifted me to his mouth. And just like that, I climaxed. But that didn't stop Win. His tongue explored places I'd forgotten I had. Relentlessly. Another orgasm shuddered through me before I even realized it had been sneaking up on me.

Win nipped the insides of my thighs and then heaved himself onto the bed next to me. His lean, lithe length stretched out like a burning oak tree.

"You taste the same. Better," he said.

I rolled until I could bury my face against his chest. He smelled the same, only better. More.

He retrieved another condom, rolled it on, and then lifted me over him.

"Your elbow," I protested. I could see the silver lines of scars where they'd done the surgery.

"You weigh next to nothing. Still," he said.

I reached between us, made an adjustment to the angle of his penis, and slowly, carefully sank onto his erection. Oh, it felt good. Like home.

His breath whistled between his teeth as he sharply inhaled. "Carrie," he groaned. He grasped my hips, fingers digging into my soft flesh. He helped me find my rhythm, and this time, I could feel every millimeter of his length inside. No pain. Just the intensity of Win. He curled up until he caught the tip of one of my breasts in his mouth and pulled deeply. My uterus contracted.

The dim light from the bedside lamp cast shadows across his face. I wanted to see him and leaned back so that he had to release my breast. His head fell to the pillow. His eyes were closed, his mouth open, and his expression seemed happy. My thighs burned. I hadn't had a workout like this since I could remember.

Win abruptly sat up. My legs locked around his waist, pulling him even deeper inside me. My breasts squashed nearly flat against his chest.

"Carrie." My name was like a sigh on his lips.

"Hmm?" I asked.

"Nothing," he murmured. "Just...Carrie."

And it was enough. For that moment. I couldn't think beyond the hotel room, beyond this early-morning tryst. My everyday life, my boring status quo faded into insignificance as Win rocked into me.

Then I was on my back again, and Win was heaving over me. He draped my legs over his shoulders, searching for total penetration. I felt the tip of his penis hit my uterus and winced.

"Sorry," he muttered and eased back a bit.

I buried my face in the crook of his neck. His skin was slick and tangy with perspiration. Yeah, I licked him. I kissed him, I nibbled on the cords to his shoulder.

He reached between us, and I tensed. I was tender, sore, and trying to get back into the swing of things after a long absence.

"It's okay," he whispered. "I promise, I'll make it okay."

And he did.

We didn't get much sleep that night. We had seven years of catch-up to do. By seven the next morning, I was so sore I could barely move. Muscles that hadn't been used since my Cortland days complained.

I awoke from the semi-doze, semi-comatose state into which Win had plunged me and winced as I tried to stretch.

"Morning," Win muttered.

"Yeah, I guess," I replied. My face heated. It was silly to be embarrassed about what we'd done. It wasn't like we were strangers or anything. Still, I was nearly as emotionally ill at ease as I was physically uncomfortable.

Win planted a kiss on my naked shoulder. "I guess we need to get going. I need to get to the stadium, get in my workout. Stuff like that."

I nodded. I knew he wasn't just feeding me a line. Pitchers are busy even on their off days. It takes a lot to stay in shape.

"Are you all right?" he asked.

I nodded, not trusting my voice. I wanted everything from him I wasn't willing to give back to him.

"This wasn't a one-night stand," he said. "And I'm not going to sneak in and out of hotel rooms."

"How can our relationship be anything but temporary again?" I asked, tears catching on a ragged edge in my voice. "You're a short-termer, Winston.

One day you'll be pitching an inning, and you'll get the call, and you won't even finish the game."

"Then come with me," he said. His huge palm cupped my cheek.

I shook my head. "I'm not a camp follower. I can't just pack up my life and follow you wherever your career takes you."

"Other women do it."

"I'm not other women, Win. If anyone knows that, it should be you."

He closed his eyes and exhaled. "I'm not going to sneak around while we're together. I want everyone to know we're a couple."

"Fair enough," I said. "I don't want to be treated like a dirty secret either."

"So we'll get together tonight after the game, right?" His thumb massaged the outer corner of my eye.

I nodded.

He kissed my forehead and then rolled out of bed.

I saw the scars on his left hamstring where the surgeons had removed the tendon used to replace the ulnar collateral ligament in his elbow. My fingers had traced that scar during the night, memorizing its contours to add to my emotional catalog of all things Win.

He swatted my flank and said, "Let's shower together."

So we did. We used to shower together all the time. The only difference was now Win was older, and I'd worn him out. Not that I could have handled another round with him.

Win was lathering my torso with a bar of generic hotel soap when he found my scar. "This is new," he said, tracing the small line down the right side of my abdomen.

I'd forgotten there were physical reminders of some very bad times in my life.

"Appendicitis?" he asked.

I forced a smile.

The rest of our morning together was uneventful. We chatted about nothing, about everything trivial over breakfast, and then Win drove me home. He kissed me. "Tonight, after the game. Meet me in the stadium office lobby."

Chapter Eight

I opened the door to my apartment. Something smelled wrong. Off.

Oh yeah. Alexandra was sleeping off her drunk in my bed.

The apartment was so silent I could hear the desk clock in the corner of the living room ticking and the hum of the refrigerator. The rooms felt empty. "Lexi?"

She wasn't in the bedroom. That was a good sign. Maybe she'd awakened and gone home.

But what was that odor? I checked my desk to see if she'd written me a note, but everything appeared just as I'd left it, as did everything in the kitchen.

The bathroom, however, was a different story.

Alexandra lay in a pale heap next to the tub. And there was blood, so much blood. Everywhere.

I screamed and raced to her side, kneeling in blood as I groped for her wrist. But the slices in the fragile skin were too raw for me to touch, so I fumbled under her matted hair for a pulse in her neck. There. Barely.

Where was my phone? In my purse, but what had I done with it? It was on the small table near the front door where I always kept it. Thank goodness for my need for order.

My shaky, sticky fingers somehow dialed 911. My voice was even shakier as I tried to be coherent enough to get an ambulance to my apartment.

Immediately. And I was crying. Sobbing. Trying to breathe with lungs that didn't want to cooperate.

After I finished with the operator, my next instinct was to call Win, because I needed his strength. But Win wasn't mine to call. And Victoria. I needed to let Victoria know I'd be late for work.

The emergency operator wouldn't let me off the phone.

"I need to help my sister," I sobbed. I put the phone on speaker and knelt next to Alexandra. I was terrified I'd inflict more damage. What if I only made things worse?

My intercom buzzed, and the operator told me I needed to open the door. Right. The door.

Sirens shrieked in the distance. I left my baby sister lying on my bathroom floor in her blood while I opened the door and watched a uniformed police officer scurry up my narrow stairs. Once he verified he was on the scene, the operator disconnected my call.

"Hurry," I said, hoping the officer could do something to help. "She's in the bathroom. That way."

"Are you okay?"

That's when I realized Alexandra's blood was on my hands and on the knees of my jeans.

The officer checked the bathroom and then returned looking nearly as pale as Alexandra.

"You have to help her!" I shouted at him. "Do something!"

"Do you have any clean towels? We need to keep pressure on her wounds until the EMTs arrive."

I didn't want to wait for anyone. I wanted someone to make my sister better. Whole. Now.

I probably should have called my father at that point, but it was his fault she'd been so drunk, so upset the night before.

And it was my fault for leaving her alone when I knew she was drunk and upset. And I didn't even want to think the word *suicide*, because suicide was illegal, and I didn't want the police to arrest Alexandra. I wanted them to help her.

I called Victoria instead. "Lexi's hurt. We're at my place."

Victoria must have run the twelve blocks from the office to my apartment, because she arrived just ahead of the EMTs. They followed her up the stairs. The police officer, however, wouldn't let Victoria into the bathroom so she could see what I meant when I said Alexandra was hurt.

That would be my memory and mine alone.

"What was she doing here?" Victoria asked, tears dissolving her mascara and creating coal-like tracks down her cheeks.

"She was upset with Dad," I explained. "He threatened to cut off her living allowance if she continued to see Marc."

Victoria's green eyes grew very round. "What happened?"

I motioned for her to come closer. The police officer was staring at me as if he knew this was my fault. That I'd abandoned my baby sister in order to fuck a baseball player.

The static-filled EMT radio and all the jargon as the medics worked on Alexandra distracted me.

Victoria started to hug me but stopped. "Is that her blood?"

I nodded. "I found her in the bathroom this morning. I think she cut her wrists."

"Oh!" Victoria's hand flew to her mouth, as if the frail barrier of her fingers could prevent further words. Maplethorpes don't react. Stiff upper lip and such.

"Why didn't you stop her?"

"I wasn't here," I said. Guilt pounded in my chest like a sledgehammer. "She showed up last night, drunk. Not suicidal. I swear."

There. I'd said it aloud. Maplethorpes didn't do things like commit suicide in such messy, obvious ways.

"I never would have left her alone had I thought for even a second she would do something like this." My entire body shuddered as I tried to contain my sobs. "She passed out in my bed."

Letting a drunk sister sleep it off in one's bed is the sort of thing good sisters did. Good sisters didn't cut their wrists in other sisters' bathrooms.

"Where were you?" Victoria asked.

"I had a date."

"After the game? Dad said he saw you there."

I nodded. "With Win." I never would have left her to be with Chandler.

"You left Lexi alone so you could be with Win?"

"How was I supposed to know she'd do something like this?"

I should have known.

I replayed our conversation in my mind. Granted, I'd been distracted by thoughts of the upcoming evening with Win, but... "I swear, she wasn't depressed or anything like that. I mean, she was crying because Marc broke things off with her, but I swear, honest to God, Vic, she wasn't depressed. She was drunk."

The police officer approached us. "What's your relationship to the victim?" he asked. "Do you know her next of kin?"

Victoria replied. She was older and seemed more in control. Of course, she hadn't *seen* Alexandra covered in blood on my bathroom floor. Hadn't touched her cool flesh. Hadn't struggled to find a pulse.

"Her name is Alexandra Maplethorpe. We're her sisters."

"What about her parents?" The cop had clearly recognized the surname. That was one of the problems being a Maplethorpe.

Victoria and I exchanged a glance, and then she offered to call Dad.

"No. Alexandra is over eighteen," I said. "And there are HIPAA laws."

Victoria jerked, and the cop turned his penetrating blue stare to me.

"You can't tell Dad what happened." My voice shook.

"Caroline," Victoria said in a warning tone.

"It's true," I insisted. Patient-privacy laws worked. I'd proved it.

Victoria's brow furrowed and then smoothed as she turned back to the officer. "We're her next of kin."

Something in my chest eased. With Victoria's calm and my devious brain, we'd figure out a way to protect Alexandra.

"Why don't you two sit," the cop suggested. "You don't look very steady." He was talking to me. Probably because my legs were shaking.

Both Victoria and I sank onto my sofa. I plucked my blood-soaked jeans away from my skin.

The officer pulled out a notebook. "What happened?"

I told him that it was my apartment and how Alexandra had shown up drunk the previous evening. How she'd passed out in my bed, and so I'd left with my boyfriend.

Boyfriend. Like Win Winston was mine. But I glossed over that part, skipping to how I'd come home to get ready for work and found her. In my bathroom. Bloody.

Victoria clutched my sticky fingers. Every once in a while I heard a whimper like a kicked dog and realized I was making that awful sound.

It seemed like we sat there forever. I was cold, so cold. My hands felt like they'd been plunged into a snowbank. My teeth would have chattered if I hadn't clenched my jaw.

Finally the EMTs emerged from my bathroom with Alexandra on a gurney. She was nearly as white as the sheets and so very, very still.

Victoria practically crushed my fingers in hers as we watched the EMTs maneuver the gurney down the narrow, steep stairs.

"Where are they taking her?" Victoria had the presence of mind to ask.

"Upstate," one of the EMTs replied.

"I'll drive," Victoria said to me.

I nodded.

She looked at my soiled jeans. "Maybe you should clean up."

"I can't use my bathroom," I whispered.

"Get some clean clothes. You can shower at my place."

I'd showered once that morning with Win. But Victoria was right: I needed to wash off Alexandra's blood. Lady Macbeth and all that.

"The family of Alexandra Maplethorpe?" a white-coated, dark-haired woman called from the door. We'd been waiting in the ER for hours.

Victoria winced. She didn't like the Maplethorpe name being bandied about in a public venue.

There was no privacy in a hospital emergency room. Everything was public. HIPAA laws be damned.

"How is she?" Victoria asked in her hushed, professional, let's-not-be-obvious voice.

"She's holding her own. We needed to transfuse her, but she seems to be stable."

I closed my eyes and whispered a prayer of thanksgiving. I'm not particularly religious, but I figured God wouldn't mind a thank-you.

"When can we see her?" Victoria asked.

The doctor gave some noncommittal answer and then started talking about psychiatric stuff.

Alexandra wasn't crazy, I wanted to shriek. She was just drunk.

Evaluation, we were told. Our choice: hospital or psychiatric center.

"We need to call Dad," Victoria whispered.

"Private psychiatric hospital," I told the doctor.

"Caroline, we can't just—"

"Yes, we can," I interrupted. "He doesn't love her unconditionally, but only when she toes his line. Well, his line is what put her here."

Victoria had never been so fed up with Dad that she just wanted to leave the whole family behind. Granted, my method at eighteen had been a lot more subtle than Alexandra's way, but the motivation was the same.

I wouldn't call Marc either.

I didn't know Marc well. Never wanted to. I tolerated him at family gatherings because he didn't seem to enjoy his mother's company any more than my sisters or I did. But he, his mother, and even Polly made my sisters and me outcasts at our father's table. And Marc certainly hadn't talked to me about Alexandra at the game. His focus had been on how my father's ire had inconvenienced him by banishing him to general admission.

It seemed to take forever to transfer Alexandra from the hospital to a private psychiatric facility—checking on bed availability and whatever else needed doing. And then Victoria and I wanted to see her. We weren't allowed much time.

At first, she wouldn't look at us. Especially me. Then Victoria started crying again, and when Victoria cries, it really means something.

"I'm sorry," Alexandra whispered. Her face was nearly translucent. Deep circles the color of day-old bruises shadowed the contours of her eye sockets. "I didn't mean to cause so much trouble."

Since I'd had time to calmly consider the circumstances, I didn't think she'd meant to kill herself. I thought it was more like an attempt to manipulate Dad.

"You were drunk," I said. Any other excuse was unthinkable.

"Doesn't matter." Her voice was hoarse, a harsh rasp that slashed through me like screams on a midnight street. "I knew what I was doing."

I reached for her hand. Her wrists were bandaged and outside the white blanket. Her fingers were cold as icicles and limp as slush. I tried to tell myself this was just her poor misunderstood artist-in-the-attic routine carried a bit too far. I needed to believe she hadn't really wanted to die.

"I was lying in your bed thinking about how Dad dictated who I could date, what I can do, where I can go to college, what I can study, and I realized there's no getting away from him. You both are still under his thumb. I don't want to live like that."

Did she really see me as one of Dad's puppets?

Victoria sniffled, then dabbed her nose with a tissue. "There are other ways to break free without killing yourself."

"How would you know?" Alexandra's tone was as cold as her fingers.

Victoria flinched.

Suddenly, I didn't want to be there in the sad little room. If Alexandra felt she would rather be dead than turn into me or Victoria, then we needed to leave her to the professionals.

Someday, maybe I'd tell her the truth of how I'd really met Win Winston. Maybe she wouldn't see me as such a meek wuss if she knew the sordid details of my past.

Yet in the end, I had bent to my father's wishes. Maybe she had a point.

My weariness caught up to me. I hadn't slept much the night before, and now I had to go home and scrub my bathroom.

A few moments later, a doctor came in and asked to see Victoria and me in his office. We learned that we couldn't visit her during the seventy-two-hour evaluation period.

"Can we stop at a supermarket before dropping me off?" I asked as we walked to Victoria's car. "I need to buy bleach. My bathroom..."

I couldn't finish the sentence.

"Sure." She sounded listless. "We need to call Dad."

Now that Alexandra was safely committed for seventy-two hours and Dad couldn't bully his way into the psychiatric hospital, we could let him know what had happened.

"Okay," I agreed. "You want to do it, or shall I?"

"You're the one who wanted to wait. I'll leave that honor to you."

I checked the dashboard clock. Six fifteen. The entire day was gone. No wonder it seemed like we'd spent hours in the emergency room. We had.

"He's probably at the stadium now. I'll call him after the game."

After the game. Oh crap. I was supposed to meet Win in the stadium lobby after the game. Except there was no way I could do that now. Especially after I told my father what Alexandra had done.

Armed with a case of bleach wipes, I tackled my bathroom. I was so weary I could hardly move. The shower curtain went into the trash. That was the easy part. Then I was on my hands and knees, scouring away the blood. The small white tiles of my bathroom floor had long ago lost their glaze, which made cleaning the soaked-in blood even more difficult.

I turned on the radio and listened to the game while I scrubbed.

Once I'd freed the bathroom of Alexandra's blood, I turned off all but one dim lamp and collapsed on the sofa. Big mistake.

I awoke to my intercom buzzing. Damn, I thought as I stumbled across the room. "Who is it?" My voice barely worked.

"Win."

Right. I'd meant to call Dad and text Win.

"Your father," a second male growled.

How had that happened?

I buzzed them in, then opened the door at the top of the stairs. Win came first, my father close behind.

The last thing I needed was a three-ring circus, but the ringmaster had arrived. And the elephant was almost in the room.

"Why did Victoria tell me to come see you?" my father asked once he hit the top of the stairs.

"Maybe you'd better sit down, Dad." I honestly had no clue how to say what needed to be said. And I certainly didn't want to blurt out family business in front of Win. "Win, will you excuse us for a minute?"

"You stood me up, and you didn't answer your phone."

I'd turned it off in the hospital and had forgotten to turn it on again. "I'm sorry." I couldn't read his expression in the dim light. "There was a family issue."

"What family issue?" Dad asked.

Win moved until he stood behind me, almost as if he were my second in my duel with my father. Heat radiated off his body and warmed me.

"Alexandra," I said. My logy brain couldn't wrap around tact. "She's pretty upset with you for separating her and Marc."

"I came over here to listen to this female clatter trap?" Dad snarled.

"No, you came over here because Victoria is too chicken to tell you that Alexandra tried to kill herself. I found her in my bathroom this morning."

Win made a sound deep in his throat and moved closer to me.

Dad waved his hand as if he didn't believe me. "Adolescent hyperbole."

I was tempted to take the garbage can, filled with bleach and bloodstained wipes, and fling it in my father's face. Instead, I clenched my fists.

"Right. That's why I just spent three hours wiping up her blood from my bathroom tiles."

Win's hand landed on the small of my back.

"That's why Victoria and I spent all day in the emergency room with her, then had her transferred to Franklin Hall."

"This is preposterous. Why wasn't I notified? I'm her next of kin. You're making this up. You've got just as much drama queen in you as Alexandra does." His words were cruel, but his voice cracked.

I closed my eyes and swayed. If not for the slight pressure of Win's hand, I might have fallen.

He must have understood this because he steered me toward the sofa. One gentle nudge and I collapsed. He sat next to me. Between me and my father. The cold burrowing into my marrow seemed to melt in Win's proximity. He took my hand and twined fingers with me.

"I wouldn't let Victoria call you," I confessed. "I wanted to get Alexandra settled first."

Dad sagged into the closest chair. "Where is she now?"

"Franklin Hall Psychiatric Center. She's there for a seventy-two-hour observation period. No visitors allowed."

"But I'm her father. I should have been notified." Dad deflated, his bluster exhausted. "All I did was tell her that if she continued this ridiculous infatuation with Marc, I wouldn't be paying any more of her bills."

"You don't have the right to tell any of us who we can see or not see. This isn't Victorian England, Dad."

Dad seemed to finally notice Win was there, supporting me, holding my hand. "You mean like you and this ballplayer?"

I wanted to sink into Win's embrace. To borrow a smidgen of his strength, his courage. "You know you're secretly thrilled that Win is here."

"But will he be here next month? Chandler won't want used goods."

Win tensed, but I squeezed his hand. "That's between me and Win."

"I can fire you from your cushy job, you know. I can cut you out of my will."

I thought about all the ways he'd already cut me—and my sisters—from his life. Money meant nothing.

"I wish you would," I replied. "Then maybe we wouldn't have to play all these messed-up games."

There really wasn't anything else to say, so Dad lurched to his feet and left. The door closed with a quiet *snick*. Maplethorpes don't slam doors.

I turned to Win. "I'm sorry. I meant to text you, but I fell asleep."

He twisted us until we faced each other, placed one huge finger under my chin, tilted my face, and then kissed me. Gently. Without the passion that usually accompanied his kisses.

I melted against him. He was as solid as a boulder. I couldn't imagine Chandler in his place. "Is your family this bad?" I asked.

"Nope. Are you okay?"

He was the first person since the police officer that morning to understand that finding my sister in a bloody bathroom might be upsetting.

"Sure," I said, although I really wanted to cry.

"Liar." He pulled me even closer. "I came over here tonight pissed that you stood me up. I'm glad your Dad got here at the same time."

"Me too." I yawned. My catnap hadn't done me much good. "But I'm exhausted. I'm afraid I won't be very good company."

"I'm not here to be entertained. Where's the bedroom?" He stood and scooped me up as if I weighed less than his glove, and held me tightly as if he were afraid a stray draft would blow me away from him.

So I directed him to my bedroom. Then we were on the bed together, and he was lifting my sweater over my head. Unsnapping my jeans and pulling them down my legs.

I was too drained to reciprocate, but he didn't seem to mind. His clothes joined mine in a pile on the floor next to the bed. Then he gathered me into his healing heat and held me. Kissed my forehead and held me. His erection was hot and pressed against my belly, but he simply held me. And that's how I fell asleep.

I overslept. I'd forgotten to set my alarm. Forgotten to turn on my phone. Forgotten about work and the gala with the Saltboilers I was supposed to organize.

I was groggy when I did awaken. Groggy and glued to Win like Polly's acrylics adhered to her nails. He had an erection, and that morning, I was alert enough to appreciate it. I was already late; I could just be later.

He touched me with intent. Lascivious intent. My body delighted in the way his fingers skimmed my flesh. He knew exactly how to caress me and where and the precise amount of pressure. No matter what he did, he was perfect.

When he slid into me gently and carefully, I felt loved. We were making love. How had I ever not known that about our physical relationship before?

When I could think again—drowsy, half-formed thoughts while lying in Win's arms—I remembered the first time he'd kissed me. On the mouth, that is. Flash was gone, and we knew he wouldn't be returning. We were down to being a couple. That's when Win kissed me. His lips had been soft. His touch tentative. Then he'd deepened the connection. His tongue brushed mine, and pleasure tingled through me. I'd never known that merely kissing could be so arousing. I also hadn't realized until the moment he kissed me that he'd never done so before. "Why did you wait until Flash left to kiss me?" I asked.

"What?"

"When we were in Cortland. You never kissed me until Flash left. I've always wondered why."

"Why would I? Until he left, you were his first."

What an odd thing to think. I smiled. "You're wrong, you know. I was never his. I've always been my own."

"It's a guy thing. He found you first. He had you first. When he left, you weren't his anymore."

"Neanderthal," I murmured.

"I told you, I didn't like sharing you with Flash. I understand why you needed me when you were with him. His name says it all." Win's arm tightened around me.

While it was true that I didn't need to supplement Win, I also knew I didn't want to depend on him for anything. I couldn't rely on him.

Having him hold me all night had been wonderful. Cuddling against him comforted me. But he'd left me alone before, the only other time I had really needed him.

His career would always come first. And he had to be that way in order to succeed in the highly competitive world of professional baseball. I understood that. I accepted that.

"I need to get going," I said, pulling away from him.

He let me go. That's the problem with Win. He talked the good talk, but he always let me go.

Chapter Nine

"You're late," Victoria said as I walked into the office. "Why didn't you answer your phone?"

"I forgot to turn it on after we left the hospital." I reached into my purse and pulled out the offending phone. I turned it on and waited for it to do its thing as I dropped into my seat at my desk. "Why did you sic Dad on me last night? If you were going to call him yourself, why didn't you just tell him about Alexandra and save him the time and aggravation of driving to my apartment?"

Victoria narrowed her eyes at me. "You said you'd call him. You're the one who wouldn't let me call him earlier. You need to take responsibility for your actions, Caroline."

"I also had a bloody bathroom to clean. Next time, you take in Alexandra when she's drunk and suicidal." I was not in a good mood.

"Dad called and asked what was going on with you and Win," Victoria explained. "You were supposed to call Dad, not hook up with your pitcher."

"I was supposed to meet Win after last night's game. He showed up at my place at the same time Dad did."

Why was everyone still so fixated on Win? Alexandra had tried to kill herself. Hello?

"You've always got an excuse as to why the rules don't apply to you."

Apparently Victoria wasn't in any better a mood than I was. Maybe if she'd been in my position, I could have understood her nastiness. But she hadn't seen Alexandra bleeding on her bathroom floor. She hadn't spent hours scouring away the evidence. She hadn't had to tell Dad that his youngest daughter tried to off herself. If Victoria wanted a catfight, that's what she'd get.

"What rules, Vic? The ones you think you have to follow to be a good girl? News flash! I am not a good girl."

"Now that's a huge surprise."

Ooh. Fighting back. Any other time, I would have thought, Good for Victoria. Not today.

"Do you ever think of anyone besides yourself?"

"Yesterday I was thinking about Lexi." I lifted my chin and dared her to contradict me. "I'm still trying to think about her. If I'd been thinking about me, I would have called in sick and slept all day. But I saw my baby sister on my bathroom floor covered with her own blood. The smell of her blood stuck in my nose... Oh, right. I'm the selfish one, the one who doesn't play by the rules. Except, you see, there are no rules, Vic. Life just is."

"This is all that Win person's fault," she said. "You haven't been like this since Mom died."

"What is that supposed to mean?" Every self-defensive instinct I possessed roared to attention. I'd already concluded I wasn't responsible for Alexandra's actions.

"Instead of sticking around to take care of your sister, you were off having sex with Win. Unless I'm terribly mistaken, that's also exactly what you did when Mom died." Victoria sounded smug.

"Why am I responsible for Lexi?" I was not going to let Victoria guilt me into taking responsibility for what had happened. That privilege rested solely with Alexandra.

"Because she came to you."

"That's like saying someone deserves to lose everything in a fire because their house burns down. Not taking on that guilt, Vic. Find someone else to blame."

Still, maybe she had a point.

Maybe sex made me crazy. Or maybe Win tapped into issues buried so deeply in my psyche that I barely acknowledged their existence. Things like resentment, abandonment, the feeling that my skin was too small for the woman inside me. The woman I wanted to be.

I picked up a folder for the gala and opened it. "Aren't we behind after missing work yesterday?" I spoke as icily as I could manage. Pretty tough considering how I was burning up inside. "And I'm going to call the hospital to see how Lexi is doing."

I turned on my computer and ignored Victoria, who stood there glowering at me. Victoria. Glowering. Wow. Red-letter day. *Mark it on your calendar, folks.*

The Internet yielded the hospital's phone number. I was listed as Alexandra's next of kin, which meant my father wouldn't be able to bully the staff into telling him anything. All information would be filtered through me.

I ignored Victoria as I dialed the phone. It took some doing to get transferred to the correct person, but I eventually made it through the labyrinth.

"She had a restless night, but they're keeping an eye on her," I told Victoria when I hung up. "It's your turn to call Dad."

Marc burst into the office. Didn't he have his own job to go to? At least he wasn't going to ask me about Win. "I just heard about Lexi," he said. "Polly told me. How is she? Does anyone know?"

I repeated what the hospital had told me. His handsome face seemed a bit haggard. "How serious are you two?" I asked.

"I thought we should cool it for a while until your father had a chance to chill. I wouldn't have gotten involved with her had I not been serious."

I turned to Victoria. "See. They're serious. Dad doesn't have the right to interfere."

"Can I see her?" Marc asked.

I shook my head. "She's in mandatory evaluation for seventy-two hours. No one except hospital personnel."

"Where is she? Franklin Hall?"

Franklin Hall was the premiere private psychiatric hospital in Syracuse. "Only the best," I assured Marc. Maybe he really did love Alexandra.

"What can I do?" he asked.

"Pray," Victoria advised.

Marc finally left. Victoria and I put aside our differences to work on finishing the details of the gala, which would be held the Saturday night before Mother's Day. The Saltboilers would play an afternoon game that day. Most of them would attend the fund-raiser. Several had agreed to be auctioned to the highest bidder.

Win called midafternoon to check on me. I didn't read anything into the call. I assured him I would be at the ballpark that evening and would meet him in the stadium office lobby after the game.

"Maybe you should back off from Win for a while," Victoria suggested. Her tone wasn't at all snarky. Then she said, "Dad's pretty upset about Alexandra. He doesn't need you screwing up too."

Okay, maybe she wasn't trying to be conciliatory.

"My personal life has nothing to do with Alexandra's issues. Nor is it up for discussion with either you or Dad."

"Your personal life is based on a lie."

"I never lied to Win."

"Caroline, he thought your name was Carrie Thorpe. If that's not a lie, I don't know what is."

"I never told Win that my name was Carrie Thorpe." And that was the truth. I had never told him my name. Period.

Caroline Maplethorpe hadn't fit on the name badge the front office issued me, so I became Carrie Thorpe. That's what everyone with the Crowns called me. It wasn't my lie. It was bookkeeping. And since I had no intention of ever seeing any of those people again, I didn't correct the misconception.

Not once had anyone asked my name. Win had seen my ID badge along with everyone else. I became Carrie Thorpe.

"There are things you don't understand about me and Win," I said. "He saw me through a pretty rough time in my life. After Mom died. When Polly got pregnant. But I never lied to him. He was my one truth."

"Truth?" She acted as if she were about to say something else, but bit her lip. "That's a funny way to describe an ex-boyfriend."

"Ex-lover," I gently corrected. "We were lovers. Nothing more."

"Yet the two of you seemed to pick right up where you left off." She sounded bitter.

Seven years ago, I'd been so absorbed in my self-pity that I hadn't given Victoria a thought. Now I wondered if there was another reason she was meekly wedding Brandon Cummings.

"Why are you marrying Brandon?" I asked.

"What do you know about marriage? It isn't all pheromones, hormones, and sex, you know."

I tried to shove aside my resentment at her judgmental attitude and focus on her actions instead of her words. Maybe if I'd done that instead of berating Alexandra for being drunk, I could have prevented her suicide attempt. No. Alexandra was responsible. Not me.

"Are you marrying Brandon because Dad wants you to?"

She didn't say anything. Maybe Alexandra's foray into disobedience had sparked some introspection on Victoria's part too.

"We're adults, Vic. We don't have to toe any line Dad decides he needs to draw. We don't have to work for the foundation. We don't have to marry the men he selects for us."

"I wouldn't disrespect Mom by quitting my job."

Which, if I thought about it, summed up my feelings. I hadn't thought it in those terms, but she was right. Maybe Dad had created the foundation to assuage his guilt over what he'd done to Mom, but that wasn't why I worked there. Nor did I work there because it was a guaranteed job for me.

I'd loved my gentle mother. The divorce had hurt me. Her subsequent illness and death had devastated me. Regardless of my father's motivation, I couldn't not work for the foundation created in her memory.

"What does Brandon have to do with Mom?"

Victoria flinched as if I'd slapped her.

"Don't marry someone you don't love with every fiber of your being just because you think it's what *Mom* would want."

Victoria's eyes glistened. "You don't understand. You've always been so much about you that you couldn't understand something else if it came up and spit in your face."

"What's going on with you, Vic? Please. Talk to me. My sisters are all I have, and I don't want to lose either one of you. Maybe I should have listened to Alexandra better the other night. Please don't let that happen between us." Tears clung to my lashes.

She shook her head. "I have work to do." Her back was stiff and her shoulders squared as she left my office.

There was definitely something going on there. Maybe I needed to pay more attention to Victoria as well as Alexandra.

Chapter Ten

I arrived at the ballpark early enough to be the first person through the gates. I went directly to my seat and waited for the magic of the game to embrace me.

The late-afternoon sun shone in my eyes, so I lowered the brim on my cap and shoved on my sunglasses.

"Incognito?" Chandler asked as he dropped into the seat next to me.

"Yes." I couldn't keep my annoyance out of my voice. This casual usurpation of my second seat was out of hand. What did I have to do to be left alone?

"How's Alexandra?"

Bad news traveled fast. Who would have told a Blandroid what had happened?

Oh, duh. Victoria would have told Brandon, who would have shared it with the other Beige Ones.

"She's resting quietly, whatever that means. We're not allowed to visit, so all we know is what the hospital is willing to dispense over the phone."

He didn't say anything. He just sat there like congealed oatmeal. At least Marc had offered a cold beer. Not that I wanted a drink. All I could think about was that this is what my father wanted for me for the rest of my life. Cold, bland silence.

"What do you want, Chandler?" I finally asked.

"I'm at the game with you," he replied.

"Um, no, you're not. Why are you really here?"

"You've had a rough couple of days. I'm trying to be supportive."

I might have believed him if he hadn't sounded so scripted. "Did my father put you up to this?"

I think his expression might have changed. It was hard to tell. His wrap-around sunglasses—some overpriced brand, I'm sure—masked his eyes. I think he Botoxed the rest of his face, rendering it immobile.

I loved all the character in Win's face.

"Is it so difficult for you to believe that I care about you?" There was an edge of bite in Chandler's tone.

"Yeah," I said. "You loathe baseball because it isn't lacrosse, and I don't exactly inspire passion in you."

"Passion is for teenagers and old men."

"Like my father?" I stared at the scoreboard, wishing I'd bought a program so I could write down the starting lineups just to have something to do that would make Chandler leave me alone. Or better yet, make him just leave.

"Well, yes."

"Why would I want to get serious with a man who's going to eventually toss me over for a trophy wife?"

My question should have shocked him but didn't.

"Because I can give you presentable children and a good life. Just because your father succumbed to Polly's charms doesn't mean that would necessarily be your fate. I'm quite fond of you, you know."

Dilemma, dilemma. Did I want to spend the rest of my life with someone who was quite fond of me and might not toss me out for a younger model in twenty years, or did I want a little time with the guy who said he'd looked for me for seven years and said he never wanted to share me again? The man who made my toes curl, my heart sing, and my mouth smile just because he wanted to kiss me.

I would be happier with a few weeks with Win than I would be in a lifetime of Blandroid Chandler.

"Is this a marriage proposal?"

"No. That's coming at the bottom of the fourth inning on the scoreboard. This game is being televised, and your father has it set up with the production people to show you accepting on camera."

He sounded matter-of-fact and sure of himself. I wanted to knee his privates to see if he'd have an honest reaction.

Instead, I asked, "What happens if I slap your face?"

"Look," he said as if he were patiently explaining a blueprint to a child or an animal. "Your father is upset with your infatuation with that pitcher. He wants to see you settled. He's even more concerned now that Alexandra has made a fool of herself over Marc Matthews."

"Dad should know all about making a fool of himself over sex," I muttered. "Especially with the Matthews family."

Chandler reached for my hand.

I sat on it. "I had Marc tossed out of that seat the other night."

"That wouldn't look good on camera. Especially when the end of the fourth inning comes around."

"Fuck the camera."

My use of the f-bomb shocked Chandler. "That's not a very ladylike thing to say."

"I'm not a very ladylike person."

"Of course you are. You're one of Kathryn and James Maplethorpe's daughters."

He dumbfounded me. For a minute, I didn't know what to say.

"You're not proposing to me tonight," I finally said. "Cancel the scoreboard. I'll reimburse your ten dollars."

"Your father arranged it."

"It won't be the first time I've disappointed my father. Trust me, he's used to it."

"I have the ring in my pocket. Would you like to see it?"

"No. I'm not going to marry you. Nothing personal."

I looked toward the dugout. I could just make out Win, sitting on the bench, clipboard in hand, ready to log the opposing batters.

"You're muddying your decision with passion." He sounded a bit contemptuous.

"You should try passion sometime. It's lots of fun."

"Just because I don't treat you like a whore doesn't mean I'm celibate," he snapped.

Wow. Was that a telling statement or what?

I fisted my hand, which was still under my bottom. Really uncomfortable. "I think you'd better leave before I get an usher and stadium security to toss you for harassment."

I bit the inside of my lower lip to keep from saying anything else.

I stood. "I'm going to get my dinner now. Please find another seat while I'm gone."

I didn't realize he'd followed me until I was in line at my favorite vendor on the third-base side of the stadium. My stomach rumbled at the aroma of the hot dogs sweating on the grill. "What are you doing here?"

"Buying your dinner." He grimaced at my choice.

"I'll buy my own dinner." I pulled several bills out of my pocket. "See?"

"I don't know why you're being so difficult. It's that pitcher, isn't it?"

"Maybe I'm not being difficult, Chandler. Maybe I'm being independent. Being an adult. I don't need my father picking out men for me to date. In fact, I kind of resent it."

The person in front of me ordered two dogs and a white hot, plus chocolate milk.

"One dog," I said to the vendor. "Well-done, please."

"Make that two," Chandler said, stepping next to me and giving the impression we were a couple.

I could create a scene or take the damn hot dog. I took the hot dog but scurried away while Chandler polluted his from the condiment pumps.

I reached my seat just in time for the National Anthem. I tossed my bag on my second seat, hoping to keep Chandler away.

He arrived after the anthem, took one look at my bag, and dropped into the seat beside it.

Great. There was nothing I could do unless I bought the ticket for the seat myself.

The usher arrived to herd the autograph seekers away from the dugout. The Saltboilers were playing a New York affiliate, so most of the other seats in my section were occupied by the parent team's fans.

"Check his ticket," I said, pointing at Chandler.

The usher did as I requested, and damn, Chandler—or my father—had bought the seat. My only option was to keep my baseball bag between us.

"Did you cancel the scoreboard proposal?" I asked as some overweight old man threw out the first pitch.

"No," Chandler replied.

"What do I have to do to make you go away?" I asked.

"You can't. You don't have your father's resources."

Oh, I didn't like the sound of that. At all. Very slowly, I turned my head to stare at Chandler. "Are you implying my father is paying you to marry me?"

"No, not at all." Chandler seemed shocked at the notion, which was a relief. "What kind of man do you think I am? I am no more a gigolo than you are a whore."

This promised to be good.

"What did my father offer you to pursue me?" I asked.

Chandler merely shook his head. "Forget I said anything."

As if I could. As if I would.

At the bottom of the first inning, I visited stadium guest services to cancel the scoreboard proposal, but Chandler was right behind me.

At the bottom of the second inning, I returned to the concourse level and went into the restroom, hoping Chandler would think I was only answering nature's call. He was standing by guest services when I came out.

In desperation, I called my father. Maybe if I told him I knew what he'd done, he would call off Chandler. But Dad didn't answer his phone.

"What if this was about Alexandra?" I asked his voice mail.

"That was cruel." Chandler fell into step beside me.

"Actually, I'm trying to be kind," I said. "Or do you really want me to embarrass you in front of the crowd?"

"You wouldn't."

"Oh yes, I would," I assured him. "Just because you and Dad made plans doesn't mean I have to play along."

"You're a Maplethorpe. You don't misbehave in public."

"I misbehave, as you so quaintly put it, anyplace and time I want. And believe me, you're triggering a craving right now."

He said nothing until we were sitting again. Then he tried to *reason* with me.

"Caroline, we'll make an exceptional couple. We'll have attractive, intelligent children. I'm on track to make department head in another year or so, so we'll have the kind of life you were meant to have. The kind of life to which you are accustomed. You can keep your job, if that's what you want. Your work with the Kathryn Maplethorpe Foundation is commendable, exactly the sort of career I'd planned for my wife."

"Are you kidding?" Chandler was definitely bringing out my inner crankiness. Pushing buttons about which no one knew. My career at the foundation was about my mother, not Chandler Goodeve or what he deemed acceptable.

"That may be the kind of life you want, but it's not my destiny." I spoke slowly, exaggerating my patience. "I'm the woman who prefers the stands at a baseball game instead of a luxury box. I'm not even sure what you do for a living, other than working for my father."

"I'm a civil engineer," he said, sounding quite miffed. Offended, even.

I was at the stadium to watch baseball, not mollify an annoyed Blandroid, but if I was to have any peace, I needed Chandler to see reason.

"Doesn't it tell you something that after two years, I still don't know what you do for a living? That's a basic let's-get-to-know-each-other fact."

He shrugged. "I thought we wouldn't get into details until we were married. You know, for dinner parties and such. Then, of course, you'll have to know about my projects so you can be conversant with our guests."

Dread filled me. He wanted me to be my mother. I loved my mother, but I wasn't her clone. And being the good wife hadn't done her much good in the end. "I don't do dinner parties."

"Don't be ridiculous. You're working on tomorrow night's gala for the Kathryn Maplethorpe Foundation right now. Clearly you *do* do them."

"That's an event," I explained.

"As will be our dinner parties."

At the top of the fourth inning, I moved. I picked up my baseball bag and left my seat. Abandoned it. Chandler's behavior was clearly harassment, and I was going to start a journal of incidences just as soon as I got home.

Well, maybe tomorrow. I planned to bring Win home with me, and writing out my irritation with Chandler moved to the bottom of my list of things I wanted to do. Mostly, I wanted to do Win.

I eluded Chandler by going to the restroom again, leaving by a different door, and then climbing to the general-admission section and working my way across the third level.

So when the bottom of the fourth came, the proposal flashed on the scoreboard, and the camera zoomed in on my empty seat, I was safely ensconced in seats behind the bull pen on the third-base side of the stadium.

The crowd cheered when the proposal came up on the scoreboard. My face burned. Okay, I probably wasn't the only Caroline in the ballpark that evening, but still. Dad should have known better.

"Caroline Maplethorpe, please report to stadium guest services."

There went my anonymity. Well, I didn't have to report. If it were a true emergency, someone would call my cell phone. Which then vibrated against my hip.

Dad. Phooey. Well, he didn't have to know I was still at the park.

"Hi, Dad."

"Did you hear something else about your sister?" he asked.

Oh. Yeah. I'd left a message. "No. But I'm telling you right now, I am not amused by your scheme with Chandler tonight."

"Where are you?" he snapped.

"None of your business," I snapped back. Sheesh. I was twenty-five years old. I didn't need a babysitter. "I'm thinking about getting an order of protection against Chandler, which will probably screw up his chances of a promotion anytime soon. Don't push me, Dad, because that's my counteroffer to whatever you offered him to marry me."

I disconnected the call.

So much for the magic of baseball.

I was the last fan out of the stadium that night. The grounds crew was doing their thing with a little green-and-yellow tractor. Security asked me to leave. I found the stairs that led to the lobby. The TV announcers, descending from the broadcast booth, were talking about the no-show marriage proposal and how the director hadn't realized right away that the seats were empty.

I emerged into the lobby. There was a seating area where the families of the players waited. Several towheaded children ran around with far too much energy for that time of night. I debated joining them, but then, I wasn't official. Better for me to wait for Win outside like any other groupie.

There were a few fans milling outside the door and no Blonderoids. I wandered over to the baseball statue to wait.

Players tended to emerge in clumps as if there were safety in numbers, but Win was the first one out.

I stepped from the shadows into the light.

He hurried toward me. "Tell me that marriage proposal wasn't for you," he growled.

I stood on my tiptoes and planted a kiss on his mouth.

"It was, but it's a really boring, really long story, and I'd rather jump your bones than go into it right now."

He laughed. "Did you say no?"

"I left before he could ask the question. Didn't even get a gander at the ring."

Win looped his arm through mine as we made our way across the players' lot. "How did you know he was going to propose?"

"He told me. He offered to show me the ring beforehand too, but I wasn't interested. In fact, I threatened to slap his face on TV."

"That might have been fun." A vehicle nearby chirped as someone used a remote to unlock its doors.

"Caroline." My father's voice traveled through the night. A freight train rumbled past the far side of the stadium, its lonesome whistle howling like wolves in the wilderness.

"Dad."

Win tightened his arm, trapping mine in his. "Mr. Maplethorpe."

"Winston." My father nodded at Win before focusing on me again. "I'd like to speak to you alone."

"I'm with Win."

"Fine. You embarrassed me tonight."

I should have known he'd twist his facts.

"You embarrassed yourself," I told him. "I did everything I could to prevent anyone being embarrassed. I mean, how would it have looked on TV if I'd slapped Chandler's face? Or if I'd even just shaken my head and said no? I tried to cancel the scoreboard twice. Don't blame me because you made plans that conflicted with my own plans."

Dad looked at Win. "Caroline has family obligations. She's going to marry Chandler Goodeve."

"Don't listen to him," I told Win. "He leads a rich fantasy life."

"Carrie needs to oblige herself once in a while," Win said. "And you don't need to worry about her with me. I'll take care of her, sir."

"What happens to her when you leave?"

"Haven't you learned anything from what happened to Alexandra?" I asked before Win could respond. "You interfered with her and Marc, and look at what happened."

"You're too much like me to do something ridiculous."

So now Alexandra's suicide attempt was ridiculous. Yeah, he'd said pretty much the same thing when she'd done it, but I'd hoped he had come to his senses.

Win squeezed my arm as I drew in a shaky, furious breath. "You're right. I am like you. You set the example. I followed."

"What's that supposed to mean?"

"You ditched Mom to marry a pageant runner-up. I'm dating a baseball player. You do the math."

"What is your sudden obsession with my marriage to Polly?"

"It's not so sudden. I never said anything before because you never tried to interfere with me. Back off, and I'll shut up."

"Carrie and I have plans, Mr. Maplethorpe," Win said, still polite.

"He's just using you." Dad ignored Win.

"He's honest about it," I retorted. "Based on my conversation with Chandler tonight, he'd just be using me too, but for my name and the connection to you. Come on, Win. I'm starving."

We left my father standing there. Alone. In the dark.

We were halfway to my apartment before either of us said anything.

I broke the silence. "Will you escort me to the gala tomorrow night?"

"Sure." He sounded distracted. There was something unfamiliar in his tone. "Do you think I'm using you?"

"Why? Does it bother you that my father thinks that?"

He was silent for several seconds, as though weighing his words. "Yeah, I guess it does. It makes me feel...shallow."

He constantly surprised me.

"I'm not using you, Carrie."

I didn't say anything.

"I'm not." His tone was firm. "A man doesn't look for a woman for seven years just so he can use her."

"Look," I said. "I don't want to talk about this now. I just want to enjoy what time we have together, okay?"

"Are you using me to get back at your father?"

"I used Flash to do that. Do we have to talk about this?"

"Your father doesn't know about Flash, does he?"

"No one knows anything." Not even you, I thought.

"I don't like your father thinking I'm using you. We're in a relationship." He sounded sure of himself. "You're coming with me when I'm called up again."

I'd already said no to him on that, and I was really tired of talking. Seemed like all I'd done all night was talk or be talked at. And ignored. I just wanted to get home, get naked, and get it on with Win Winston. I'd think about what would happen when he left after he was gone.

Chapter Eleven

Saturday's game started at noon. I smeared myself with sunblock as I watched Win sign autographs for a swarm of kids. He was great with his fans, and watching him warmed me.

When the Buffalo outfield was coming back to the dugout at the bottom of the first, the second baseman tossed a ball into the stands near me. I caught it and handed it off to a young girl wearing a New York hat sitting in the row behind me. I liked it when players paid attention to kids.

The second baseman winked at me. I smiled because I'm polite. I checked my program roster to see who he was. Swanson Crabtree. When he came to bat, the Saltboilers pitcher retired him on a called strike, and as he sauntered back to the dugout, he stopped and asked my name. I shook my head, indicating that I wasn't interested.

He persisted in the middle of every inning and whenever he was at bat.

I glanced at the dugout where Win should have been taking notes for the next day's game. I couldn't tell, but it felt as if he was glaring at me through his sunglasses.

I'd driven myself to the game so I could leave early and begin preparing for the gala. It was a formal event, and I liked to do the pamper-myself thing beforehand.

A long bubble-drenched soak in the tub, scented lotions on my feet and legs, pedicure, manicure—yeah, I do my own—the works. I needed to put on the very best face possible for the Kathryn Maplethorpe Foundation. This was our biggest fund-raising event all year.

Most women tend to wear black at these events. Oh, there would be two or three blondes in red—I think that was the color of the gown Alexandra had planned to wear—but I'd found a shimmering smoke-gray sheath that fit like a second skin. I usually didn't go for sexy, but I wanted Win to see me at my finest. The dress had some kind of built-in contraption that not only made a bra unnecessary but also pushed my breasts into a magnificent display of cleavage.

I dabbed a little perfume in a couple of strategic spots. Silver shoes and bag. My bobbed hair is a classic style that can go from the ballpark to the ballroom with a swipe of a comb.

Win was picking me up at six thirty. The gala started at seven. I probably should have arrived earlier, but Victoria was so organized there wouldn't be anything to do.

My intercom buzzed at six fifteen. Without checking, I opened the downstairs door and then the upstairs door. I plucked my spangled silver shawl from the back of my sofa.

"You're early," I said when I heard footfalls coming into my apartment. "You're lucky I'm not one of those fussy women." I whirled around, draping the shawl across my shoulders.

My smile wilted when I saw Chandler standing there, looking stuffier than usual in his tuxedo. "Why are you here?"

"I'm escorting you to the gala," he said. "You look lovely."

I shook my head. "We never discussed you being my escort tonight. I have other plans."

"I'm your fiancé," he snapped. "Who else would escort you?"

Whoa. The Blandroid had teeth. That didn't, however, change anything.

"We're not engaged." My voice shook. I was upset. No, I was furious. "Win will be here any minute, and I don't need you complicating things."

"I was good enough until he showed up."

"His showing up has nothing to do with how I feel—or don't feel—about you. I've had a really crummy week, and you haven't helped at all."

"Only because you've shut me out."

My earlier good mood evaporated. It was my own fault Chandler was in my apartment. I had the intercom for a reason, and I needed to use it all the time.

"Chandler, I am not going to the gala with you. I'm going with Win, which is good PR because he's a Saltboiler, and this is a joint Saltboiler-and-foundation event."

Trying to explain this to him was like explaining it to a boulder. Maybe in a million years, my words would have an effect and create a dimple in the immovable density. In the meantime, my incredible control prevented me from stomping my feet and howling.

"I don't understand what you see in him. Yes, he's in his fifteen minutes right now, but I never figured you for someone whose head would be turned by fame." Chandler sounded genuinely perplexed.

I wasn't going to explain anything to Chandler. I didn't owe him even a thought. "You need to leave. Now."

"No."

Why had I ever considered Chandler meek? He was as stubborn as I was, which was okay in me but not in him.

"What's your deal with my father?"

He clenched his teeth. A muscle in his jaw worked. His pale brown eyes narrowed. "You misunderstood what I said."

"You better hope I did. And even if Win weren't in the picture, we would not be getting married. What do I have to do to get you to drop this nonsense?"

He didn't even hesitate. "Marry me."

I shook my head, thinking I hadn't heard him. "What?"

"Marry me. Have a discreet affair with your pitcher, if you must, but marry me."

My brain blanked. Chandler was insane.

The intercom buzzed again. Dazed, I forgot to confirm who rang.

I kissed Win at the door. I hadn't applied my lipstick yet for that very reason. I wanted to cling to him, to steal some of his sanity.

"You look fabulous," Win said.

"So do you," I replied.

And he did. Some men were born to look good in a tuxedo, and Winslow Winthrop Winston the Whatever was one of them. He already had the tall, dark, and handsome cliché down pat. That was the easy part. But the intelligence shining out of those obsidian eyes, the strength in his jaw, the sensitivity in his calloused hands, and his lean strength made him a fantasy package. My fantasy package.

Chandler cleared his throat.

Win jerked. "What's he doing here?"

"I thought he was you when he rang the buzzer."

"Not even close."

"No kidding," I muttered.

"There seems to be a mix-up," Chandler said. "Apparently Caroline believed she was free to ask you to escort her to the event this evening when, in fact, she was not."

"You're saying you've got dibs on Carrie?" Win asked.

Chandler's nostrils flared as if he smelled something foul. "Yes."

"The last guy who thought that got hit in the head with a line drive."

Flash. Win was talking about Jordan "Flash" Gordon.

"Is that a threat?" Chandler's tone never varied. He wasn't emotionally engaged. He was inconvenienced, not angry.

"I never make threats," Win replied. "Always seemed pointless to me."

"Agreed," Chandler said.

Chandler, Win, and I ended up walking to the Urban Renaissance Building together. I had the weirdest sense of déjà vu and had to keep reminding myself that Chandler wasn't Flash, and that when the evening was over, Win would be the only man in my bed.

The gala was starting to hum when our trio arrived. A band in the minstrel gallery overlooking the first-floor lobby provided tunes for couples jostling on the dance floor. Servers wove through the guests offering hot hors d'oeuvres. The crudités table was already depleted, and there were long lines at the cash bar.

Chandler's clinging added a surreal touch to an already bizarre situation. My father and Polly acted as if there was nothing awkward about the past. Victoria flitted about, making sure everything occurred the way it should. I mistook Marsha Lee for a 1970s refrigerator, resplendent in harvest gold with moldy-avocado-green fringe. The woman hadn't purchased new clothes in decades. Marc was there too. Solo. Most of the Saltboilers were present. The only person missing was Alexandra.

A flashbulb went off nearby. Lots of press. Excellent.

Win and I examined the merchandise donated for the silent auction. A pair of Saltboiler season tickets captured my attention until I reminded myself that if I did have another pair in order to create a bubble of privacy, my family, satellites, and Blandroids would consider use of the seats their due. I'd have even more of them bothering me.

Besides, I'd earmarked my budget for the evening for something else.

Win swung me onto the portable dance floor for a slow number. We'd never danced together, but that wasn't a problem. We knew how to move in sync.

Chandler tried to cut in, but I left the floor, pulling Win with me. Swanson Crabtree—the Buffalo second baseman—asked me to dance as Win and I headed toward the bar, but I declined.

At nine o'clock, the bar closed, the food vanished, and the band took a break. Foundation volunteers herded the attendees into the theater.

It was time for the main event. A bachelor auction that featured several unattached Saltboilers—including Win. Each bachelor had donated a preset "date" for his highest bidder. Some of the married or otherwise spoken-for players had scheduled things like private batting lessons or an inning in the dugout.

I thought the entire idea had been a stroke of genius on my part. And I intended to bid on Win myself.

The men being auctioned were quarantined in the backstage dressing rooms.

"Why aren't you auctioning yourself?" I asked Chandler when he sat next to me in the audience. Just because he didn't appeal to me didn't mean someone else wouldn't want him.

"I'm not available. And please remember what I said to you earlier about discretion."

Victoria introduced the men, including a local TV news reporter, a firefighter, a chef, and several Blandroid-like men, five Saltboilers, and two hockey players from Syracuse's minor-league team. Even the Buffalo second baseman, Swanson Crabtree, put himself on the block.

Bidding was brisk. The foundation coffers grew. My father bought a Saltboiler inning in the dugout for Matthew.

Win was the final man up for bid.

Victoria read his professional stats—an alphabet soup of initials meaning nothing to most of the women there. Except his LIPS. That's how Victoria read the stat—Win Winston's lips. His *late-inning pressure situation* batting average was pretty impressive for a pitcher. It was a good thing someone from the Saltboilers front office had compiled the bios and other pertinent information for us.

A woman a couple of rows behind me started the bidding at two hundred fifty dollars.

Win had quite a following in Syracuse, because the media had made such a big deal out of him rehabbing there. Add that notoriety to his devilish good looks, and he was bound to be our top earner for the evening. I certainly planned to do my part to encourage it. I wasn't about to share him any more than he was willing to share me.

That thought sharpened my dislike of Chandler.

Someone in the balcony bid three hundred dollars. The woman behind me immediately responded with three hundred fifty.

I didn't get into the action until the bid was at five hundred dollars. Then, to my utter shock, Chandler bid six hundred to top my five hundred fifty.

"What are you doing?" I asked in a furious whisper.

"Raising money for the Kathryn Maplethorpe Foundation," Chandler calmly replied. "And trying to provide a united public front showing that Winston is *our* friend, not *your* lover."

The man was crazy.

The woman in the balcony, followed by the woman behind me drove the price to seven hundred dollars.

"Seven fifty," I said.

"Eight," Chandler immediately countered.

"Even if you win, which you won't, you're not going to stop me and Win from being together." I didn't care what "people" might think.

"Thank you, Chandler Goodeve," Victoria said.

"Eight fifty," I snapped.

The other women forced Chandler to one thousand dollars.

I rolled my eyes. Yes, I wanted Win to raise the most money for the foundation, but Chandler was being petty.

"Eleven hundred," I said, ignoring the gasp that went through the theater. No other bachelor had gone for such a high price.

"No wife of mine is having an intimate dinner for two with the likes of Win Winston," Chandler muttered.

"You have to be married before you can make a statement like that," I reminded him.

"Fifteen hundred," Chandler called.

"I don't play for your team," Win called out to Chandler, generating a laugh from the rest of the audience. "Five thousand on myself."

Chandler slumped in his seat.

What could Victoria do but accept? She said something to Win. He shook his head and then kissed her on the cheek.

Ten minutes later, we were in the lobby again, the band was playing, the bar was open, and the guests were decimating the dessert tables.

Win draped his arm over my shoulder, and we smiled prettily for a photographer. Chandler stood on my other side. I hoped the photo didn't include him, although the bidding war would likely make the news.

The reporter interviewed Victoria and Brandon. Vic was lovely in a pale pink gown that shimmered over her curves. Brandon wore a bright pink cummerbund with his tux. Silly, I thought, even at a breast-cancer-awareness event.

I studied Victoria's face. She looked exhausted. She'd busted her back on this gala, and the weekend wasn't over yet. We all had to appear at the Saltboilers game the next day. And unfortunately, it was an afternoon game.

I was bushed too. I wanted out of my shoes and out of the cleavage contraption.

"One final dance. Then let's get out of here," Win whispered. His breath was warm, his tongue hot as it traced the contours of my ear. "My curfew was an hour ago."

"I have to stay until the end. You go. I'll catch a ride with Victoria." As much as I wanted to be with him, I did have obligations.

Win scowled but didn't argue. He was scheduled to pitch and needed his sleep. So we danced a slow number, and then he brushed his lips over mine, murmured that he'd see me tomorrow, and left.

I longed to accompany him.

Finally the musicians packed their instruments. The caterers loaded their gear into vans. Chandler hovered.

I excused myself and headed for a second-floor restroom.

Chandler wasn't outside the door when I emerged, but he stood in one of the alcoves overlooking the first floor. He stepped forward as soon as he saw me. "Are you ready to leave?"

I shook my head. "I'm going home with Victoria."

The dim light cast deep shadows across his face. His mouth thinned to a severe line. "Why are you acting like a tramp?" He fixed his gaze on my cleavage.

The dress really did create an impression of *more*.

"Don't you realize Winston is using you to kill time?"

I pulled my silver-spangled shawl across my chest. "It's none of your business, Chandler. It's very sweet of you to be concerned, but it's none of your business."

"Your father says differently."

"My father does not dictate to me. I can't believe you let him bully you."

Chandler's gaze traveled down my body, and I wished the dress wasn't quite so clingy. "You're just enthralled by Winston's fame. The little bit of glamour he's bringing to your life. It's an illusion, Caroline. You're going to wake up one morning and be all alone."

As if I wouldn't be alone if I married Chandler. As if I hadn't already known the bone-deep loneliness of Win's absence.

I clutched my evening bag tighter and then adjusted my shawl for maximum coverage. "Good night, Chandler."

"I'll walk with you."

I sighed. Short of murder, I didn't see how I was going to get rid of him. I tried anyway. "I'm going with Victoria and Brandon."

"I've already explained to them that I'll walk you home."

I looked for them, but they'd vanished.

Chandler took my arm.

We didn't speak for the entire eight blocks between the Urb and the Susie Buddha Café. I punched in my security code. "Thanks for walking me home," I said.

"Aren't you going to ask me in?"

"No."

He reached past me and opened the door. "Fine. Then I'll invite myself." He crowded me into the entry and closed the door to the street.

I reached for the handle to open the door again, but he shoved me against the wall. I could feel the fragile fabric of my gown snag on the rough brick.

"I'm tired of your games, Caroline. I've tried to do the right thing by you, but you've forced my hand."

He crushed my mouth beneath his, and I thought I was going to vomit. I bit down on his lower lip and jabbed my elbow into his stomach. He doubled over, and I fumbled with the doorknob.

I opened the door and somehow managed to shove his wheezing, gasping self to the sidewalk, where he lay writhing like the worm he was.

The final day of the Kathryn Maplethorpe Foundation's big weekend was clear and warm. The gala had been Victoria's gem. The baseball diamond was mine.

I was in a rotten mood.

I wore a Second Base Club T-shirt, a Saltboilers hoodie, and my pink cap from the previous season. New hats would be handed out today courtesy of the Kathryn Maplethorpe Foundation. I shoved the pink-ribbon file folder containing the stadium announcer's speech into my baseball bag and drove to the stadium instead of taking the bus.

The concourse was busy with interns handing out hats. The vendors dispensing information about breast cancer were active. The Second Base Club kiosk was mobbed.

Polly sang the National Anthem. She did a credible job, but all my old resentments were entrenched. It was Mother's Day. Once again, Polly had usurped my mother's rightful place.

Victoria and I stood on the field while the announcer read the speech I'd prepared about too many mothers lost to breast cancer. Alexandra should have stood with us. The hole inside me grew with her absence.

Dad threw out the first pitch, just like he'd thrown out my mother. His involvement in this event was as much a travesty as Polly's participation.

After the on field ceremonies, there was a first-inning command performance in Dad's box. I missed Win's opening pitches. I wasn't happy about that.

Things worsened when Marsha Lee loudly berated me for my Second Base Club T-shirt. "Vulgar" was one word she tossed around.

I ruffled Matthew's hair and told Marsha Lee I didn't give a rat's rump what she thought and if she wanted a definition of "vulgar," to look in the mirror.

Victoria raised an eyebrow at me, but I was possessed of the same jittery craziness that had defined me seven years ago. Chandler tried to shush me. As if he had rights. I didn't know why he was there, even if Dad had invited him. Hadn't I been blunt enough last night? Next time, I'd knee him in the testicles.

Time to leave the box. I didn't bother saying good-bye to anyone. Not even Matthew, who'd been bugging me to take him to my seats. I told him his probationary period wasn't over.

I needed to be alone. If anyone in my family, the satellites, or a Blandroid showed up, I'd have an usher deal with them.

There was nothing I could do about Swanson Crabtree. I was sitting right there, behind the visitor's dugout, and Crabtree apparently had been looking for me.

"Hey, pretty lady," he called to me at the bottom of the first. "I see you missed me."

I had no idea what he was talking about. I figured he was trying to distract Win by flirting with me. Then the Buffalo third baseman asked me what I had against third base.

My face heated as I realized I hadn't zipped my hoodie, and my Second Base Club T-shirt was visible.

Crabtree was the second batter in the inning. Win struck him out in three pitches. Did the same thing to the third baseman. His game was flawless.

My phone vibrated. Polly wanted to know if Matthew could sit with me, because he was driving everyone in the box crazy. I told her no.

Polly sounded annoyed with me, but I really didn't care. Enough was enough. I turned off my phone.

Win came to the plate at the bottom of the third. He held a pink bat—something some players did to show their support for the cause.

A lump gathered in my throat. Why was he even batting?

He looked at me and nodded as he stepped to the plate.

My vision wavered as tears brimmed in my eyes. I knew in my heart that he'd ordered the pink bat for me. And his intro music. Home-team batters pick their own if they want it. I was surprised Win had chosen a song. He hadn't batted all season. His choice was like a punch to my solar plexus. Don Henley's "Boys of Summer." A man promising his love will stay even after "the boys of summer have gone." It could have been our song.

Win bunted the second pitch and actually made it to first base. Pitchers aren't known for their hitting skills.

The next hitter advanced him to second. Crabtree moved closer to the bag. I could see them conversing, but they were too distant for me to read their lips.

The exchange appeared rather heated, although neither man looked at the other.

The pitcher walked the next batter, advancing Win to third. Bases were loaded. The next batter swung at the first two pitches.

The next pitch was a fastball, ninety-three miles an hour, and the hitter connected at the sweet spot. The Saltboilers fans surged to their feet and watched the ball sail over the right-field fence. Grand slam. Beautiful.

I cheered as loudly as anyone when Win loped across the plate followed by three other runners.

The Saltboilers scored three more runs in the inning.

After the third out, Crabtree trotted toward me. I mean the dugout. Except he stopped to speak to me. "Why are you sitting here if you're Win Winston's woman?"

I was too stunned to answer. What had Win said to him?

"I'm staying at the Clubhouse Inn," Crabtree continued. "In case he lied."

Win retired the side in order again. He was in stunning form.

Swanson Crabtree came to the plate at the top of the sixth.

Maybe it was just me, but the tension seemed to intensify. I couldn't see Crabtree's face. I didn't know if he did something to annoy Win. But Win pitched high and inside. Chin music. Only fast footwork on Crabtree's part kept him from being hit by the ball. My ego whispered the two of them were arguing over me.

Win grinned at Crabtree. Not like he'd grinned at me the night before but rather, a scary grin. More like a grimace.

I'd hoped they would be professional, but Crabtree started fouling off every pitch, jacking Win's count to where he'd have to leave the game soon. Very valid strategy, especially on a rehabbing guy. After about ten of those, Win lost it. The next pitch, a ninety-five-miles-per-hour fastball (according to the radar), hit Crabtree's ribs. He went down like an anvil, clutching his side, writhing in the dirt.

Win stood at the mound, rigid and alone, despite the way the infield converged to surround him.

Buffalo stampeded from the dugout. The Saltboilers followed suit, and for several moments, it looked as if there might be a brawl.

I wondered if anyone else had seen what had gone on while Win was at second base.

Finally, Crabtree staggered to his feet, favoring his right side. The ump tossed Win from the game, and Buffalo put up a pinch runner.

I saw the coach talk to Win in the dugout during the bottom of the inning, probably expressing concern about how hard he was throwing.

A middle reliever took over the next inning. The rest of the game was a blur. I looked for Win in the dugout but didn't see him.

I figured he was cooling off somewhere, and I'd see him after the game. If the Saltboilers managed to hold on to his lead, he'd be in a great mood. We could celebrate together.

But there was no sign from him after the game. It was as if he'd vanished. I looked for his SUV in the players' lot, but it wasn't there. I stood with the fans at the players' door, and that's how I found out: Win had been called up to Columbia during the game.

Chapter Twelve

The news was like a hundred-miles-per-hour fastball to my heart. He couldn't have texted me?

It was, to quote Yogi Berra, like déjà vu all over again.

I'd thought I would be better prepared this time, and I tried to pretend I was. I even managed to drive home without getting into an accident.

Once there, I checked my phone to see if I'd somehow missed a call. And belatedly remembered I'd turned it off after arguing with Polly.

Win had left two voice messages—"I've been recalled. I'll touch base later," followed by, "Where are you? Why won't you pick up?"—plus a *Call me* text. My family wondered where I was, why I wasn't at the postgame celebration, and if I'd run off with Win.

I didn't want to talk to any of them. My mother was still dead, and the man I loved had left me again.

I barricaded myself in my apartment, looking at the newspaper photos from the previous evening. I studied Win's precious face.

I was a big girl now, the adult I hadn't been seven years ago. I'd resumed my relationship with Win knowing we were temporary.

I debated returning Win's calls. I'd reached out to him when he'd left before. I'd needed him, and his lack of response had undermined me like nothing else could have. Maybe it was best to admit he was gone.

I fixed myself a can of soup and went through the motions of eating. Watched my terrarium grow. Called the hospital to check on Alexandra and was told she was being released the next day.

I tried to be cheerful about that. I wanted her out and well, and surely they wouldn't release her if she were still suicidal. I needed to be strong for her in the ways no one had been for me in my dark hours.

When my intercom buzzed, my heart lurched into my throat, and I raced to the speaker. "Who is it?" I knew I sounded too breathless.

"Victoria."

Heart thudded back into place.

I buzzed her in, bracing myself for an unpleasant scene.

"Are you all right?" she asked. She was alone, thank goodness. "We heard about Win at the bottom of the seventh inning."

I nodded. "I knew it was temporary."

"But are you all right?"

Did she think I'd pull an Alexandra? Things had been much worse the last time, and killing myself had never crossed my mind. "I'm fine."

"He didn't ask you to go with him?" Victoria plopped onto my sofa.

I dropped onto the other end. "Even if he did, it would still be temporary," I said. "I won't uproot my life for temporary. Besides, I can't leave now. Alexandra is getting out of the hospital tomorrow."

"What does that have to do with you and Win?"

"There is no me and Win." I struggled to keep my sadness out of my voice, but I guess I didn't succeed.

"Anyone who saw the two of you together would call you a liar." She gestured toward the newspaper on the sofa table, folded to the picture of me dancing in Win's arms.

"I'm not Win's plaything."

Well, I was, but Victoria was tactful enough not to mention it.

"Gotta set a good example for my younger sister," I added.

Victoria seemed grateful for the change of subject. "What are we going to do with her? She can't go to Dad's house."

"She can stay with me," I said, although I hadn't done such a great job the last time she stayed with me. "I'm sure you and Brandon don't want her underfoot."

Victoria shrugged as if Brandon didn't matter.

I was glad I wasn't so mired in my own misery that I was insensitive to my sisters. They were all I had left of my mother.

"What's wrong?" I asked. "I thought last night was a masterpiece, and today was fabulous, even if I do say so myself."

"We were very successful," Victoria agreed, but she didn't sound happy about it. She inhaled deeply, as if bracing herself for something distasteful.

"But?" I prompted.

"I was a little jealous of you last night," she admitted in a small voice. "You and Win. You were both radiant."

"Huh?" I'd never been radiant a day in my life.

"It's obvious that you two have something going for you. I was envious."

I started listening to her. "You don't feel radiant with Brandon?"

Beige wasn't radiant, but some people liked it.

Victoria shook her head ever so slightly. "I suppose I shouldn't complain. At least he's still in town." The corners of her mouth twitched as if she knew she should smile but was too preoccupied to give it her best shot.

"What are you doing with him if he doesn't make you feel special?"

"Not everyone can have a man look for her for seven years."

"Win claimed. Doesn't mean it's true," I reminded her.

"Do your toes curl when he kisses you?"

"A lot more than my toes," I admitted.

"What's it like?" She sounded...wistful.

Wait a minute. Why was she asking me these things?

"Your bones don't melt when Brandon kisses you?"

Another barely perceptible shake of her head. "I looked at you and Win last night and realized something is missing with Brandon. Win couldn't take his eyes off you."

I wanted to cry, but this wasn't about me.

"One long, last look," I tried to jest, but it wasn't funny.

Victoria reached for my hand. Covered it with her smooth, pampered one. "I'm sorry. The way he stood by you when everything was happening with Lexi and you had to deal with Dad's nonsense... Well, a casual guy doesn't do something like that."

My fragile composure verged on shattering.

"Let's not talk about Win, okay? Let's talk about you and Brandon." I slid my hand from beneath hers in order to cover hers. "What's wrong?"

She heaved a sigh. Victoria rarely sighs, and when she does, they're very ladylike and genteel. Maplethorpe. She *never* heaves. Something was definitely wrong.

I didn't know Brandon well, but I couldn't see Victoria happy with him. She's a smart, gregarious, outgoing woman, yet proximity to Brandon dampened her sparkle. They made a striking couple, but that didn't mean the relationship was right. Was she supposed to be a political asset or boost his negligible masculinity?

"I'm jealous, just like I told you," she admitted. "So I'm having second thoughts about Brandon, and it's not just prewedding jitters."

"Have you set a date?"

"No, but he's pushing me to. He wants to get married before the campaign season for county legislature kicks into full swing."

"That's very practical, but where's the romance? The magic?"

She closed her eyes for a moment, as though wincing at my words. When she opened them again, she said, "Exactly. Sometimes I feel like Brandon wants to marry me because—"

"Dad wants him to."

She shook her head. "I mean, there is that, but there's more. It's just a sense, but—"

"He looked nice in his pink cummerbund and bow tie last night," I said in a soft voice. It was a murky hint, but given all the clues she'd been dropping, I might not be out of line thinking Brandon didn't want a wife so much as a beard.

Her face colored nearly the same shade as the aforementioned cummerbund.

"A man has to be either very secure in his masculinity or gay to be that comfortable in fashion-doll pink, even at a breast-cancer-awareness event," I continued.

She nodded, which meant only that she agreed with me.

"So which is it?" I asked.

"I don't know," she admitted in a low voice.

"Guess," I suggested.

Tears glittered in her green eyes so that they resembled shards of a broken beer bottle. "Gay," she whispered. "I don't know anything for certain, but sometimes..." She broke off. Shrugged.

"Listen to your gut," I said. "If this feels wrong, don't go through with the wedding. Break off the engagement now."

"I can't. Dad sent an announcement to the paper last week. It would be such an embarrassment." A tear trickled from the corner of her eye.

"Better a month of embarrassment than a lifetime of misery." I squeezed her fingers. "I'd trade in toe curling for embarrassment any day."

"But Dad—"

"Ditched Mom and married his toe curler."

Victoria opened her mouth as if to refute me and then closed it and pursed her lips.

"You haven't set a date. You haven't bought a dress. You haven't even asked Lexi and me to be in the wedding party. Canceling now is easy."

"We've looked at venues," she said in a wavering voice.

"Have you put down a deposit?"

"I don't think so. Dad is paying for everything."

Of course. The event would be more about Dad's status than Victoria's happiness.

I braced myself to be blunt. "There's nothing wrong with being homosexual. Unless you're trying to pass for straight and marry someone from whom you're keeping it a secret. Then it's a crime. No, it's a sin. If Brandon really loves you, he'll tell you the truth."

"What if he doesn't know the truth?"

This conversation was getting too awkward. I wasn't helping. "I know it's none of my business, but do you have a sex life?"

Her face colored. "Brandon wants to wait until we're married."

Well, crap. How could I fault a guy for having morals?

Or he's using morality as an excuse, evil Carrie whispered to compassionate Caroline.

I was starting to dislike Brandon intensely. If I thought he truly believed a couple should wait until after the vows before falling into bed, I could respect him. But he was in my father's pocket and had political aspirations. The pink cummerbund only added to my sense that all was not right in my sister's universe.

"Maybe your toes don't curl because he's inexperienced," I offered.

"Maybe." But Victoria looked and sounded skeptical.

"I didn't come over to talk about me and Brandon." She squared her shoulders and smiled at me. A fake, perky smile. Victoria was *never* perky. The Maplethorpes don't have perky genes. "I'm worried about you."

I'm sure my smile matched hers. "I'm a survivor, Vic. You know that."

"I don't know anything, not really," she replied.

"This isn't the first time Win's left to go to the next level in his career. I survived it last time; I'll survive it now." I spoke with confidence.

"You love him."

"Of course. Did you ever doubt it?"

"Does Win know?"

"He doesn't need to know. He's gone. I'm here." I shrugged as if I were more concerned about baseball stats than Win Winston.

"But he said he'd looked for you for seven years."

"It's a great line, isn't it?" I swallowed hard, trying to dislodge the lump in my throat. It was one thing to think in those terms and quite another to admit aloud.

"Win always shows up when I'm involved with the wrong guy," I explained. "Not that I've ever seriously considered a future with Chandler, but Win helps me see why the other man isn't right for me."

"Because Win is the perfect man for you."

I changed the subject again. "Chandler is not taking my hints, though. I don't know how to get any clearer than 'we have no future together.' I almost had to give him a crotch shot last night. He said he'd back off when I matched Dad's offer. When I asked him if he meant money, he refused to talk about it."

"Dad's *offer*?" Victoria's pale eyebrows shot up her forehead.

I nodded. "Any idea what that means?"

She shook her head.

"I'll bet Brandon knows."

Her gaze met mine and stayed. "You're probably right," she said after a lengthy pause. "The question now becomes, do I have the courage to ask him?"

Ask him if he is gay or ask him about Dad's offer?

Victoria stayed a few more minutes and then left me alone to wallow.

No. I refused to wallow.

I poured myself a glass of wine, lit a vanilla-scented candle, put on a Bob Dylan mix I'd made myself that I called "Dylan Says It Best"—the ultimate in "fuck you" music—and cranked the volume. I was so into "The Idiot Wind" that I didn't hear my phone right away, and when I did, I didn't rush to answer it. There was no one to whom I wished to speak.

I glanced at the screen. Win. I debated not answering for all of half a second. "Hi."

"Hi."

Gee. That was worth rushing across the room.

"Why didn't you answer your phone?"

I said nothing. Win's departure was old news. Real old. I got over it before; I'd get over it again.

"You're pissed," he said.

"Why would I be angry?" Indeed, I had no reason to be upset. Hadn't I always known Win would be going to Columbia sooner rather than later? Any irritation I might have felt was directed at myself.

"Carrie." His voice rumbled across the cellular technology to lodge in my chest. "Don't do this. Don't cut me off like you did last time."

Time must have warped his memory.

The wine hadn't done its work. I wasn't numb. I needed to be very careful about what I said. "I didn't cut you off."

"I miss you," he said. "I want you to come to Columbia."

I sat back and closed my eyes. "No."

"Why not?" He sounded petulant.

"Let's start with the fact that you're not there half the time. I'm not going to disrupt my entire life for a part-time lover. I have obligations here."

"Chad?"

"It's Chandler, and no. But my sisters both need me right now."

"I need you too."

I almost said that what he thought he needed from me he could get from any woman, but that would cheapen what I felt for him, so I didn't. I didn't say anything.

"Are you going to let your sisters dictate every move you make for the rest of your life?" He sounded impatient now.

"My sisters have a better chance of being in my life six months from now," I retorted. "I'm your summer fling, remember? You flinged. Flung. Whatever. Now it's over. Why are you trying to drag it out?"

"Who said we were just a fling?" Definitely impatient and more than a little peeved. "You're my good-luck girl. I need you. I can't win without you."

Lucky me, relegated to the status of a rabbit's foot.

"Win, I'm really tired," I said. "Call me tomorrow, okay?"

I wasn't going to hold my breath. I'd been down this road with Win Winston before. This time, I wasn't nearly as vulnerable.

Chapter Thirteen

Alexandra looked wan as she smiled at Victoria and me, but she was smiling. That was the important thing. "I didn't mean to create such havoc," she said in her usual voice.

For some reason, I had expected her to be contrite and humble when she was released from Franklin Hall.

"You're entitled to your emotions," I said. She was. I understood her feelings on a lot of levels and needed to share my own black moment with her, but not in front of Victoria. "Only next time, don't express yourself in blood in my bathroom. Okay?"

"You're a writer," Victoria added. "Next time you feel desperate, journal about it."

"Next time, I'm going after Dad," Alexandra said.

We'd made it to Victoria's condo after a tense ride from the hospital.

Some converted factories are as gloomy as a grave, but Victoria had painted her former-shoe-factory brick walls a buttery yellow that brightened the atmosphere. Sunlight spilled through large windows hung with white sheers. Pale pink peonies cavorted across the creamy upholstery of her cushy sofa. Rose-scented potpourri lingered in the air. Everything was pastel and gentle, much like Victoria. We draped ourselves over the light, tasteful furniture, acting as if nothing were wrong. Victoria even served minted lemonade in blush-colored glasses, reinforcing the impression that I was at a garden party.

In a way, it *was* a party. Alexandra was out of the hospital, and Victoria and I were going to spend the day with her.

"Does Marc know where I'm staying?"

Victoria and I exchanged a glance. Neither of us had called him. Our agenda was simple: get Alexandra out of the hospital and move her in with Victoria. Marc didn't figure into our scenario.

"Maybe you two should cool it for a while," Victoria suggested.

"So Dad can sic Andrew on me?" Alexandra's laugh was strained. "Not likely. If he starts turning up again, I'm going after him too."

"I'll help," I muttered.

"What's going on with you and the pitcher?" Alexandra asked.

I wanted to keep my most recent conversation with Win to myself for a bit so I could nurse it like a spark threatened by a blizzard.

"The pitcher was recalled to the mother ship," I said. "In the middle of yesterday's game, no less."

"And you just let him go?" Alexandra sounded like herself. Feisty. Outspoken. Overly emotional.

How could she sound so normal after what she'd done?

"I didn't know he'd gone until after the fact," I explained. I did not want to have this discussion again. I wanted to close my gritty eyes for a moment's rest. I hadn't slept at all. "I don't want to talk about it right now. I have other things on my mind besides Win Winston. Like you. I've been worried sick about you."

"We all have," Victoria added.

"Including Dad?"

"He hasn't said much to me," I admitted.

He hadn't. But what he had said wasn't very...loving. His anger because *he* hadn't been notified was his most tangible reaction, and I wished it was based in some kind of affection.

"He's upset," I said. That was true too.

"We'll have lunch in a bit," Victoria said, changing the subject. "But first, we need to set some parameters."

Alexandra rolled her eyes. "Look, I'm sorry. I was drunk. I never would have done it"—she raised her bandaged arms—"otherwise."

I didn't understand how she could be so cavalier about slicing her wrists and scaring me and Victoria the way she had. Her casual demeanor irritated me. I reminded myself she had issues, that I needed to be compassionate, not pissed.

"Catch me up on everything," she commanded. "How did the gala go?"

"We missed you," I said. "You should have been there and at the Mother's Day Game."

"Well, I wasn't, and the world didn't come to an end."

I opened my mouth to say something to put her in her place, then remembered Alexandra the drama queen. Maybe she wasn't all bravado. Maybe her mouth was a form of armor.

"Now tell me all about your pitcher."

"He's not my pitcher," I replied.

"But he's replaced Chandler, yes?"

"Chandler was never placed. Win just made it clear to everyone else."

"Cool. That's how I feel about Marc and Andrew." Alexandra turned to Victoria. "How about you and Brandon? I see you're still wearing his ring."

Victoria's smile was tight. Forced. "Dad sent the engagement announcement to the paper."

"So? Engagements can be broken, and Dad may be a three-letter word ending in *D*, but he's not God. My therapist just said so."

"Not everyone has your flair." Victoria's tone was dry.

"I don't know." Alexandra tossed her head so that her long blonde curls flipped behind her shoulders. "Caroline's doing pretty good with her high-profile pitcher."

"You have no idea," Victoria muttered.

"Then fill me in, and take notes for yourself."

I wanted to squirm as Victoria told Alexandra about the foundation's gala, the dancing and bachelor auction, about Chandler's insistence that he was betrothed to me, and about Swanson Crabtree getting hit by a pitch.

"That was an accident," I protested, even though I suspected Win's throw had been intentional.

"A photo of Win and Caroline dancing at the event was picked up by a wire service," Victoria concluded. "It's very telling."

"What? I didn't know that." I didn't want the world to know about my relationship with Win.

"It's great publicity for the foundation." Victoria's smile was genuine, and she sounded pleased.

"And it sounds like Caroline stuck it to Chandler but good."

"I didn't stick it to anyone. I don't want to talk about this. I think we need to discuss parameters."

Alexandra stiffened. "You two don't have custody of me."

"You tried to kill yourself three days ago," I reminded her. In case she'd forgotten or something.

Her green gaze clashed with mine. "And your point is what? You want me to beg your forgiveness? Well, I don't need anyone's forgiveness except my own."

I didn't think my irritation stemmed from wanting her to beg my pardon. "Should I have just left you there?"

She flinched as if I'd slapped her.

"Do you want us just to ignore everything that's happened to you in the past seventy-two hours?"

"Yes." Her chin tilted up, daring me to say more, but I glimpsed tears in her eyes.

Victoria escaped to her kitchen. We could hear her banging around, fixing lunch for us. I thought I heard a quiet sob. *Maplethorpes don't cry in public.*

"What's up with her?" Alexandra asked as soon as Victoria was out of sight. As if everything was exactly the way it was before she'd shown up drunk on my doorstep. "The only thing she talked about was you and Win."

"I don't think all is well in the Blandrom."

Alexandra snickered. "He's gay."

"Did Marc tell you that?"

"What do you have against Marc?"

Lots of things. He's a leech. He's using Dad's marriage to Polly as a livelihood and looks to ensure it by latching on to you.

I brushed a strand of hair off my cheek. "I think you need to learn some life lessons your own way. If that includes bonking Marc's brains out, that's your prerogative. You're like me. You learn from your own mistakes."

"And you think Marc is a mistake."

I chose my words with care. "If he is, he's your mistake, just like—" I started to say *Flash* but caught myself in time.

"Win?" Alexandra asked.

Win would never be a mistake. The mistake was how I'd handled things then, how I was handling things now.

I shook my head. "Drifting along in Chandler's wake," I replied. "My apathy led him to think there was more to our relationship than there is or ever can be."

"You're different since Win showed up," she said.

"It's the sex," I said, and she laughed like my little sister, Lexi Lou.

Maybe she was okay.

"Sleep with Marc if you must," I continued. "But finish your novel and finish school. Don't tie yourself to something you might regret in seven years."

"That sounds like experience," Alexandra said.

"Lunch is ready," Victoria called from the dining area, saving me from having to respond.

After we ate, Alexandra pulled out her phone and excused herself.

I'd wondered how long she could go without a Marc fix.

"She thinks she's in love with Marc," I told Victoria. "I guess she needs to learn from her own mistakes."

"Like you did?"

The question startled me. "Of course," I replied. "Do I come across to you as thinking I'm perfect?"

"Sometimes."

Ouch.

I smiled anyway. "Good. Means I'm covering up pretty well."

"And damn the consequences."

Was she going to start with that crap again? Because if she was, I was so going to be history, even if we had promised the day to Alexandra.

Victoria didn't sigh aloud, but one was there in her body language. "Sorry. It's just that I'm jealous of you. You and Win."

"There's nothing to be jealous about." My voice was steady, as was the gaze I kept on her. Inside, I was shrieking, quaking, tearing out my hair. "Win's not here. I'm not with him."

"Have you spoken to him?"

I paused before nodding. Apparently Win was more important than Alexandra.

"What did he say?"

"He asked me to come to Columbia," I admitted.

"And?"

"And nothing. He's not there half the time. I'm not going to uproot my life, everything I've worked for, just to have sex every couple of weeks."

"Toe-curling sex," Victoria corrected.

"Toe-curling sex," I agreed. My body flushed just remembering his kiss. I didn't dare recall anything else.

Our entire relationship was based on nothing more than sex.

Alexandra rejoined us.

"How's Marc?" I asked.

"Fine. He's coming over after work."

"Do you think that's a good idea?" Victoria asked.

I didn't, but I kept my mouth shut. I'd said what I needed to say.

"I don't care what either of you thinks," Alexandra told us. "I love Marc. He loves me."

She sounded more grim than happy.

My cell phone chirped from my purse. I couldn't imagine who would be calling me in the middle of the day. Dad knew Victoria and I had closed the office to take care of Alexandra. He had enough sense not to interfere in what he had called *"damned female foolishness."*

Win. Calling me. I'd figured he'd called last night out of guilt and that would be the last I heard from him.

"Hi," I said, walking into the foyer for privacy.

"Hi." His voice was like a welcoming beam of spring sunshine after a long Syracuse winter.

I waited for him to say something else. Small talk. Something.

I wasn't prepared for what he did say.

"What do I have to do to get you to come to Columbia?"

"Will you be in Columbia next week?"

I already knew the answer: sixteen straight games on the West Coast—as far away from South Carolina as their team could get.

"Ever been to LA?" he asked.

"Yes. I hated it." I did. Too bright, too populous, too vacant. Hollow. There hadn't been anything under its glossy surface.

"Me too," he said. "Come keep me company."

"I'm sorry," I said. And I was, a little. "My sister just got out of the hospital."

"You're on suicide watch?"

"I suppose you could call it that." But I didn't want to.

"Where are you now?"

"Victoria's place. Alexandra is going to stay with her for a while."

"Good," he said. "I'll call you after the game tonight. It'll be late."

"When do you pitch again?" I needed to figure out how I could watch the games in which he pitched. Televised baseball in Syracuse was limited to the New York teams, and the game of the week.

"Friday. I'd love to have you in the stands for my comeback game."

"I can't," I said. I could hear my sisters' murmurs as they carried on without me. "Alexandra needs me."

I half expected Win to tell me that he needed me too, but he didn't. He didn't need anyone. He just wanted me. And after a few weeks back in the bigs, he'd forget about me again. The only difference this time would be that he'd know where to find me.

Maybe I should have told him not to call. I didn't want to anticipate nightly contact. I knew myself well enough to picture long evenings clutching my cell phone whether I was at my apartment or at the stadium. That's what I'd done the last time.

Did I want to go back to being that girl?

No. Emphatically no.

I needed to be a role model for Alexandra, whether she liked it or not.

"How long do you think your sister will need you?"

"I don't know." His question irked me, but I couldn't figure out why. Maybe because you couldn't put a radar gun on emotion. On life.

"Look," I said. "I've got to go help clean up from lunch."

I ended the call and rejoined my sisters.

Chapter Fourteen

No one bothered me at the ballpark that night. It was as if everyone had finally heard me.

Except Swanson Crabtree. Buffalo was still in town, and Crabtree tried to take advantage of Win's absence.

Ignoring him wasn't difficult. He wasn't playing, probably due to sore ribs. I slipped Salty the Mascot ten dollars to stand on the roof of the dugout and shake a finger at Crabtree.

I couldn't focus. I wanted to blame Crabtree's antics for stealing the magic from me but, in a fit of brutal honesty, had to admit my state of mind was my own doing. I missed Win.

My cell phone vibrated in my jeans pocket during the seventh-inning stretch.

"Is Lexi with you?" Victoria sounded harassed.

"No. Why?"

"She's not here." I could barely hear Victoria over the final strains of "Take Me Out to the Ballgame."

"Where's here?"

"My condo!" Victoria shrieked.

"Hey!" I said, rather sharply. "Calm down. Take a deep breath." I thought I heard a sob. "Vic? What's going on?"

"Brandon and I went out to dinner. She wasn't here when we came home."

There was no reason to panic. "Have you tried her cell phone?"

"Of course! She's not answering."

I don't think I'd ever heard Victoria sound quite as frazzled.

"What about Marc?" I asked.

"I don't have Marc's number. Do you?"

"Let me see if Dad has it," I said.

"Don't let him know she's missing!"

How stupid did Victoria think I was? "Let me see if Dad's here," I said. I couldn't think of anything else. As much as I didn't want to talk to him, finding Alexandra would go a long way in helping me sleep later.

"Call me right back." Victoria disconnected.

I pulled my binoculars from my baseball bag and trained them on Dad's box. Dark. Which didn't mean anything except I would have to walk up there.

The crowd was thinning. The trip didn't take long, but it was in vain.

I leaned against the wall in the hall outside the empty box and called Victoria. Since Dad rarely left a game before it was over, it was safe to assume he hadn't come to the park. Maybe Alexandra was with him.

Victoria answered on the first ring. "Dad's not here," I said. "Are Lexi's things still at your place?" I wished I'd thought to ask earlier.

"I can't tell. Some stuff is here."

"Okay. Call Polly for Marc's number."

"I never call Polly," Victoria protested. "How could I call her now without arousing suspicion?"

"Better you than me," I replied.

"You're Matthew's favorite sister. Call him."

"It's past his bedtime."

"Then stop in on your way home."

"I took the bus!" I was starting to be as exasperated as Victoria.

"Why do you have to take the bus when you have a perfectly good car?" Victoria snapped.

I hung up on Victoria, gathered my courage, and called Polly. "Do you have any idea what time it is?" Dad asked instead of answering the phone like a normal person. "Has something else happened to Alexandra?"

That answered one question. "I need to talk to Polly," I replied.

"Polly?"

I never called to talk to my stepmother. "Yes, Polly." I didn't choke on her name. Hadn't in years. I could have asked Dad for Marc's number, but I figured Polly was female and might be more sympathetic.

"Why do you need to talk to her? If you're going to abuse her the way you've been digging at me—"

"Will you just put Polly on the phone?"

Dad hung up on me.

I muttered a couple of words I save for special occasions and dialed Victoria. "I tried to get Marc's number from Polly, but Dad wouldn't let me talk to her. I did, however, find out that Alexandra isn't there." I slid down the wall and sat on the cold concrete floor. "Did you look for a note?"

"A suicide note?"

"Any kind of note! Do I have to do all the thinking here?"

"There's no note."

I heard the tears in Victoria's voice. She was supposed to take care of Alexandra and had failed. I took a deep breath. Summoned compassion. "I'll be there just as quickly as I can."

By the time I made my way to the concourse level, the game had ended. People trickled out of the stadium and meandered toward the bus. A taxi wouldn't have been faster.

Half an hour later I was at Victoria's condo.

"I need a beer," I said as I walked through the door.

Victoria was pale and tense, and I remembered how awful I'd felt only a few days ago when I'd found Alexandra in my bathroom.

Brandon wrinkled his perfectly ironed expression. "We need to keep our heads," he said.

I ignored him and plopped on the love seat next to Victoria. We hugged. "This isn't your fault."

"She said she'd be fine."

"Brandon, make yourself useful and get Marc's phone number from Dad or Polly," I said. Why hadn't one of them thought of that? Victoria was a savvy business woman. I was surprised at how easily she'd fallen apart.

He reached into his pocket and pulled out his *super phone.*

"You think they're together?" Victoria asked.

I tried to remember everything we'd talked about that afternoon. "Running off with Marc is exactly something Lexi would do."

I reached for Victoria's hands, which were as cold and frail as snowflakes. The dim light in her living room cast deep shadows on her face, turning her natural loveliness into something else. I wondered how much of the haggard look was over Alexandra and how much was over her relationship with Brandon.

Brandon said something into his phone and then swiped his finger across the screen. "I have Marc's phone number," he said to Victoria. "Do you want me to call him?"

Victoria nodded, and I kept my sarcastic thoughts to myself.

We waited as Brandon stood there, phone pressed to his ear. His stance said he was in charge. "Marc. Brandon Cummings. Call me when you get this message."

He did the swipe thing again, then pocketed the phone.

"Should we call the police?" Victoria's voice wavered.

Brandon shook his head. "Your father wouldn't appreciate bringing the authorities into Alexandra's present peccadillo. If it comes to needing them, I have someone I can call who will be discreet."

"What if she's done something really stupid? Like going to one of the insurance towers downtown and jumping off?" Victoria asked. "Or plans to hurl herself onto the railroad tracks?"

Brandon made a sound of impatience. "You're as melodramatic as your sisters. Stop being ridiculous."

Maybe Victoria's scenarios were a bit extreme, but her concern was valid. And where did a Blandroid get off calling anyone ridiculous?

My cell phone vibrated in my pocket. I pulled it out. Win.

My heart surged, and for a moment, I resented the constraints placed on me by my family.

"Hi," I said. I lurched to my feet and wandered into Victoria's foyer. "Can I call you back in a little bit?"

"What's wrong?"

I really didn't want to get into all the family angst with him now. He was gone. These phone calls were merely a phasing out of our relationship. I couldn't let them be anything else.

"Alexandra has disappeared," I admitted. "She was supposed to be staying with Victoria, but when Victoria and Brandon were out to dinner, Alexandra...vanished."

"You don't sound panicked."

He was right. I wasn't frantic. I was more annoyed at Brandon than anything. How dare he not take Victoria's concerns seriously? Training for his political life, I guessed.

"Panic won't help," I told Win. "Can I call you when I get home?"

"If you don't call in an hour, I'll call you again," he said.

I was glad. I needed counterbalance to Brandon's indifference.

It took me another forty-five minutes to break free. There wasn't anything Victoria or I could do, so it didn't make sense for me to stay at her condo.

Brandon supported my theory that Alexandra was with Marc, and again, annoyance flared. I didn't want him on my side.

All the way home I tried to justify calling Win. If I were a good sister, I wouldn't tie up my phone for who knows how long talking to him, but if Alexandra tried to call me, she could be a good sister and leave a message if I didn't pick up. But I would pick up. I always did.

Once home, I changed into an oversize T-shirt and crawled into bed with my phone.

Win beat me to it. "Are you home?" he asked.

"Yes." I told him the skeleton of Alexandra's latest crisis.

"Seeing you in action with your family makes me glad I don't have any siblings," he said.

He never spoke of his family. The topic had never come up when we were in Cortland, and we had other issues these days. I asked him to tell me about them—his family, not our issues. I learned about his father, a corporate type like my own, his socialite mother, and about growing up outside of Cleveland in Shaker Heights. His parents had supported his baseball dream despite not understanding his passion.

Win didn't sound close to them, which surprised me. He spoke fondly of them but seemed...disconnected.

I stifled a yawn and snuggled deeper into my bed.

"I'm keeping you awake," Win said.

"It's okay."

It was. I loved the timbre of his voice, deep and steady. It vibrated against my eardrums before winding its way through me, into my chest, curling into my heart. He remained a sanctuary from the turmoil of my life.

"Are you in bed?" he asked.

"Mmm."

"Wish I was there with you."

"Wish you were too," I murmured.

"I'd love to kiss you right now."

"I probably wouldn't get much sleep."

He chuckled. "You're right. You wouldn't."

Then his tone turned serious. "What do I have to do to get you to come with me?"

Why did he have to keep harping on this? "You're rarely in one place for more than four nights in a row six to eight months of the year. Do other women travel with the team?"

"Sometimes. I'll settle for sometimes, Carrie."

And that was the problem. Sometimes equaled temporary to my way of thinking, and our temporary affair was over. He'd moved on, just as I'd always known he would. Dragging it out was pointless. All I'd earn would be a deeper hurt.

I opened my mouth to tell him that but couldn't. I wasn't quite ready to sever our relationship. Long distance would be a good way to ease back to my regularly scheduled life.

"**S**he eloped with Marc," Victoria said, her tone flat.

"What?" I sat up and switched on the bedside lamp. My alarm clock read six thirty a.m. I put the phone on speaker and rubbed my eyes.

Why was Victoria calling me so early? It seemed like I'd barely gotten to sleep. Win and I had been on the phone for at least nine innings.

"Didn't she text you?"

I scrubbed my face with my palm. "I dunno." My voice was little more than a croak. Pale gray light edged the window blind. It was a good thing Victoria had called, because it looked as if I'd forgotten to set my alarm. "They eloped?"

"As in ran off and found a JP," Victoria confirmed.

"I thought there was a waiting period in this state," I mumbled. "One day or something."

"How would I know?"

I yawned. Stretched. Rolled my shoulders. "I guess that makes her Marc's problem now, doesn't it?"

"How can you be so blasé?"

There were a million and twelve reasons, I was certain, but at that moment I couldn't think of a one. "Sorry," I mumbled. "Late night."

I pictured Victoria rolling her eyes.

"But off the top of my head, I think a husband is supposed to take precedence over sisters."

"So if he beats on her, we're supposed to ignore it?"

Okay, now I was awake. "Marc beats on her?"

"I don't know. I was asking a hypothetical question."

"If he beats on her, we kill him," I replied, thinking about the Dixie Chicks and a guy named Earl.

"Fine. Whatever. It just sounded like you're glad to be rid of her. That you're washing your hands of her."

I sank against the pillows propped along the headboard of my bed. "I didn't mean that at all, and I'm very hurt that you thought that."

Victoria wasn't the only who could play a guilt card.

"I just meant that Marc obviously loves her and wants to take care of her," I said. "I mean, he works for Dad, and he knows Dad does not condone his relationship with Lexi. Yet he married her anyway."

Victoria was silent for a moment, as if thinking. "Okay. What do we do now? Throw them a party? A bridal shower? What?"

"How about nothing?" I suggested. "She didn't care enough to have us there or even tell us until after the fact. Why should we fuss over her?"

I was actually starting to feel jealous. My younger sister had the guts to run away with the man she loved. I didn't have the courage to fly to the West Coast to watch the man I loved pitch six innings.

How pathetic was that?

"Does Dad know?" I asked.

"How should I know?" Victoria replied, more than a hint of snark in her voice.

"Well, I don't think we should tell him," I said. My brain was finally kicking into gear. "There has to be a waiting period after they get a license, and they don't have a license yet."

I swung my legs out of bed and grabbed the phone. My laptop was on my desk in the corner of the living room. I could run a web search on my questions.

"What are you talking about?"

"You're the blushing bride-to-be," I reminded her as I padded barefoot across the cold wooden floors.

"Brandon is handling all those sorts of details," she muttered.

Yet another sign that her heart wasn't in her relationship with Brandon, but I didn't say anything. Not now. This was about Alexandra.

"I'm pretty sure both parties have to arrive in person to get a marriage license, and Marc and Lexi haven't had time. Either you or I were with her from the time she left the hospital until city hall closed."

"Right. So we could go stake out city hall and stop this."

My laptop took forever to boot.

"I'm not so sure I want to stop them," I admitted. "I think our big concern is how to keep Dad away from her. He was pretty adamant about wanting to see her."

"So he can bully her?"

"I can't think of any other reason."

My computer finally connected to the Internet. God bless search engines. I had what I wanted in less than two minutes.

"Okay," I said to Victoria. "Both parties have to apply in person with their birth certificates. Do you know if Lexi has her birth certificate?"

"No idea."

"Then there's a twenty-four-hour waiting period. Okay. That means Lexi and Marc are holed up somewhere together. She tipped her hand by texting too soon."

"You sound as if you condone this."

I thought about it for all of ten seconds. "Yeah, I do."

"Because it will annoy Dad?"

"Ooh, bonus points," I said. "Nope, because she has the courage to follow her convictions."

"She just got out of the psychiatric hospital," Victoria pointed out. "I wouldn't trust her motivations."

"But she was in the hospital because she loves Marc and—"

"She was in the hospital because she didn't get her own way about Marc, and Dad threatened to cut off her college funding."

That was harsh.

"Dad's going to do more than cut off college money when he finds out about this. Marc works for him, remember?"

Okay, she had a point.

"I suggest we do Dad-avoidance," I said.

"Why?"

I rolled my eyes at my terrarium. "Because you know how you envy the way you think Win looks at me? Well, I'm jealous of Alexandra's courage." I barely had the nerve to admit that aloud. "And right now I don't want Dad to dampen my enthusiasm. I don't want his brand of persuasion hammering, yammering at me. Let's take off. It's a pretty spring day—"

"We've taken off too much time lately," Victoria reminded me. "Yesterday, last week—"

"And we—you—pulled off our big event anyway. And we worked all weekend. Let's call it comp time."

"You have an answer for everything, don't you?"

If I did, I would know what to do about Win.

But I didn't share that thought with Victoria.

"I do need to start looking at wedding dresses," she said. Her tone was hesitant.

I didn't push. Girlie stuff like clothes shopping wasn't high on my list of enjoyable ways to spend my time. Victoria and Alexandra were Dad's froufrou daughters. Me, I went to baseball games.

"Or maybe I'll elope too."

I worded my response with care. No suggestion of perhaps finding another groom. "I can't see an aspiring politician not wanting a lavish affair of a wedding. Perception and all that. And Dad probably expects an event."

"It's supposed to be the bride's day," she reminded me. "I'm not going to let anyone steal that from me."

"Good for you," I said, and I meant it.

"Dad suggested I wear Mom's wedding gown."

I wasn't sure my voice would work when I responded. "That's a really bad idea."

"It is." She cleared her throat. "I said no. Looks like you might be the one wearing it."

"I doubt it." I kept my tone as light as I could, even though my father's insensitivity appalled me. I was surprised the dress still existed. Someone should have tossed it when Dad threw out our mother.

"I'm going to work today," Victoria continued. "I need the distraction."

"Even if it means Dad haranguing you?"

"He has the right to know what's going on. Alexandra is his daughter. We never should have kept her...accident from him."

Accident?

"Her injuries were intentional," I reminded Victoria. A flash of my bloodied bathroom made me wince. "She was drunk."

Maybe Victoria had a point about me fabricating an answer for everything.

"Alexandra needs to learn there are consequences to her actions." Victoria was starting to sound like she had a stick up her ass. "Maybe you need a refresher course. I expect you at the office at your usual time." Her tone was frosty.

"Nope," I said. "I'm calling in sick." Not a lie. I was sick of all the family drama.

"You don't have sick days," my sister, the boss, reminded me.

"So dock my pay. Good-bye, Vic."

I disconnected and closed my eyes.

I was regressing to the girl I'd been at eighteen, and wasn't sure I liked that.

Win in my life disrupted my molecular structure or something. Made me more than a little crazy. Woke me up. Heightened all my senses. Kept me on an emotional razor's edge. One slip could be fatal, and I didn't know if I could survive it again.

So staying involved with Win was detrimental to my health. He was gone. Back in the stratosphere in which he belonged. He was major league, and I was the girl in the bleachers of the hometown team.

I shouldn't answer my phone the next time he called. Or if I did answer, I should tell him—gently, of course—that we needed to reassess our relationship. Not that we had a relationship.

Our affair. Yeah. That's what it was. An affair. Not a tawdry, nasty thing, but a convenience for Win. I didn't mind, because I'd learned it wasn't something lacking in me that kept me single and not interested in changing that status.

Chapter Fifteen

I worked at home that day. The miracle of the Internet assisted me. I ignored phone calls from my father and Victoria. I also read and deleted the text message from Alexandra announcing she'd eloped. Disregarding the incessant buzz of the intercom was more difficult, but I figured it was my father trying to bully me when bullying Victoria netted him no answers. That assumption was confirmed a while later by a call from Susie Buddha, who hung up before my father could snatch away her telephone.

I also discovered every baseball game was streamed on the Internet every night, so I'd be able to watch Win pitch.

Which was silly, because I planned to ease him out of my life. Even a long-distance relationship wouldn't work. Too much history stood in the way.

Win called at three in the morning.

"I miss you," he said. "I wish you were with me now."

"Things are still rough here," I replied, falling back on my current excuse: my family. "My sister eloped."

"Which sister: the suicide or the beard?"

Everything in me went very still. "Beard?"

"Your older sister is dating a gay man. Don't tell me you didn't know."

"Just because he wore a pink cummerbund to the foundation event—"

"Carrie, he's gay," Win interrupted.

I released a breath I didn't know I'd been holding. "Yeah, I think so too, but the other sister eloped. The suicide, as you so rudely called her."

I was annoyed with his flippant remark. Alexandra was my baby sister. He had no right to make snotty comments, no matter how true.

"She finally got in touch with you? Good. I know you were worried."

"I'm still not sure marrying Marc was a good thing, but at least we know she's okay."

"Focus on that," suggested the King of Focus.

"I am. That and her attitude. I kind of admire the way she went after what she wanted." Those words were difficult for me to say aloud, especially to Win.

He didn't say anything for a couple of seconds, as if he was digesting my confession. When he did speak, it was in a low, rough voice that rasped along every nerve in my body. "That's even better news." I neither confirmed nor denied his analysis.

"What are you wearing right now?" he asked.

"A batting-practice T-shirt from last year and a pair of panties," I replied.

"A BPT?"

"Yeah. The Saltboilers have a garage sale every year where they sell used stuff, and I bought a batting-practice T-shirt."

"Whose number?

I shrugged, even though he couldn't see me. "Forty-eight." The number meant nothing to me and would mean even less to him. It was just an oversize T-shirt I'd bought for ten bucks.

"No bra?" he asked.

My nipples tightened under the silky texture of the shirt.

"I don't wear a bra to bed," I reminded him.

Of course, the nights I'd spent with him, I'd worn nothing but beard burn.

"Good," he murmured. "Don't you want to know what I'm wearing?"

I laughed, sounding shaky. "Probably nothing at all."

"A big smile," he corrected me. "And a hard-on."

What could I say to that? I was already warm and tingly from talking to him.

"If you were here with me right now, I'd kiss you." His voice deepened; the rasp became harsher. "Softly at first, just savoring the taste of you. You know, I never forgot the taste or scent of you."

My breath hitched.

"Imagine I'm kissing you. That my tongue is in your mouth."

My eyes closed. I wished I had one of his T-shirts or something permeated with the fragrance of him.

"Now I'm working my way down your neck. Your neck, your throat has its very own flavor. Did you know that?"

I shivered, wishing he were there in my bedroom, matching action to word.

"My hand finds your breast. You have the prettiest breasts I've ever seen. I wish I could look at your breasts all day, every day for the rest of my life. Touch them. Flick your pretty pink nipples. You do it. Flick your nipple."

I froze.

"Carrie, please." His breathing seemed a little heavier. "Put your phone on speaker, okay? And I'll do the same."

The tingling and heat inside me increased. Spread.

My fingers shook as I placed the cell phone on my night table and activated the speaker. This was...weird, but I wasn't completely uncomfortable. That was even weirder.

"You with me?" The hollow, echoing effect of the speakerphone enhanced the smoky roughness of Win's voice.

"Yeah." My throat was so tight I could barely whisper.

I dragged a thumb across an already raspberried nipple. It felt...good. Not as good as Win's touch, but not as shameful as I'd thought it would.

Yeah. Me. Feeling shameful about sex. Wild, huh? But until Win had walked back into my life, I'd been celibate since the day he'd walked out.

"Leave your shirt on, okay?" Win continued. He sounded like he had some experience with...this. "Is the BPT black with white numbers and the logo over the left breast?"

"Yes."

"I'll bet you look sexy as all hell in one. Play with your nipples, Carrie. Pretend it's me pinching, rolling, tweaking."

"If you pretend I'm doing the same to you." My voice felt as gravelly as his sounded. Win had very sensitive nipples, small and brown but extremely responsive. "Pretend I'm licking your nipples," I said as a rubbed my own.

"Oh Jesus," he said on a heavy exhale.

My nipples tightened into little knots of aching need.

"I'm taking one into my mouth now," he said. "Just a nibble. Just my tongue flicking back and forth."

Something deep inside me pulsed. Quivered. My thighs relaxed; my knees splayed. I might have moaned. I slipped my hands under my shirt so I could feel flesh on flesh, imagining Win's mouth, his calloused hands on me.

It was nice. Hot. Very hot.

"Do you still have on your panties?" he asked.

"Mmm," I replied.

"Take 'em off. Slowly. Use only one hand. Run your palm down the side of your ribs, slowly, lightly. Just skim. Dawdle at your hip. Spread your fingers."

I followed his direction, lightly brushing the warm flesh covering my hip bone with the pads of my fingers. I knew they weren't Win's fingers, because his were calloused from pitching.

I wished I could return some of the heat to him. "I'm kissing my way down your chest," I said. "You smell fabulous. You taste like my favorite food."

His breath whistled. He wasn't the only one whose words could tantalize.

"My tongue is rimming your navel," I told him.

He groaned.

I imagined kissing the thin, taut flesh between his navel and the root of his penis. Inhaling the musk of his sex.

"Pull off your panties," he told me. "Draw them down your legs very slowly without touching yourself at all."

Easier said than done. "I'm licking your lower belly now," I said as I slipped my panties over one ankle. "Your penis is erect, huge, brushing against my chin, my cheek."

"Are your panties off?"

"Yes."

"I'm spreading your legs now. Kissing the insides of your thighs. You're so soft. So perfect. I want to give you a hickey right where your legs join your body."

"My tongue brushes the tip of your cock," I replied. "Touch the tip of your cock and rub in the precum."

His groan was a little louder now. I felt...powerful.

"Part your pussy lips. Find your clit."

I was wet. Very wet.

"Rub your clit. Pretend it's my tongue. I'm licking you, sucking your clit. Slipping a finger into you. God, you're so wet. So hot. So ready."

My breath was coming faster now, heavier, matching his.

"I'm going to push my cock into you now," he said. "God, you're so hot, so tight, so wet, so perfect. Use your fingers, Carrie."

My hips moved as I remembered how perfectly he filled me. I thought I heard the squeak of bedsprings coming from his end of our connection.

"Faster, baby," he groaned.

My orgasm spiraled from the heat in the soles of my feet, climbing my legs like flames, igniting the rest of me. I gasped—lost sense of everything else going on and let the waves throb through me.

Win's groan brought me back to myself, back to my lonely, cold bed.

His breathing was harsh, heavy.

"Holy shit," he said after another moment. "That was...amazing. Did you come?"

"Yes," I admitted in a small voice. I pulled my sheet up to my chin as if he could see me.

"Me too."

I didn't want to think about what some poor chambermaid had to deal with in his room in the morning.

"I miss you so much," he said. "I'd rather you were here with me."

It took all my self-control not to offer to fly out to LA that evening. "I miss you too," I admitted.

"Have you ever had phone sex before?" he asked.

"No. You?"

"No. I'd rather have the real thing."

I snuggled deeper under my covers. "Me too." I was afraid to talk, afraid of what would come out of my mouth.

"Maybe we should get webcams and Skype this."

"No cameras," I said.

"It might make it more...intimate."

"No cameras," I repeated.

"I love to watch you climax," he whispered. "I love the way your eyes close. The way you try to take as much of me as you can."

It was time to change the subject. "I figured out how I can see you pitch," I told him.

"The Internet," he said, as though he'd known all along.

I yawned. It was after four in the morning my time. "I'm sorry. I didn't mean to do that in your ear."

"That's okay. It's late," he replied.

"How do you do it? Bouncing from time zone to time zone and still stay on your game?"

"It's tough. I try to stay on my own schedule anyway. But you've got to get up in a couple of hours. I'll talk to you tomorrow night."

I didn't bother trying to sleep.

As soon as I got to work—I went in early so Victoria couldn't complain too much—I checked the Gems' upcoming schedule. They'd be home after the West Coast tour and then in Philly for a three-game stand.

Philly. Philly was doable. I could drive. I could take a train or even a bus. Foolish as it was, I wasn't ready to resume the life I'd created after Win left the first time. I wanted more of him. I'd be fine, I assured myself. I knew it was temporary. I was much better prepared this time around.

Victoria arrived just before nine. She simply raised an eyebrow at me before disappearing into her office.

I got up and closed my office door. I needed privacy for my next bit of craziness.

I called my doctor and scheduled an appointment. No chances. I was getting my butt on birth-control pills before I ever got to Philly.

"**Y**ou were right about the waiting period," Victoria said, leaning against the door frame of my office.

"Huh?" I was thinking about what my doctor's office had told me about going on the pill. Even if I was able to go on it before Philly, I'd still need to be careful for a month.

"About Alexandra and Marc. They went to Connecticut. I searched it on the Internet. There's no waiting period to get married."

Alexandra. Right. "Did she text again?" I asked, reaching for my phone. I had three unopened texts. How did I miss them coming in?

"Yes," Victoria said. "I tried calling her to see when she was coming home or even if she'd let Dad know, but she's ignoring me."

"She's a newlywed," I murmured as I looked to see who had texted me. Alexandra and two from Win. My insides went all soft and squishy.

"You call her. Maybe she'll pick up for you."

"I doubt it," I said. I really wanted Victoria out of my office so I could read Win's messages in private.

I opened Alexandra's text. Yep. She'd eloped to Connecticut. I replied with, *You go girl! Call ASAP, OK?*

"I don't want to be the one to blindside Dad with this," Victoria continued.

"Then don't mention it to him," I said. "That's Marc and Alexandra's responsibility. He must know Marc hasn't been to work for a couple of days."

"You didn't have to deal with him yesterday." Her tone was bitter. "He called and demanded to see Alexandra. It was all I could do to put him off without actually lying to him."

I glanced up from my cell phone and grinned at her. "You lied to Dad?"

"I won't conceal Alexandra's behavior. I can't believe you condone it."

"I don't care whether you condone it or not," I said. "I'm one hundred percent behind Lexi. Well, except for the wrist-slashing stuff."

"I'm so glad you qualified that."

"Hey, sarcasm. Congrats." I flashed a phony smile at her.

"This is not funny," Victoria snapped.

"No," I agreed, "it's not. But it's also not the tragedy you're making it out to be. Our twenty-one-year-old sister fell in love with a somewhat acceptable man and eloped with him. Who did she hurt? And in the end, if the marriage doesn't work out, she's the one she's hurt. No one else."

"What about Dad?"

"Bad publicity might hurt his plans to build an amusement park or another mall, but I sincerely doubt any emotion for Alexandra plays into what he does."

"Are you saying he doesn't love her? That he doesn't love us?"

I studied her face before I answered. For some reason, my father's love seemed to matter to Victoria. She was willing to marry Brandon because Dad wanted her to.

How odd that we came from the same gene pool and environment.

Me, I was still being realistic. If Dad could toss out the woman he'd vowed to love until death separated them for a pageant runner-up, how could I or my sisters trust him not to do the same to us?

And then there was the whole Blandroid thing. Dad treated us like commodities, not daughters.

"I'm saying that I believe Dad's love sometimes seems conditional, and if we don't...if we disappoint him, then he withdraws affection. And that's not enough for me, and maybe it's not enough for Lexi either. Maybe we want to be loved for ourselves, flaws and all."

Victoria looked as if I'd slapped her.

I realized what I said wasn't just for her but for me too. If someone couldn't love me, flaws and all, I didn't want the affection.

God knew I'd certainly made some pretty horrible mistakes in my life. Who was I to pass judgment on my little sister?

"There's no talking to you." Victoria sounded disgusted.

"Talk to me all you want, but don't expect me to come around to your way of thinking. I'm never getting married—especially not to make Dad happy. If you think marrying a man you don't really love will make Dad love you more, go for it. I want you to be happy, and if that makes you happy, I'm happy for you."

"Is that all you ever think about? What makes you happy?"

"Hey." My tone was sharp. "Life's too short. What else is there besides happiness?"

It occurred to me that I needed to listen to myself. Maybe my relationship with Win was temporary, but so was life. I needed to seize the moment, live it to its fullest extent, and if that meant flying in and out of strange cities in order to be with him while I could, then I guess I'd be earning some frequent-flier miles.

I pulled up the Gems' schedule on my computer again, as if I didn't already have it half-memorized. "Life's too short," I repeated. "Do you think Mom did everything she ever planned to do before she died?" I asked. I glanced at Victoria, whose face was completely drained of color. "What do you suppose her dreams were? Her secret wishes? Did she want to go rock climbing? Take opera lessons?"

"Stop." Victoria sounded as if I were choking her.

"Or did she just want to grow old with Dad and spoil her grandchildren?" I inhaled deeply. "Yeah. Life's too short. I've spent the past seven years living 'safe.' No more."

I typed in the web address of a travel site and started looking for deals on airfare to Philly. I wasn't going to be a coward about Win, but I still didn't feel right about flying to Columbia to be with him. Maybe that was a little high school-esque on my part, but my current bravado was very new.

I couldn't let Victoria's need to please Dad rule me. Alexandra clearly didn't need my help, and her elopement went a long way in assuaging my guilt over what she'd done.

What *she'd* done. I shouldn't feel any guiltier over her plea for attention than Victoria should feel about what I'd done for attention seven years ago.

Well, gee. Wasn't I just a font of inner wisdom that morning?

I smiled at Victoria. "You know, everything is going to work out."

Chapter Sixteen

Over the next several days, nothing bothered me. It was spring, the sun shone, flowers bloomed, baseball was in season, and I was in love.

When the Saltboilers were home, I sat in blissful solitude in my seats. I was persona non grata as far as my family was concerned. Except for Alexandra, of course, who was too busy being a newlywed to bother with me. I'd rush home after the Saltboilers games to watch the Gems on their West Coast schedule and await Win's nightly phone call and our phone sex.

I decided to wait until Win was back in Columbia before telling him I'd be in Philly. The time apart forced us to talk to each other, not just about our pasts or our families, but our day-to-day trivialities and our essences—our favorite colors, music, and movies.

Work was rough. I was exhausted from the late nights. On the other hand, I was getting a pretty accurate picture what the life of a professional player's wife was like. Lots of telephone time. Lots of longing. Phone sex was adequate but lacked the intimacy I craved. I wanted to see him face-to-face. Touch him. Savor his unique scent. Taste him.

And then there was Chandler. He called me at work a couple of times, asking me to lunch. I declined. Politely. Never said, *Maybe another time*. I couldn't accuse him of stalking or harassment or anything because his calls were always very civil, and it's not illegal to ask a woman who refused to marry you out to lunch.

Finally. Win's West Coast trip was over. He'd picked up two wins. We were in the same time zone. Which made it difficult for me to watch the Gems play while I was at Saltboiler Stadium. Which meant I was getting to sleep a little earlier in the evening, because both games tended to finish around the same time.

"I'm coming to Philly next week," I told Win his fourth night in Columbia. "If you still want me to."

"You have to ask?"

Yeah, I did, but I didn't admit it aloud.

"When? I'll get your plane ticket, arrange for a limo to pick you up at the airport, and bring you to the stadium. Oh, and a room. I'll get you a room on the same floor as the team and let Skip know you're in town."

Players at Win's level didn't rate their own rooms on the road. Only superstars who had it written into their contracts didn't have to share.

He sounded like a little kid on Christmas morning, and that warmed me. Intensely.

"I've already got my plane ticket," I said. The rest of the stuff—the limo, the hotel room—yeah, I'd let him pay for that. I knew he'd have tickets to the games too, so I figured I'd use those.

"You should let me pay for your plane," Win said.

"You can pay for everything else," I replied.

He paused and then asked, "What are you wearing?"

I didn't pack anything fancy, just an extra pair of jeans, a pair of khaki cargo pants, and a couple of black T-shirts. Everything fit in my oversize silver-quilted purse.

A uniformed chauffeur held a sign with my surname on it as I emerged from the jet bridge. My real surname.

Dad had taken me to a couple of big-league games a long time ago, so the Philadelphia stadium wasn't a total shock to me. I picked up my ticket at the will-call window as Win had instructed, and then made my way through the throng.

My seat was behind the home-plate net, a bit toward first base. Several women already occupied the section, some with children but mostly solo. My seat was between a Hispanic-looking woman and a blonde.

"Hi," the blonde said. "You must be Carrie. I'm Tammy Lammers. My husband, Wayne, is the reserve catcher and Win's roommate."

"I'm Milagros Santos," the dark-haired woman said in a slightly accented voice. "My husband, Diego, is a relief pitcher."

I smiled and sat, suddenly terrified. I had no business sitting with the players' wives. "Then I guess I didn't get lost."

"You didn't," Tammy confirmed. She had a touch of the South in her voice. "And Win asked us to watch out for you."

"He's really happy you came today," Milagros added.

He talked about me?

I don't know why that bothered me, but it did. I mean, I didn't want to be his dirty little secret, yet on a couple of levels, I was. It was different at home because what happened in Syracuse didn't really matter, but this was the pinnacle of any ballplayer's career. The Show. Life under a microscope. A-Rod being dissed because Cameron Diaz fed him popcorn at the Super Bowl. Joe DiMaggio and Marilyn Monroe.

And he'd told these wives I was Carrie, not Caroline.

I inhaled deeply and made sure my smile hadn't slipped.

Win, using that built-in Caroline-GPS thing he'd developed, spotted me right away.

Worries of all sorts tried to sabotage my mood. Then Win waved at me, and I felt better.

Tammy and Milagros chatted about inane things—their children, the hassles of having an absentee husband—things that would never apply to me. I was seizing a moment, and Win was reliving his wild youth. That's all. His elbow injury had reminded him of his mortality.

We sat quietly for the most part, because we were surrounded by home-team fans. Rowdy fans. I made the mistake of cheering a bit too enthusiastically when Win got on base. At least, that's what the jerk behind me must have thought before he dumped his cold beer down my back. I gasped at the shock of the icy liquid on my spine.

"Stay calm," Milagros muttered.

Then the verbal jabs started. There were several other Columbia wives, girlfriends, and even players' children sitting in our section. The hometown crowd didn't seem to care. The language used was appalling.

I can drop an f-bomb as well as anyone, but there are some words I just don't like, and I really didn't like it when the jerk who'd dumped his beer on me called me one of those words.

He must have liked the sound of it, because he didn't stop. Auto racing must be popular in Philadelphia, as several others joined in to refer to me as Winston's...cup. Yeah. Cup.

I debated asking the jerk if he kissed his mother with that mouth.

"We'll pray for their souls," Tammy whispered.

My T-shirt dried, but I smelled like a brewery.

When the Gems actually won (with Win as the pitcher of record), the rudeness increased to abuse. No one came out and directly assaulted us, but a beefy elbow against the back of my head had me seeing stars for a few minutes. Tears filled Milagros's eyes when someone yanked on her long hair.

By the time we reached the hospitality suite, if there'd been any food, it was long gone. Two bottles of tepid water sat on a table stuffed in a dark corner. Like the rest of the stadium, the suite seemed intent on humbling us.

I felt completely out of place. The others appeared to have at least a nodding acquaintance with one another. I stood near Tammy and Milagros, listening and trying to keep track of who was who.

"I saw that jerk dump his beer on you," a tall, slender black woman said to me. "I hate this stadium."

"The fans are the worst," Milagros agreed.

I kept my mouth shut. It seemed safer.

It was nearly an hour before the players started trickling in. I tried not to be too anxious about seeing Win. All my senses went into overdrive the moment he entered the room. He spotted me immediately and closed the gap between us in a few long strides. "You made it."

I nodded. "You were great," I said in a low voice. It was one thing to talk to him on the phone after a game, quite another to stand in a room filled with his teammates and their families and gush. What I really wanted to do was throw my arms around him and hold him close, bury my nose against his skin, and inhale. Taste him. But touching was going to have to wait. Until we did this team thing, whatever that was.

Win's nostrils flared as he moved closer. "Spill your beer?" he asked.

"Something like that." No point going into how unpleasant the fans had made my visit. That was over. I wanted to avoid anything negative. Our time together was so sparse. I wanted only good things.

"I have to take the team bus back to the hotel, but you've got a seat in the limo with Milagros and Tammy. We'll catch a bite to eat later, okay?"

This was a whole new world for me. Tammy and Milagros were nice enough, although Tammy wore a little too much perfume and seemed more religious than most people I knew. She reminded me of my first college roommate, a woman I hadn't particularly liked.

Once we were on the road, I noticed Tammy looking at me strangely.

"What is it?" I asked.

"You're not wearing a ring," Tammy replied in a concerned voice. "I don't condone sex before marriage, but I thought you and Win were serious. Why aren't you wearing a ring?"

Heat rolled into my face in hot, surging waves. Tsunamis.

"Aren't you and Win in a serious relationship?"

I opened my mouth and gaped like a fish stranded on land after the flood receded. "We've just reconnected after a long time apart," I replied in a soft, broken voice. "We're working things through." Not that what Win and I did was any of Tammy's business.

I thought she might argue with me, but frigid silence and distasteful glares were her weapons of choice. So I had time to think about why I was in Philadelphia after I'd sworn I wouldn't be a camp follower or a stalker. Our limo beat the team bus to the hotel, where a gauntlet of sweet young things loitered outside the lobby doors.

"Groupies," Milagros explained.

"Shameless hussies," Tammy clarified with a sniff for them and a glare for me.

I recognized them without their definitions. Body-hugging clothes, gold chains, too much makeup, deep tans. Blonderoids. I wondered how many players succumbed to the temptations so blatantly on display.

I followed Tammy and Milagros to the front desk and gave my name. Win had made my reservation and paid. All I needed to do was sign in and take the key card. Milagros and Tammy waited for me. We needed to use our room cards to access the elevator.

"Restricted floor," Milagros explained. "We're on the same floor as the team. It's just extra security."

The first thing I did when I reached my room was head for the shower. I didn't know how far behind us the team bus would be. I was starving, and I couldn't go out sticky with beer.

I'd just rinsed my hair when the shower curtain opened. I didn't have time to scream or anything before Win covered my mouth with his. Panic mode to aroused mode took about ten seconds.

"Great idea," he murmured when he came up for air. "I love when you're all wet for me."

"You scared me," I said.

"Sorry." And he kissed me again, his tongue doing things to the inside of my mouth that probably weren't legal in states below the Mason-Dixon Line. But you didn't hear me complain. Nope. Those moans and sighs were rooted in pure pleasure.

His fingers slid down my ribs, across my belly, and lower. My hands mirrored his movements. That's when I discovered he was already wearing a condom.

His groan echoed in the confines of the shower. He cupped my butt with both of his huge hands and lifted me until I could sink onto his erection. He filled me, stretched me, and completed me. I buried my face against his neck and inhaled his aphrodisiacal scent.

"Wrap your legs around me," he said.

I didn't think it was possible, but he went deeper into me.

"Hang on," he said.

As if he needed to tell me. I climaxed about two seconds after he started thrusting, and he wasn't that far behind me. It was over so quickly it was almost a waste of a condom.

An hour or so later, I was curled up against Win in the king-size bed, seeking his warmth in the artificial chill of the hotel room.

"Hungry?" he asked as my stomach gurgled beneath his hand.

"I could use some food," I admitted.

"Didn't you eat at the ballpark or in the hospitality suite?"

One of his hands rubbed my tummy like I was a good dog or something. My butt was pressed against his groin. He was so lovely. Heated.

"No," I said. I didn't want to discuss the hostility, even in the alleged hospitality suite, so I told him one version of the truth. "I was too excited to eat. Did you make plans with anyone?"

"The only plans I have involve keeping you naked in this hotel room for as long as possible."

Worked for me.

So we ordered burgers and beers from room service.

I couldn't believe I was holed up in a hotel room in a strange city with Win Winston. It was the sort of thing one read about in supermarket checkout tabloids, or saw on those celebrity-gossip TV shows broadcast on minor cable networks.

I couldn't think of anywhere else I'd rather be.

Chapter Seventeen

"Where have you been?"

I made the mistake of answering my cell phone when it rang as I was unlocking the upstairs door of my apartment. Silly me. I should have checked to see who was calling instead of assuming it was Win.

"Hi, Dad," I said, forcing cheeriness into my reply. "I was out of town."

"You couldn't answer your phone?" He sounded crankier than usual.

"I was busy," I replied.

Victoria would have called if there were a family emergency. I would have answered—or at least eventually responded—to a message from her. Dad's definition of "emergency" was when he didn't get his own way. Which, come to think of it, is where Alexandra inherited it. I'd never before realized how much alike they were.

"What's up?" I asked, determined to stay cheerful. I also wanted this conversation over quickly so I could call Win.

"Polly and I have something we need to attend tomorrow night, so Matthew needs to go to the game with you."

"No," I replied just as easily as Dad stated his expectation. "I have other plans. Where's Marsha Lee?"

"Marsha Lee doesn't like baseball."

"Then Matthew will have to do something else," I said. I didn't want to get into why Matthew was banned from my seats. I was, however, going to have to explain it to Matthew. Again. The fact that Win and I were together, however temporary, had no bearing on what Matthew had done. Another situation might not have been so harmless.

"Why are you being difficult about this?" Dad snapped.

"I'm not being difficult. I can't watch Matthew tomorrow night, so you'll have to find another sitter. Try Victoria or Alexandra."

My phone beeped, signaling another incoming call.

"I have to go, Dad. Love you. Bye." I hung up before he could detain me any longer.

"Hi. You made it home okay?" Win asked when I answered.

"Yeah."

"I miss you," he said.

The words tugged a place deep in my psyche. "I miss you too."

"What are you wearing?"

The week went downhill from there.

Between two sisters, a father, and the man to whom he wished me wed, plus a six-year-old half brother, I was on the verge of screaming, committing murder, or running away. So I did the only thing a sane woman could do: I told Win I'd go to St. Louis for the weekend.

Neither Tammy nor Milagros was there, but another player's normal girlfriend was. She and I bonded quickly. The weekend was wonderful.

We fell into a pattern for June and early July. I spent weekdays in Syracuse, working and avoiding my family and satellites as best I could, but if the Gems played anywhere in the eastern or central time zone on the weekends, I joined Win.

I learned that when he played at home, we stayed in his small town house. Other players lived in the apartment complex, but it was a lot more private and a lot more relaxed than being on the road. Win stocked my brands of toiletries in his bathroom. It was almost as if I lived there. And we had sex. Mind-boggling, soul-searing, satisfying sex.

But it wasn't only sex. I know that sounds like a lie, but after all those years, we were starting to get to know each other. Our face-to-face conversations were a natural offshoot of our late-night phone fests. But the sex was better.

The press was anxious to snap photos of Win and me. Not like they'd hound an Alex Rodriguez or Derek Jeter, but Win was definitely paparazzi fodder. Ever since the fund-raiser for the Kathryn Maplethorpe Foundation, we'd become something of an item. Pittsburgh promised to be no different from any other series. I flew into town late Friday afternoon, checked into the hotel, and then took a cab to the stadium. I'd finally convinced Win I didn't need a limo. I could have driven to Pittsburgh, but that would have tired me. I wanted to be fresh for him.

I claimed my ticket at the will-call window—there was a ticket with my name on it at every Columbia Gems game—and made my way to the visiting-friends-and-family section. I inhaled the beloved aroma of grilling hot dogs and popcorn, of hot, greasy fries, and cotton candy. A baseball stadium smelled like home.

Three people were already seated in my row: a middle-aged couple and a young woman about my age. The younger woman was blonde but not in a Blonderoid type of way. She was polished, but she didn't glitter like a cheap carnival toy. No layers of gold on her neck, her wrists, or her fingers. Her hairstyle was very similar to mine, a basic bob, but hers was shorter. The temperature had to be in the upper 80s, but she wore a twinset and a lightweight skirt in a pastel floral pattern. Pearls studded her earlobes.

I didn't mean to eavesdrop, but they were right next to me.

"I can't thank you enough for inviting me, Mrs. Winston," the girl said.

My heart plummeted to my stomach.

I surreptitiously studied the middle-aged couple. Win's parents? I couldn't see a resemblance, but then they both wore sunglasses. *Oh boy.*

I didn't want to scrutinize the young woman, because that would mean I was wondering who she was and how her presence might affect me. I did notice that her toenails were tinted a tasteful shade of pale pink. She reminded me of Victoria in many subtle ways.

"Does Win know we're here?" the young woman asked.

"He always leaves tickets for us," Win's father replied.

I considered introducing myself but didn't want to seem forward. My mother had taught me manners, even if it felt like I hadn't used them much lately.

I settled back to watch the game and to focus on Win's performance. I tried not to listen to the Winstons and their guest, who was everything I wasn't.

Win had told me his parents were well-off, but that he wasn't close to them. His father reminded me of my father.

Which made me wonder more about the girl.

Was she the Winston version of Blandroid?

The Gems lost the game.

I debated texting Win to meet me back at the hotel instead of the friends-and-family suite. But that was the coward's way out, and I'd surrendered my cowardly ways when Win reappeared in my life. I steeled myself for major awkwardness and made my way to our meeting spot.

Several of the Gems' wives greeted me. I was becoming known, even if I did tend to keep to myself. Most of the women were friendly. In fact, one of the wives was involved in the breast-cancer community in her hometown and had approached me about doing a breast-cancer-awareness event in conjunction with the Gems. I fit in with these women.

I stayed as far away from the Winstons and their guest as possible. I was torn between pleading a headache and returning to the hotel or brazening it out. I'd overheard Win's parents' plan to take him out for a late supper. If I hung around, either the girl or I would be the embarrassing fifth wheel.

But Win had stuck to me in the face of my father's irritation and Chandler's stubborn insistence that we were a couple. Payback time.

If Win wanted me.

He greeted me first. His father said something, and I thought I heard a muttered curse when Win saw the trio. His grip on my hand tightened.

"Mom. Dad. Glad you could make it. Hello, Olivia. It's nice to see you." His voice sounded funny. Smooth. Bland.

Olivia smiled at him and then glanced at me.

I smiled back.

Win shook his father's hand and air-kissed his mother's cheek, never releasing my hand. My face muscles ached from my forced smile. "I'd like you to meet Carrie. Caroline, actually. Caroline Maplethorpe."

Win *never* called me Caroline.

"Carrie, these are my parents, Winslow and Vanessa, and the daughter of one of their friends, Olivia Meredith."

I murmured appropriate things, all the while sending prayers of thanksgiving to my mother for raising me right. I would have shaken hands, but Win wouldn't release mine.

"You're the woman in the picture," Olivia said. A shadow of discomfort skittered across her face. "The breast-cancer photo."

I reminded myself that Win had invited *me* to Pittsburgh.

"Awkward" didn't begin to describe the situation. I opened my mouth to make my excuses, but Win squeezed my fingers.

Win's father—Winslow the Third—decided we'd all go out together. I thought Vanessa looked a little...desperate. My presence was seriously kinking her matchmaking plans.

I wasn't dressed for the restaurant Win's parents chose, nor did I have time to change. Not that I'd packed anything but the basics. I vowed that going forward, I'd make sure I packed a skirt or at least some dressier slacks.

Party of five. Clumsy. And as I should have expected, I was grilled.

Eventually, it came out that my background was very similar to Win's. My daddy was acceptable to Win's daddy, and my job wasn't something embarrassing like posing naked for glossy magazines or Internet porn sites.

Now I knew how Win felt when my father got pissy because we were together.

By the time the evening ended, Win's mom asked me to call her Vanessa, Win's dad asked me to call him Winslow, and Olivia and I had a lunch date the next time I was in Cleveland.

As soon as we got back to the hotel, Win grabbed me, kissed me, and apologized. "I'm so sorry. My agent always arranges for tickets for them when I play in Pittsburgh."

"Olivia seems like a nice girl."

Win backed me toward the bed. "She's okay, but she's not you. You're a hot woman." He buried his face against my neck as we fell to the mattress together. "You're my hot woman." He nibbled on my throat. Shivers skittered along every nerve in my body. "Mine, right, Carrie?"

"Mmm," I replied.

He propped himself up on his elbows and stared down at me. "What kind of answer is that?" He acted as if my response mattered. Really mattered.

I said nothing, but I also didn't look away from him.

I was his in ways I'd never confess, but I knew this wasn't forever. Someday he'd go home to Cleveland and marry an Olivia, or he'd find some glitzy, glamorous girl, and they'd have children together. I was temporary.

"Do not tell me you are even considering marrying that Chad guy." Win's words came out like a low, rough growl.

I blinked.

"You couldn't possibly be engaged to him and here with me." He didn't sound certain, as if my past were catching up to us.

No, not *my* past but ours. He'd been there too.

I shook my head. "Chandler belongs to my father, not me." I didn't say another word about Olivia.

"Marry me."

When I didn't respond, he said, "Hello? I just asked you to marry me."

My heart expanded in my chest, cramping my lungs.

"Yeah," he continued. "That will solve everything. Your father will quit throwing Chad at you, my folks will stop bringing around Olivia clones, and you won't have any excuse not to move to Columbia with me. I should have thought of it sooner."

Shrinkage of the heart is painful. I tried to squirm out from under him, but Win was a big man. Tears prickled my eyes, but I'd be damned if I'd let him see me cry. I braced my palms on his shoulders and shoved.

"Hey!" He rolled to his side, but he didn't let go of me. "Is the thought of getting married so awful?" He had the audacity to sound hurt.

"I need to use the bathroom."

"You're not going to hide there and cry. Shit. I thought you'd be happy. Aren't women supposed to be happy when a guy proposes?"

"Getting married to get our parents off our backs is a lousy reason," I snapped.

He looked as if I'd sucker punched him. "My parents aren't on my back," he said. He studied me, his deep brown gaze never leaving my face. "I did this all wrong, didn't I?"

He released me and rolled off the bed.

I sat up, intending to bolt for the bathroom, but he dropped to one knee next to the bed and grabbed my hands. They felt so very small and fragile inside his huge, calloused paws.

"Caroline Maplethorpe, will you marry me?"

I tried to inhale but was so close to tears that my breath was more of a shaky, silent sob.

"Shit," he muttered. "You're going to make me say it, aren't you? You're a chick, and chicks need the words. It's not enough that I searched seven years for you, that I'd never forgotten you, or that I can't stand being away from you. That I dream about you, even when I'm holding you while we sleep. You need the damned words."

Just like that, my heart inflated again.

"I love you, Caroline Maplethorpe, Carrie Thorpe, hopefully soon-to-be Winston. I want to grow old with you. Look up when I'm pitching and see you in the stands, cheering me on, believing in me. I want to make babies with you. I want my home to be in you, wherever I end up as a ballplayer and after, because you're the place that makes me whole inside. I love you. Okay, you've got the words." It must have really cost him to say all those things. He looked incredibly uncomfortable.

"Okay," I said.

"Okay? Just okay? You make me get down on my knees and spill my guts, and I get an 'okay'?" He sounded flabbergasted.

"Okay, I'll marry you."

Guilt tugged at me as I spoke the words. I had things I needed to tell him, things that might change his mind about wanting me to be his wife and mother of his children. And there was a lot of lingering guilt over seven years ago that sometimes threatened to swamp me ever since Win had walked into the Susie Buddha Café that fateful April evening.

But right then, that night, I wanted to marry Winslow Winthrop Winston the Whatever more than I wanted anything else in my entire life. There'd be time between tonight and the actual marriage to talk.

Besides, Win seemed through talking. He leaped onto the bed, knocked me onto my back, landed on top of me. My breath whooshed from my lungs. I barely had time to replenish it before his mouth came down on mine. I felt his penis grow hard as he pressed it against me, while my girl parts seemed to soften.

"Let's find a JP tomorrow," he muttered when he finally came up for air.

"Can't," I whispered. I didn't want to talk. I wanted to make love. I would have started undressing him, but my arms and hands were pinned by him.

"Why not? Don't tell me you and your sisters made some kind of family-wedding promise."

"No, silly. When Alexandra eloped, Victoria and I researched waiting periods in neighboring states, and Pennsylvania has a three-day waiting period after you get the license. And where will we find a license on Saturday?"

"Well, shit," Win said. He propped his upper body on his elbows and stared down at me. "I guess we'll just have to fuck until Monday."

Chapter Eighteen

The next morning, we looked at a calendar and decided to get married in Syracuse during baseball's July break. We—I—had three weeks to pull together a wedding. I didn't need big or fancy or showy, although I had a sinking feeling that my father and the elder Winstons would want an extravaganza. Well, if they didn't like casual, they didn't have to come.

We went to a mall, where Win bought me an emerald-cut diamond set in white gold. The stone was obscenely huge.

The next few weeks were crazy. Win flew into Syracuse so we could get our license, then flew to Cincinnati for a game. Thank goodness he wasn't pitching that night.

There was no time to talk to him about the things I needed to tell him.

I tried. Really, I did. But some things can't be said on the phone, and our weekends were filled with baseball games and just being together.

I tried in Chicago.

"I need to tell you something," I said once we'd returned to the hotel after a late dinner following the game.

"Whatever you do about the wedding is fine with me. Just tell me when and where, and I'll show up."

"No, this is about before."

He narrowed his eyes. "I know about Flash. I was there, remember? And whatever happened after I left, well, I don't need to know all the dirty details about your sex life. But I'm also not going to share you again."

"I don't want you to share me, and I had no sex life after you left," I said. He was making my confession more difficult. "In fact, you've been my only sex life since we've met."

He dropped his shirt onto the chair. "What? Are you trying to tell me that from the time I left Cortland until we ran into each other a couple of months ago, you were celibate?"

I nodded as I studied his chest, memorizing the whorls of dark, curly hair.

"Are you kidding? Are you crazy?" His voice rose at the end of each question.

I shook my head. "Not interested."

He sat on the foot of the bed as if his legs couldn't support him.

"But that's not—" I started to say, but he interrupted.

"Carrie. Are you serious?"

I refused to be embarrassed. "Look, I did the casual-sex thing with Flash, and that was enough. Okay? Stop looking at me like I've grown a second head, will you?"

"C'mere." He reached for me, his voice husky.

I stepped between his legs and let him embrace me. "That's not what I wanted to—"

He interrupted me again. "We need to make up for lost time." He lifted the bottom of my T-shirt, exposing my fish-belly-pale stomach and plain beige bra.

"Seven years." His breath was hot against my skin. He unsnapped my capris and slowly unzipped the fly. My boy briefs were more comfortable than sexy. He rolled down the wide elastic band, exposing my navel. His tongue dipped, circled the indentation, and dipped again.

I shivered. "Win, we need to be serious."

"I'm completely serious here," he said, cupping my left butt cheek in his enormous hand. His fingers kneaded the soft globe. He used his other hand to encourage my capris to fall until they puddled at my ankles in a mud-colored pool of twill.

My knees trembled. If he hadn't been holding me, I would have fallen. Instead, I somehow ended up on the bed next to him, all desire to tell him anything gone.

The last game before his break finally arrived. I flew to New York, where a limo drove me to the stadium.

Columbia and New York split the four-game series. Win won the fourth game, an afternoon game, so we were both pretty upbeat as we left the clubhouse. It was a gorgeous, hot July Sunday. The sun was still shining. Life was fabulous. Our limo awaited to take us to the airport. Win cupped my elbow as we headed toward the car.

"Excuse me." A chubby, balding man with bloodshot eyes stopped us. "Caroline? Win?"

Something cold coiled in my stomach. Something about the man raised my hackles. Something bad was going to happen.

"Or maybe I should say, Carrie," the man said as he reached for my free arm. "Carrie Thorpe."

I jerked away, and Win stepped in front of me. "Flash," I said.

"For a minute there, I didn't think you'd recognize me." The man sounded jovial.

Flash had once been a golden flame, blazing bright and hot. Apparently he'd burned out since I'd last seen him.

"I didn't," Win growled.

"Yeah, well, not all of us got lucky after Cortland." Bitterness poisoned Flash's tone. "That line drive finished my career."

I will never forget the crack of the ball smashing into his skull.

"I thought you were finally getting yours when you threw out your elbow a couple of years ago," Flash said.

"What do you want, Gordon?" Win asked, a dangerous undercurrent in his voice.

That's when I noticed Flash clutched a grimy, worn manila envelope, the clasp of which was broken. The cold in my gut coiled tighter.

"You know, all the publicity you two are generating made it real easy to find you." Flash spoke as if he didn't have a care in the world.

"I haven't been hiding," Win pointed out.

"But Sweet Caroline has been." Flash grinned, a dim shadow of his former glory.

A blizzard of white spots cavorted in my vision.

Win moved closer to me, his body heat bouncing off the shell of ice that had encased me. "What do you want?"

Flash...leered. "I'm feeling left out."

"Forget it." Win's tone was flat. Final.

Flash snorted. "I didn't mean left out that way, although now that you mention it, a quick fuck for old time's sake might be fun. No, I'm not talking about sex." He held up the envelope.

"Money," I whispered. My lips were as numb as the rest of me, but I somehow managed to form the word.

Flash winked at me. "You always were quick, Carrie."

I don't know about quick, but I was definitely nauseated. "You're trying to blackmail us."

Win's grip on my arm tightened. I'd wear bruises at our wedding.

"Blackmail is illegal," Flash said.

Win hustled me toward the limo.

Flash thrust the envelope at me. "I'll be in touch." He turned and sauntered into the crowd that still edged the stadium as Win shoved me into the car. He closed the privacy panel, isolating us from the driver.

I handed Win the envelope, too afraid to open it myself. I didn't like to think about those weeks with Flash. What if he had photos? But no one had a camera. Unless there'd been someone else in that damned closet. Like Pedro Cruz, the catcher Flash had wanted to join us.

I closed my eyes and shrank into the corner of the seat.

I could hear the rustle of paper as Win opened the envelope. He said nothing for a very long time, while I played ostrich. The ice in my gut melted and turned to molten fear.

Win reached for my hand.

I opened my eyes but wouldn't look at him. The scenery between the stadium and airport was deadly boring.

"We've got trouble," Win said once we were back in Syracuse.

We sat at opposite ends of my sofa. Sweating bottles of water dripped onto the coffee table. Time for our reality check.

"Pictures?" The word barely emerged from my throat. A long swallow of cool water didn't ease the tension or relax my larynx.

"Just one." Win's voice was soft. "It's really grainy, like a cheap cell phone shot that's been saved to a computer too many times. The rest of what he gave us reads like a *National Revealer* tabloid article."

We both stared at the envelope, which lay on the coffee table between our water bottles.

Tonight wasn't supposed to be like this. Win and I were getting married in two days. I was supposed to be happy, not sick to my stomach.

"What should we do?" I asked.

Win was the one in the limelight, not me. He had to be used to extortion attempts. Right?

"I haven't the faintest idea."

"Let's call the FBI," I said. "Or a hit man. Do you know any hit men?"

"No. Maybe my agent does."

More silence. I tried to focus, but I was too upset. Shaky. Livid.

"What's the worst thing that can happen if we let him go public?" I asked, shifting my gaze to Win.

He gave a little half shrug. "A lot of nasty publicity. Pay-per-view porn sites on the Internet, like Pamela Anderson and that rock singer."

"We could take the site operators to court and win residuals," I said.

"You're kidding, right?"

"I'm trying to focus. If we give in to Flash, we're cooked anyway. Do we want to be randomly cooked or cooked on our own terms?"

"I don't exactly need opposing players offering to help me fuck my wife," Win snapped.

I hadn't thought about how it would affect him—only me. And really, what did I have to lose except my secrets? I mean, did I want photos of me having sex with two men made public? Absolutely not. But eventually, the hoo-ha would die down. Win couldn't even remember the name of Pamela Anderson's rocker. Blackmail never ends.

"I think we should call the FBI," I repeated. "Blackmail is a crime. He didn't tell us not to contact the authorities."

Win rolled his eyes. "That's because he hasn't done anything illegal. All he's done is hand you an envelope of his alleged memoirs and a crappy snapshot. If we go to the authorities now, he can claim he just wanted to make sure someone else didn't post it on the Internet or something."

Damn. I hated it when Win was right.

"So maybe he isn't going to blackmail us." I couldn't keep the hopeful tone out of my voice.

"I wouldn't hold my breath."

I heaved a sigh. "What do you want to do?"

"How the hell should I know?"

He sounded pissed. At me. I hadn't done anything. Except take my clothes off for Flash seven years ago. After that, we were all culpable. Win was the one hiding in the closet. Win was the one who'd asked Flash if it was okay to join us. I could have said no, but that simple word might not have stopped anything.

I reached for the envelope. Whatever it contained wouldn't be anything new to me.

"Are you sure you want to see that?" Win asked.

I nodded as I pulled a sheaf of regular computer paper from the grimy envelope. Maybe I should have used the disposable gloves left over from cleaning my bloody bathroom. "I need to. I need to know exactly what we're up against."

"I'm a guy," he said, so softly I nearly didn't hear him over the rustle of the paper. "I'm a ballplayer. I'll be forgiven, if not exempt, from condemnation."

The chills stalking my veins pounced. Win's gaze clashed with mine.

"And I'll be branded a slut." Amazingly, my voice didn't tremble as I pronounced the truth in our world. "Tammy Lammers will declare herself a prophet."

Win didn't contradict me.

After several agonizing heartbeats, I glanced at the sheaf of papers I held in my too-steady hands.

The three of us had experimented that summer. No one had much experience, and we turned that motel room into a free-for-all. There'd been oral sex. There'd been anal sex. There had been traditional sex in a smorgasbord of positions.

Flash had written it all out, like a *Penthouse* fantasy. No need for exaggeration. Grammar check, yes, but not exaggeration.

I saved the photo for last.

My gorge rose. I knew exactly what I was looking at. Someone had been hiding in the damn closet.

In the photo, I was astride Win while Flash entered me from behind.

The next night, Flash pushed to bring in a fourth party, Pedro Cruz, their catcher, but Win supported me in my refusal. Even then I already regretted those few weeks of madness.

"Do you miss it?" Win asked, snapping me out of my reminiscing.

I shook my head.

"Did you stay celibate for seven years because if you couldn't have two men at once, you didn't want any?"

My head went light. Black spots danced before my eyes. The skin on my face felt so tight that if I tried to speak, I was certain my flesh would split.

I couldn't believe Win was asking me these questions. I thought that if anyone would understand what had happened that summer, he would. That he wouldn't condemn me. He'd been there. He knew how relieved I'd been when Flash left.

"The only person I missed was you," I said, my voice as low and rough as a growl.

He took the photo from my hand and tossed it on top of the other pages on the coffee table.

"No one else—including Jordan Gordon—is man enough for me," I continued as Win pulled me close. His mouth came down on mine, not soft, not gentle but hard and demanding.

I met his fierceness with my own. "I've never wanted to be with anyone else besides you," I said when he came up for air.

"You don't need anyone except me," he replied.

"Always you. Only you."

He pressed me against the sofa, pinning me as his hands freely roamed. Roughly roamed, as if he intended to put his mark on me so Flash would never—could never—again claim me.

Win's touches became more deliberate as we shed our clothes. The photo had brought back too many memories, and Win seemed determined to make me forget them all.

"It's more than the sex," I whispered against his ear as his fingers stroked between my legs. One finger pressed into my anus. I didn't like that, and I told him.

"Do you have any lubricant?" he muttered against my neck.

I tensed. "No. I don't need that kind of help with you."

He flexed his fingers, and I squirmed.

"Am I hurting you?"

I didn't know how to answer. There was no physical pain, but I didn't like his attitude.

"Yeah," I said. "Because you don't believe me about Flash and everything that happened."

"I don't want you remembering Flash. I want you to remember *me*, to think only of *me*."

"How many other women have you been with? Tell me there have been no other orgies in your life since you left me the first time."

"There are no damned pictures threatening to pop up on the Internet."

Okay. Now I was pissed. No longer in the mood. I pushed at his shoulders. "So this is about a double standard? News flash: You're in this photo too."

"No, this is about you and me, babe, and exorcising ghosts."

I really hated being called *babe*. "I am so done here."

He kissed me again, as if trying to change my mind.

I turned my head to avoid his mouth. "No! Stop!" When he didn't, I shoved at him.

He stopped. "Carrie." The single word sounded like a plea.

"Let me up."

"I'm sorry." He rolled off me and then helped me sit up. He raked his fingers through his hair. "Shit."

I reached for my T-shirt, feeling far too vulnerable sitting there completely exposed. The photo had drifted to the floor, mingling intimately with my clothing as if trying to hide that Carrie from this Caroline.

Win reached for his discarded khakis.

I pulled my T-shirt over my head, sending my hair flying every which way. He tugged the hem over my belly, his fingers brushing the scar on my lower right abdomen.

Yeah, and I still hadn't told him about *that*.

"I would never do anything to hurt you," Win said. "This stuff with Flash just makes me crazy. It made me crazy then. It makes me crazy now."

So we were coming from the same place. That was a good thing. I reached for my panties.

"What do I have to do to make you believe that I don't want a second person, man or woman, in my bed? Our bed?" I asked.

He shook his head. "I do believe you. I guess Flash showing up all of a sudden brought back all the frustration from the old days. Every time I tried to get you alone, he somehow sensed it and interrupted."

"I thought I'd imagined that," I said, surprised he remembered those times the same way I did.

"I wanted to kill him," Win admitted in a soft voice. "When Pedro Cruz hit him in the head with that line drive during batting practice, I wanted to throw a party." He rested his elbows on his knees and buried his face in his hands.

I very nearly asked him why he hadn't called me after he left if he felt that way, but now wasn't the time to start that argument.

"Me too," I admitted. "Why did we never talk about this back then?"

"I was scared you'd want to bring in someone else."

When I opened my mouth to argue, he held up his hand. "I know you protested bringing in Pedro when Flash suggested it, but that didn't mean I felt confident that you wouldn't do to me what you did to Flash."

"What? What did I do to Flash?"

"Me." He sounded grim.

"You were his idea, not mine," I reminded him.

"But you agreed. If you were happy with Flash, you wouldn't have said yes."

"I would have said yes because I was crazy. Acting out."

"Then why did you say no when Flash wanted Pedro?"

I wouldn't have known how to answer that question seven years ago, but I did now. "Because once you were added to the mix, I knew I didn't want anyone else. Including Flash. I just didn't know how to end it with him. Besides, I thought you wanted him there, and if I had to be with him in order to be with you, then that's what I'd do."

Win slid his arm around my shoulder. "We should have had this conversation years ago." He tugged me closer until my head rested against his chest.

"You left. You never called me. Eventually I realized we were too young. We wouldn't have worked."

"True." His voice rumbled beneath my ear. I noticed he didn't offer a reason for not calling, and figured it was just youth. That's what I'd assumed then. He's a guy. Guys always say they'll call and then never do. Clichés are usually rooted in truth.

"There's something else I need to tell you," I confessed.

I'd already waited too long. We couldn't start our marriage with a huge secret between us.

He tensed ever so slightly and muttered something that sounded like *disclosure time.*

And that's when my doorbell rang.

Was I relieved? Yeah. He'd been so quick to judge my celibacy that I was a little leery about arming him with more ammo. No matter how often I told myself he was the one who hadn't called, I'd always known where to find him.

I looked out the window.

Victoria stood outside the Susie Buddha Café. "It's my sister."

Win grabbed his clothes and headed for the bedroom. I checked myself to make sure I was decent. Victoria buzzed again.

"Hold your horses." I glanced at the coffee table. Win must have grabbed Flash's papers. The sudden tightness in my chest eased a fraction. I buzzed Victoria in.

"Your timing stinks," I called down the stairs as she trudged up them.

"Aren't you waiting for the honeymoon?" she asked.

I rolled my eyes.

"Or are you getting nervous?" she said as she entered the living room. "Where's Win?"

He exited the bedroom as if cued. "Hi, Victoria."

She dropped her bag to the floor and plopped into my rocking chair. "Who is Jordan Gordon?"

My throat closed, and I looked to Win to respond.

"He played on the Cortland Crowns at the same time I did."

"Why is he calling the foundation looking for Caroline?"

It was a good thing I was sitting on the sofa, because my legs were no longer capable of supporting me.

Win perched next to me. "Because he's a troublemaker."

The darkness in Win's tone chilled me.

Victoria scowled and leaned toward the coffee table. "What is... Caroline?" Her voice soared a couple of octaves.

Oh, dear heavens, Win hadn't removed the photo.

I reached for the paper to snatch it away from her, but it fluttered to the floor.

She stared at me, her eyes dark in the ghostly pallor of her face. "Is that you? And Win? And someone else?"

I tried to inhale a calming, yoga-inspired breath, but that wasn't working too well.

"You're having sex with two men."

No one said anything for several long, painful heartbeats. Then Victoria shook her head. "You make me sick, you know that? The Teflon sister. You do something like that, and it doesn't matter."

She grabbed her purse from the floor and flounced from the apartment.

"Victoria! Wait!" My voice barely functioned. I stood at the top of the stairs long after she closed the street door behind her.

"Will she keep her mouth shut?" Win asked.

I was too numb to speak. To think.

Everything was falling apart.

Chapter Nineteen

Win's agent, Marty Fiscoe, arrived in Syracuse midafternoon the next day. Win had merely uttered the word "blackmail," and Marty had hopped a plane.

I'd met Marty when I'd signed the prenuptial agreement. He was young, energetic, and exhausting to be around. He was also very, very good at what he did.

Win buzzed him into the apartment, and Marty headed for the kitchen as if he lived there. He must have followed his nose to the coffeepot, because he helped himself to a cup and then sat at the table. "Talk to me, kids."

Win dropped Flash's envelope on the table in front of Marty. "To use a cliché: a picture's worth a thousand words."

I winced.

Win leaned against the counter, a mug of coffee at his elbow. He looked haggard.

We'd discussed showing the article and photo to Marty. Win was reluctant. He didn't want his agent to see me like that. Not that I wanted anyone to see that picture, but Marty needed to know exactly what Flash could do to Win, to us, and that meant showing Marty everything.

He studied the photo at length, then read the pages.

The only sounds in the kitchen were the hissing and sighing of the coffeepot and the hum of the refrigerator. My face grew warm, my breathing was shallow, and I was light-headed.

Marty stacked the pages together and returned them to the envelope. He sipped his cooling coffee.

Win couldn't take it any longer. "Well?"

"How much of the story is true?"

"Pretty much all of it," Win admitted.

Marty sipped his coffee again. Swallowed. "I'd say you have every reason to be concerned about blackmail." He looked at Win as he spoke. "Did either of you have any idea someone was taking pictures?"

"No."

"Carrie?" Marty didn't flicker an eyelash in my direction, for which I was grateful. He'd already seen too much.

"No." My voice came out in a croak.

"In fact," Win continued, "Flash suggested we invite another player to join us, but Carrie and I both said no."

"So that picture was taken expressly against your wishes?"

"I don't remember Flash ever asking if he could take pictures."

"Carrie?" Marty asked.

I would have shaken my head, but Marty hadn't looked at me since I'd handed him the envelope. "I never would have consented. I was crazy, not stupid."

"Crazy?" Marty's head jerked in my direction, but still no eye contact.

"Crazy," I confirmed. "I was under a lot of stress at the time I consented to...multiple partners."

Marty noted something on his smartphone. "So you did consent to having sex with two men."

"No."

Win's gaze shot to me. His scowl would have made a wolverine cower. "I heard you say yes."

"I consented to have sex with two specific men," I softly clarified. "I was already having sex with Flash, and I agreed to make love with Win."

Win's scowl melted. We stared at each other until Marty cleared his throat.

I loved Win, damn it. We'd run a gamut of emotion since Flash reappeared, but the circle had closed itself. Our connection was too strong for us to walk away from each other again.

"You should have called me as soon as Gordon approached you. I'll try to file an injunction, but I think you should postpone the wedding."

"He nailed us yesterday," Win said. "As we were leaving the stadium. And we don't want to postpone."

"You don't want to give Gordon an excuse to go public right now," Marty told him. "If there's news about your marriage, he might be tempted to cash in on the publicity."

Marty was right. Coattails and all that.

"We can postpone," I said, my voice a lot steadier than my insides. I couldn't remember why we'd thought the All Star break was such a good idea. Our wedding anniversary would always be in the middle of the season. "I'm going to shower," I said, thinking they'd want to be alone to discuss strategy or for Marty to cut Win a new one for being a foolish rookie.

Both men looked relieved.

I canceled the judge. The rest of the folderol—flowers, food, venue—I still had to pay for all that. Fortunately, Susie Buddha was my caterer. I suggested she have a Canceled Wedding Special at the Café. She loved the idea, and it saved me some cash.

Next on the list of people to notify were our families. Win's parents were supposed to fly in late that afternoon, but he was able to get hold of them before they left.

Then there was my family.

We had a faux rehearsal dinner scheduled at a pretentious restaurant in the burbs. Polly had suggested the Galeville Coach Stop Inn to Win's mother, who, because she was in Cleveland, let Polly handle everything except the bill. Silly woman.

Since his parents weren't coming, Win said he'd foot the tab. We'd make one announcement with everyone present.

Win and I timed our entrance at the restaurant so that we were the last to arrive. Family and satellites milled around the parlor of the private suite Polly had booked. A predinner cocktail hour put everyone in a good mood. It was a pleasant half hour or so. Even my father behaved.

I wondered how long that was going to last.

Then Polly asked where Win's parents were.

That meant we had to make our announcement a little earlier than I would have liked. On the other hand, I figured I'd be able to eat without nervous apprehension knotting my stomach.

And of course, Dad decided that just because we said we'd decided to wait to get married wasn't a good enough reason. He wanted a better explanation.

Win and I exchanged a glance.

"I want a wedding anniversary I can celebrate every year," I said. "The end of October or early November is safe."

I thought it sounded good. Victoria rolled her eyes, and Alexandra said she didn't blame me. Even Polly got a little misty. Sometimes I'm such a good liar it scares me.

"Foolish female nonsense," my father muttered.

"You're not paying for it, so chill," I said, raising my glass of far too expensive champagne to my mouth. Vanessa Winston had spared no expense in planning this evening.

"You should have thought of that sooner," Marsha Lee said. She wore a rust-and-harvest-gold shiny suit that wasn't quite old enough to be chic. Hopefully refrigerator colors from the early 1970s never would be. "Everyone had to rearrange their schedules to accommodate your middle-of-the-week impulse, and now you're telling us it was for nothing?"

"I don't remember inviting you," I said.

Win pressed his palm into the small of my back.

Alexandra snickered. Marsha Lee was also her mother-in-law. Poor kid.

Of course, my comment ticked off everyone, but I'd only spoken the truth. Apparently my family preferred my lies.

I hadn't invited Marsha Lee to my wedding. I'd wanted only immediate family but had included Polly, Marc, and Brandon because I had to. Marsha Lee was nowhere on that list. I didn't even know why she was at the rehearsal dinner.

Because Win was paying for the rehearsal dinner, I was the hostess. I briefly toyed with the thought of kicking Marsha Lee out of the suite. She could wait for us in the bar, which in a less elitist establishment would be a suitable venue for her.

"Marsha Lee is right," Dad said.

"Why don't you tell everyone the truth?" Victoria interjected. She'd been steadily sipping her champagne and might have been a little tipsy. "It's all going to come out eventually if Jordan Gordon has his way."

Win stiffened beside me.

"Jordan Gordon has nothing to do with why we're postponing the wedding," I lied.

"Who's Jordan Gordon?" Dad asked. "He's been calling and leaving messages at the office. He's connected to you?"

I was going to yank every one of Victoria's blonde curls out of her scalp by the roots. Then I'd do her eyebrows and lashes for her.

"I played A ball with him in Cortland," Win said.

"I was involved with him before I met Win," I added. "No big deal."

Victoria peered at me over the rim of her crystal champagne flute. "Yeah. I saw the picture. No big deal is right."

"Victoria, shut up." I raised my glass of champagne and glared at her as I swallowed.

Just because she was miserable with Brandon and jealous of what I had with Win didn't give her the right to reveal my secrets. She was nothing but a thief. A secret thief.

"No. I'm sick and tired of you getting away with doing whatever you want while I toe the line."

"Then ignore the line," I snapped. "I think you've had too much to drink."

That cued Brandon to take away her champagne. Mustn't have the wife-to-be publicly shnockered.

"What picture?" Dad asked.

"A picture of Flash and me," I said.

"And Win," Victoria added in a snide tone. "Don't forget Win. Who *is* a big deal."

Win's cheeks darkened as he blushed.

"Of course Win Winston is a big deal," Matthew piped in. "He's a Columbia Gems."

Damn. Couldn't Victoria have waited until the kid wasn't in the room?

"Maybe Matthew doesn't need to hear all this," Win said.

Fortunately, I wasn't the only adult who thought this conversation wasn't suitable for a six-year-old. "Marsha Lee, why don't you take Matthew down to the bar for a Shirley Temple or something," I suggested. Two birds, one rock.

"And miss this?"

If she could be honest, so could I. "Since it's none of your business, yes."

My father finally sided with me. "Marsha Lee, take Matthew down to the restaurant," he growled.

Marsha Lee started to argue, but Dad was in CEO mode. Underlings quaked, not argued, when James Maplethorpe spoke.

The rattle of plates and cutlery reached into the room when Polly opened the door to hustle out Matthew and Marsha Lee.

"It's no use," Win muttered. "We'll have to tell them."

I wanted to cry. I wanted to lunge at Victoria and claw her lettuce-green eyes out of their sockets. Rip her pouty pink lips off her porcelain face.

Instead, I cleared my throat. Chose a flower woven into the center of the carpet as my focal point. Inhaled deeply. Win's hand lightly pressed the small of my back. "Win wasn't my only lover when we were in Cortland. Jordan Gordon—everybody called him Flash—kind of introduced Win to me."

I sneaked a glance at Victoria, who was as pale as the cream-colored center of the carpet flower but who wore a snarky, triumphant expression.

Another deep breath. My insides quivered. Hot chills caroused through me. *No details. Just the basics.* I focused on the peach and mauve wool petals at my toes.

"The three of us were together for about a month."

I heard a gasp from Alexandra. My gaze remained on the carpet. "Then Flash got hurt. Win and I stayed together."

The pressure of Win's hand on my back increased. Warmed me in the air-conditioned chill of the room.

I raised my chin. Looked my father in the eye.

Alexandra whimpered. I glanced at her. She'd pressed her fingers against her mouth. Her eyes were wide.

I looked back at Dad, whose face seemed a little gray. "I'm not trying to hurt you," I said in a soft voice. "I'm just telling you so you'll know. I never would have told any of you anything, except Win and I ran into Flash yesterday."

Hard to believe it had been only yesterday.

"Actually, he approached us," Win clarified. "With his memoirs. And a picture."

My father's complexion was undeniably gray.

"We think Flash plans to blackmail us," I said.

"Why now?" Alexandra asked.

"Because he didn't know Carrie's real name until the wire service picked up the photo of us at the gala," Win explained.

"And Carrie Thorpe was nobody," I added. "Unlike Caroline Maplethorpe."

I was getting concerned about Dad. He really looked crappy.

"Why are you telling us this tonight?" he asked. He sounded as awful as he looked.

I inhaled deeply again. Looked every assembled person in the eye. Win's arm slid around my waist. "We aren't going to let him blackmail us, so there's a chance he'll go public."

I thought if I listened closely enough, I could pick out each individual's heartbeat.

Victoria smirked. Brandon's face registered nothing. Politician poker face. Alexandra's eyes shone, but I couldn't tell if the brightness came from malicious interest, such as I saw on Marc's and Polly's faces, or from tears.

Dad was definitely pasty. "And you expect me to do what about this?" he finally asked.

"Nothing." I wasn't certain he was making an offer, and frankly, I didn't want him to do anything.

"I'm not going to sit back and do nothing," Dad snarled. "You couldn't have come to me privately instead of telling the whole world at once?"

I had to unclench my teeth to respond. "I didn't tell the whole world. I told my family. The people who stand to be hurt the most by this. And only because Victoria forced it."

"If I thought there was any other way to handle this, sir, I would," Win added.

"Don't you have an agent or a publicity person to run interference?"

"Marty is working on it," Win said.

"Marty?" Dad asked. "Marty Fiscoe? He's good. What's he planning to do to control damage?"

"How will this affect Matthew?" Polly asked. "Caroline, if you've done anything that will hurt him in any way—"

"This isn't about Matthew," I said. Leave it to Polly to make this all about her and hers. Well, if that's what she wanted, I was more than happy to oblige. "You were getting pregnant by a man old enough to be your father when all this happened, so we were basically doing the same thing at the same time, Polly. Glass houses and all that."

"You know"—Alexandra added, smiling at Polly—"if you want to get picky, we could blame you for everything that went on that summer, so if I were you, I wouldn't say anything."

Marc seemed surprised that Alexandra wouldn't side with his sister. If he thought she would change allegiances just because he'd married her, then he didn't know Alexandra well at all.

"Leave Polly alone," Victoria said. "She wasn't the only one who got pregnant that summer, was she, Caroline? The real question is, does Caroline even know who fathered her baby?"

Chapter Twenty

The room went dark-green-and-maroon paisley except for a tiny pin-prick of light.

"Baby?" I heard Win say, even as I tried to echo the word myself.

"You thought I didn't know?" Victoria's voice was a mix of half-hysterical laughter and self-righteous contempt.

I tried to respond, but my throat was sealed.

"What baby?" Win asked.

"Caroline was pregnant when she started college," Victoria explained, slurring her words a bit. "Her roommate was concerned and called me."

I'd never liked the sanctimonious bitch I'd roomed with my first year.

"You were pregnant? With my baby?" Win sounded shocked.

My vision cleared enough for me to see his face. He no longer touched my back and seemed to loom over me.

"What makes you think it was yours?" Victoria asked. No one else even breathed. Inhaling or exhaling might cause them to miss something. "Judging by the picture I saw, it could have been anyone's."

"It was mine," Win said.

At least he didn't doubt that.

"Say something, Carrie." His voice shook. "Tell me. Where's my kid?"

My mouth was so dry I couldn't speak. Tears prickled my eyelids.

"Didn't you think I'd care? That I'd want to know?"

I shook my head. What else could I believe? I'd called him as soon as I'd confirmed I was pregnant. He had never returned my call.

This wasn't how I'd planned to tell him. Not with a fresh argument over Flash still dogging us. Not with my sister sitting judgment on something she didn't understand. Not with my entire family and their satellites surrounding us with shocked silence.

"Were you ever going to tell me?" He sounded disgusted.

"Yes." The single syllable hurt my throat.

"When?"

"You don't understand," I said, but I wondered if he even heard me.

"Adoption or abortion? How did you get rid of my kid?"

The room swayed. Tilted.

"How many more lies am I supposed to take from you?"

A flash of anger overrode the agony. "I never lied to you."

"Carrie. Thorpe." He could have merely spat and saved his effort.

Reality-check time. "I never told you my name was Carrie Thorpe. Caroline Maplethorpe was too long for the badge, so the clerk wrote it out as 'Carrie Thorpe.' You and Flash assumed that was my name. Neither of you ever bothered to ask me. You're the one who lied. You said you'd call me, and you never did. Even when I swallowed what was left of my pride and called you to tell you about the baby. You didn't pick up! I left you a message to please call me. That it was important, but you never called!" I was shrieking by the time I finished. "How did *I* lie to *you*?"

Win looked as if I'd slung a hundred-mile-an-hour fastball into his athletic cup. "I couldn't call you. I didn't have your number. It was in my phone, which was stolen. And I had a disposable phone back then, so I couldn't carry over the number. When I called the Crowns' office to track you down, they told me there was no such person as Carrie Thorpe. Besides, you had other ways to contact me. My whereabouts have never been a secret."

"I thought you'd moved on." My voice was cold and bitter.

"Jesus, Carrie. I loved you."

Loved. Past tense.

"Do you have any idea what I was going through? I was alone, Win. My mother was dead after my father discarded her, and he was too busy sleeping with someone the same age as my sister to give a damn about what happened to his daughters."

My father made some sort of strangled sound as Win said, "Don't you try to turn this onto me."

I guess I knew where I stood with Win. He was ready to condemn me before he knew the facts. Before he knew anything.

Since we were telling it all, he was going to hear it all. They all were. "I almost died trying to have your baby."

Win went very still.

"You know that appendicitis scar? Well, guess what? Not appendicitis. Ectopic pregnancy. You know what that means, Win? It means the baby was in my fallopian tube, not my uterus, and the tube exploded. As soon as I found out I was pregnant, I did everything I could to keep your baby safe. I took vitamins. I stopped drinking. I read books. I made a doctor's appointment. And none of it mattered because it all just blew up."

Tears flooded my face. My chest heaved with the effort of breathing.

"You abandoned me. My family was in shambles. I was alone. I lost my baby. I lost fifty percent of my ability to conceive another child. Tell me, Win. Tell me again how *evil* I am because I lied to you."

I lifted my chin. I heard someone crying behind me. Maybe Victoria. Maybe Alexandra. It didn't matter. They were just tears. Tears renew, regenerate themselves. I had proof.

The expression on his face was horrible. Kind of like the condition of my insides. Hollow, echoing, a vast nothingness. His eyes were dry. Empty.

The only sound in the room besides my sisters' soft sobs and my father's labored breathing was the frantic thrumming of my heart.

"Alexandra, can you give me a ride home?" I asked. I wanted to be alone. Any concern on Win's part was seven years too late. Same with Dad. And Victoria? Well, this meltdown was her fault. I would never forgive her.

"Sure," Alexandra said.

Win's head drooped as if it were too heavy for his neck.

I wanted to lean back somewhere, close my eyes, and let the waves of despair and mourning wash over me anew. I'd never intended to reveal most of what I'd just blurted. Heck, I hadn't even known that some of those emotions were still so raw.

"I'm sorry." I barely heard Win's voice over the rush of my blood against my eardrums.

This wasn't as simple as Flash. Sorry? When I couldn't bear my sorrow?

"The baby exploded," I whispered. "And it hurt. It hurt so much. I lied to my family, told everyone it was appendicitis. The doctor, the hospital couldn't tell anyone the truth. And now, I might never be able to have a baby. I'm scared that even if I did try, the same thing would happen on the other side. I can't go through that again, but I guess it's a moot point."

"Carrie." Win's voice cracked. "Let's go home."

"No. I don't want to be with you right now."

Not after the hideous things he'd said to me. Not when he really believed I was heartless. Selfish. I'd wanted my baby more than I'd ever wanted anything, even my mother. Even Win.

Win motioned to Marc, who slipped his arm around Alexandra's waist. "Let them go," Marc said.

Alexandra looked as if she wanted to argue, but Marc shook his head, and she acquiesced.

Win took my arm, and I found myself too weary to fight him. I could mourn in his rented SUV as well as I could in Marc and Alexandra's vehicle.

I don't remember the ride home at all. I barely recall allowing him to follow me up the stairs to my apartment. I do know there was a tiny seed of wanting to injure him as badly as he had hurt me.

I don't know how long we sat in my dark living room, silent and boneless. Locked in our private shells of misery. It was a warm night, but I was chilled to the marrow.

At some point, Win carried me to bed. My brain was fuzzy, but I recognized his scent. I started to protest, but he hushed me and cuddled me until I slept again.

My next memory is of waking up in my dark bedroom, Win curled around me, his rough palm resting hotly on the scar on my abdomen.

I tried to roll away from him, but he held me close. "I'm so sorry. I'm sorry for everything I said. Every stupid thought I had. For not trying harder to track you down seven years ago."

I was talked out. I was *listened* out. I had nothing left.

"I'm going to tattoo your phone number on my dick so I never lose it again."

Too little, too late.

"If you can't get pregnant by fucking, then we'll do that in vitro stuff. You still have all your eggs and stuff, right? And we know I've got swimmers. So we do it that way. I can afford it."

A little while later, he said, "Our kid would have been just a bit younger than Matthew." Win's whole body trembled as he exhaled, his warm breath stirring my hair. "That has to be hell for you."

My eyes burned in the dark. Someone had replaced my eyelids with emery boards.

"Talk to me, Carrie, please."

How could a man who professed to love me *think* such things about me? Those hideous, unforgivable things.

I remembered his reaction when he'd thought Matthew was our child. He'd been nasty that night too. Proof he was predisposed to believe the worst of me. Evidence I'd ignored.

The man who professed to love me didn't trust me. He didn't trust me to remain faithful, and he didn't trust me when it came to potential children. Because some clerk had been too harried to write out my full name on an ID badge seven years ago.

"This is what you kept trying to tell me," Win whispered. "But I didn't want to know. Anything. Because I just wanted you without complications. Because sharing our secrets might destroy what we have."

I didn't trust myself to speak. In case I started crying again. In case I started spewing emotions about which I was not consciously aware. In case I said something to Win I would never be able take back. Like the things he'd said to me.

I could forgive him for doubting my fidelity. We'd made no promises. But I'd thought we'd moved past those two crazy kids to something more mature this summer. Something lasting and true. Silly me.

Win was born to break my heart.

"I always felt that if I could find you, we'd be okay, the way we were after Flash left. We've always been a couple, even if we were temporarily apart. I always knew being apart was only temporary," Win said.

"Maybe I didn't want to be found." My voice felt rusty. Sounded weak. "Maybe you never should have tried to find me. You said it yourself: I've always known how to find you."

"You don't mean that," he whispered. "Look, I was wrong. I never should have said—"

"You never should have *thought* what you thought. If you loved me, really loved me, you would know I wouldn't have…" I couldn't even repeat his accusations.

"I was stunned. Blown away. Reacting, not thinking."

As if that excused him.

"I've been thinking so much about having a family, even though we never discussed it. A couple of kids. I hated being an only child, and I envy the relationships you have with your sisters and Matthew. I have this perfect life plotted out for us. A fantasy of being married to you, making babies with you, spending forever with you, and hearing that you'd been pregnant and had never told me, I felt shut out of my dreams."

Welcome to my life.

"Imagine how I felt when you didn't return my call."

"I can't," he said. "And I will never be able to make that up to you. But if I could go back and change things, I would change everything. I wouldn't share you with Flash. I would put your phone number someplace else besides my cell phone. I would have asked you your name."

I reached deep inside for a response and couldn't find one.

That didn't stop him. "If you could go back, would you have tried harder to track me down when you found out you were pregnant?"

"Probably not." I shifted away from him, but he followed. "I was operating on the theory that all men were scum. My father ditched my mother for a younger model, Flash wanted to share my body with anyone who expressed interest, and you never returned my phone call.

"I thought you'd outgrown me. I was just the girl you slept with while you were in A ball, and if I persisted in trying to track you down, I'd be a stalker. I had enough crap in my life without adding another rejection."

"I should have taken you with me when I was called up."

"I wouldn't have gone," I told him.

"I was just a summer fling?"

"Yeah."

If that truth hurt him, let him bleed. He wasn't the only one who could be cruel. Life was cruel.

I'd protected myself by sealing off deep emotion. Until Win delved beneath my facade looking for Carrie Thorpe.

Oh, I was functional. I loved my sisters, had grown to love Matthew. I even tolerated Polly and made an effort to get along with my father. And I knew it was silly to begrudge a lack of a phone call from a guy. I mean, it was a cliché. How could I work up a righteous anger over a stereotype?

Except I'd been pregnant. And I'd wanted Win to make it tolerable. He'd been the one thread of sanity, of normalcy that summer, and I'd wanted him to bind me, weave me into a life other than the one with which I'd been stuck. I'd wanted a prince on a white steed to make everything better and had been devastated to learn that Win was merely mortal.

Like my father.

The rising sun reddened the edges of the slats in my bedroom blinds, turning my windows into mouths of bloodied, predatory teeth.

This day was going to bite me in the ass.

I tried to swing my legs over the side of the bed. Win's arm anchored me firmly to him and the mattress.

Win. Holding me as if that could change anything. Did he really think that words could erase other words? Words are like toothpaste. Once they're out, they can't go back into the tube.

And even worse than the words were the sentiments behind them. Okay, I should have told him about the baby when we first started getting serious again. I should have tried harder, not let him distract me. My bad. But he never should have even *thought* the things he thought. Not if he loved me.

He clearly didn't know me. He remembered great sex from a crazy girl, none of which had anything to do with me—the real me, Caroline Maplethorpe. Nothing from this summer had revised his memory of that girl. Of Carrie Thorpe.

"We don't know each other. We have memories of a couple of crazy kids and a few months of trying to recapture that, but we never tried to get to know each other. It was another summer fling. Maybe Flash did us a favor. At least we don't have to file for a divorce."

"Don't say that." His voice was hoarse.

"I can't marry you."

"If this is about the fertility thing, I already told you what we'll do." He sounded a little desperate. "If you didn't love me, if you didn't know that I am your one, then you never would have stayed celibate for seven years. You would have given another guy a chance."

"Who wants half a woman?" The words slipped out before I even thought them.

"Would you say that to a woman who'd had a mastectomy? Who you are isn't the sum total of your body parts. Look at me. My elbow's been rebuilt with part of my ass."

"You have doubts about me." My voice shook. I was angry because he didn't understand how important mutual trust was to me. "You're always going to wonder if I'll be faithful to you while you're on the road because you don't think you're enough of a man for me. Well, you're right. You're not. A real man would be so secure in his woman's love that he wouldn't question it."

He tensed, pulling me against him. My back pressed his bare chest. When he spoke, his tone was cold.

"Reality check. Maybe fairy tales work in your corner of the world, but not in mine. Half of my teammates are married and fuck around on their wives while they're on the road. I've seen 'em chip in to pay for abortions for groupies who don't know which one of 'em knocked 'em up. I've seen grown men devastated to learn that the kids they thought belonged to them were really just the by-product of bored, lonely wives. So don't preach to me about real men, because the real men I know don't fit your definition, and I know a hell of a lot more about men than you do.

"Do you have any idea how much it hurt me to think you were just another groupie, getting rid of a kid—my kid—because a kid wasn't convenient? I was being honest with you, which is more than you can claim."

I didn't say anything. What could I say? He was right about the honesty part.

"I love you," he whispered. "In the end, that's all that should matter."

Chapter Twenty-One

I t rained the day I was supposed to get married. Steam rose from skillet-hot sidewalks and sun-fried lawns and then mingled and hid within the low mist clinging to trees and shrubberies.

Marty showed up early, and the three of us holed up in my apartment. Win and I were civil. If Marty sensed tension between us, he didn't mention it, at least not to me.

He set up his tablet at my kitchen table. I offered him the use of my desk, but he insisted that he preferred the kitchen. Closer to the coffeepot, I guess, because he consumed massive quantities. "Gotta file that injunction now," he kept muttering.

Fortunately, it was the middle of the week. Unfortunately, it was July, a very popular vacation month. It took some doing, but Marty managed to find a lawyer who knew a judge who would help us on short notice and who happened to be a Columbia Gems fan.

Assembling our team, however, turned out to be the least of our problems, or so Marty claimed. No one knew where Flash was. Couldn't serve papers to a ghost.

We would have to wait until he contacted us again and hope like crazy that he wouldn't grace the Internet with our presence while we waited.

Marty also embraced the lie I'd told my family. Win and I had decided to wait until after the postseason to get married. He liked the logic; he liked that it was optimistic. That was the statement he issued to the press. He definitely earned his 15 percent.

Win called his parents and asked them to keep an open mind about anything they heard, and said he would explain when he had a chance. Better for them to be prepared than blindsided.

I curled up in the window seat in the living room and stared at the wet, gray landscape. The stop sign on the corner twitched in the wind. Raindrops wedged themselves into the mesh on my window screens and glittered like shards of glass, even in the murky light. Most of the umbrellas bobbing on the sidewalks were black. Every so often, I'd see a red one or a silk-screened flower, but black ruled. Like my mood.

"Carrie." Win spoke in a low voice. He sat on the sofa. He knew better than to try to touch me. "We need to talk."

"I think we've said enough." I spoke as softly as he did. Marty, still in the kitchen, didn't need to know everything.

"Clearly we haven't, or we wouldn't be keeping secrets from each other." He sounded annoyed.

"I don't have any secrets left," I replied. Empty. He'd emptied everything from me.

"You're not the only one in this relationship," he said. "And now it's my turn."

I teetered on the edge between exhaustion and agony and really didn't care about what he had to say. All that remained was returning his ring and ridding my apartment of him and his agent.

Win cleared his throat. "I'm adopted."

He paused, as if waiting for a reaction from me. When none came, he continued. "It's a hot button for me. When I see a guy paying a girl to have an abortion, I wonder if some guy tried to pay a girl to abort me."

That explained his gut reaction. He'd lashed out from pure emotion.

"And you weren't the only crazy one in Cortland that summer."

I was so damned sick of that summer in Cortland.

"I didn't know I was adopted until right before I signed with the Gems. One of my mother's sisters let it slip at my graduation-slash-going-away party." His tone turned bitter. "I overheard her speculating about the identity of my biological parents. Probably Hispanic, she thought, because I was so dark and that would explain the whole baseball thing. Like baseball was a disease or something."

I didn't know what to say. I didn't know what he wanted from me. Sympathy? Comfort? So I said nothing, because I had nothing to give.

But I watched his reflection in the rain-spattered window.

"Everything I believed about myself was a lie. And when I asked my parents, my mother cried, and my father called me son—wasn't I Winslow Winthrop Winston the Fourth? Like that proved anything."

Four used to be my lucky number.

"Whatever," I muttered. "You changed your name to Winslow Winthrop Winston the Whatever. It wasn't a joke. It was your reaction."

"Exactly. And you're the only person who gets it."

A gust of wind rattled rain against the window, blurring my view of Armory Square. And of Win's reflection.

"When I had my team physical, I was terrified they'd find something wrong, something mysteriously genetic that I couldn't answer."

I turned away from the window to face him. He wasn't looking at me but rather at something on the coffee table.

"I don't know who I am. If I ever need a kidney or bone marrow, I don't have anyone I can go to for a possible match. It's like being in limbo. And I wonder about when I was a kid, when I misbehaved—did my parents ever want to send me back because I wasn't good enough?" He cleared his throat and met my gaze for a moment. "I wondered if that was why you didn't try harder to get hold of me. Because I wasn't good enough to be a father to our baby. If something in me kept the baby from getting to your uterus and caused all the problems."

That was utter nonsense. But he was spilling his guts, so I kept my mouth shut. It was most definitely his turn. My big, oversize, amazing pitcher shouldn't have these feelings of inadequacy.

Then I realized I was caring about him, about his feelings and tried to burrow into a cave of emotional distance. Caring made me vulnerable, and I'd survived enough of my own crap. I didn't want to care. Not about Win.

"I debated telling you about being adopted, because I didn't want it to matter to you. The unknown thing. I didn't want it to make a difference."

"You have no more control over being adopted than I did about losing the baby." I sounded so...reasonable. I didn't want to be reasonable. I wanted to be angry.

I turned back to the window. Tiny rivulets of rain channeled the glass like tears streaking the cheeks of someone who could feel. Not me.

"That's true. And I know I should have told you when I proposed, but nothing you could have told me seemed as bad as my secret."

"That's what you meant last night when you said keeping secrets." Some things were starting to make sense.

"Yes."

Win and Marty left for the airport a couple of hours later. Marty went back to New York City, and Win had to be in Washington for a game the next afternoon. He refused to take my ring and promised to touch base with me.

My apartment felt empty, like part of its heart had withered. I watered my terrarium and scrubbed the bathroom. I called for takeout from Susie Buddha, but after I picked up the cup of zucchini soup, I couldn't eat it. I couldn't swallow. All the muscles in my throat seemed to have atrophied.

My eyelids, too, ceased functioning. I lay in bed that night, cataloging the irregularities in my ceiling.

Win texted me when he arrived at his Columbia apartment. At least he'd had the sense not to call. Unlike my sisters. Thank goodness for technology that allowed call screening. I finally turned off the damned phone.

If I never laid eyes on Victoria until she was in her casket, it would be too soon, and the only reason I'd be at the funeral would be to wear scarlet and dance. I hoped she married Brandon and was perfectly miserable for the rest of her days.

Susie Buddha was the person who got through to me. "Your family is making me crazy," she said. Her gaze met mine, steady and calm, like the eye of a hurricane.

She'd delivered lettuce soup and a yellow-bean salad. Rings of red onion decorated both. My kitchen smelled like an inner circle of heaven, but the food remained uneaten.

"I understand why you're hiding. A broken heart needs time. But honey, this apartment isn't a cloister. And Win Winston is a good man."

I agreed.

"Listen to him," Susie Buddha counseled. "The man is crazy in love with you. I've never seen two more compatible auras."

Susie Buddha was a good friend, but sometimes she took her paranormal spirituality *woo-woo* too seriously.

"And you need to have some contact with your family. Not Victoria. If you want me to fix something that will make her really sick, just say the word. But you need to talk to Alexandra or your father."

I didn't bother asking how Susie Buddha knew anything. All I'd told her was that the wedding was postponed, which had happened before Victoria made her drunken accusations. Susie Buddha had her ways.

"And then there's the press."

Now she had 100 percent of my attention. "What?"

"Win and your father have been 'no commenting' all over the TV, radio, newspaper, and Internet. Win's agent issued a statement about postponing the wedding. Check out the Internet, but call Alexandra, okay?"

As soon as she left, I beelined for my desk and laptop. I prayed there were no photos.

There were. Mostly recycled shots from the gala. Not Flash's picture. Some of the pressure in my chest eased.

I turned on my phone and texted Alexandra. *Susie Buddha told me to talk to you.*

Three minutes later, Alexandra called.

"What's going on with the media?" I asked.

"Polly." Alexandra sounded disgusted. "You breaking off your engagement to a famous baseball player is the best thing to happen to Polly since her last pageant."

I stared at Win's ring, still on my finger. "Postponed."

I didn't stop to wonder why the nuance was so important to me.

"Polly doesn't care. Dad, however, is furious. With her. Oh, and Brandon broke up with Victoria."

I tried to feel something. Sympathy, glee, anything, but that trigger seemed to have malfunctioned.

"He says he can't afford to be affiliated with a family with a porn star."

Victoria must have given him quite a description of the single photo she'd glimpsed.

Two days ago, I might have quipped that if that's all it took to break their engagement, I was happy to be the sacrificial lamb. I didn't much feel like quipping anymore. I wasn't even glad I could return the favor for her.

Later that night, when Win texted me, I called him. He answered on the first ring.

"I'm sorry I've turned your life into a media circus," I said. I had a feeling this was only a taste of what was to come. "I never intended for this to happen."

"You didn't do anything that wasn't going to happen anyway." His voice was rough as gravel. "Besides, we're in this together."

"No," I said. "We're over, Win. Too many people's lives are being torn apart by what we did. It's like my father and Polly all over again. Victoria was right." Admitting that aloud depleted me.

"I love you," he said. "Doesn't that count for something?"

"Do you want Marty to make the announcement, or should I have my father's machine construct a press release?"

Chapter Twenty-Two

I didn't go to work the following day. My anger toward Victoria was still rampant, and my situation was already ugly enough without me bitch-slapping her. But I did log in to my business e-mail and try to create an alcove of normalcy. My terrarium was getting tired of all the attention.

Several hours later, I checked Sports Website Headlines and saw an ambush interview with Win. He pushed his way through a pack of reporters, issuing his prepared statement of, "No comment."

Then he stopped. He towered over most of the reporters. He stared straight into the camera, his dark eyes glittering, and spoke. "Seven years ago, I met a wonderful woman. I asked her what her sign was, and she said, *'Squeeze play.'* I fell in love. That's all."

The reporters laughed.

"Ask me about my pitching, okay? Because that's what's public, not my personal life."

For the rest of the afternoon, I forgot why I was upset with him.

Susie Buddha was right. I needed to get out of the apartment. So that night I went to a baseball game. The Saltboilers were in town. I had season tickets. I would be fine. I was the anonymous one in our relationship, and this was Syracuse and the minor leagues. Nobody cared.

The air was heavy and the humidity high. Rain started pelting the stadium in the fifth inning. I opened my umbrella and huddled deeper into my seat. I was okay until the lightning arrived. Management ended the game.

I was halfway to the bus when someone grabbed my arm. I twisted to find Chandler looming over me like a 1950s radiation movie mutant.

I tried to wrench out of his grasp, but he merely tightened his fingers. "Hello, Caroline. Let me give you a ride home."

I shook my head. Strands of my hair clung to my cheeks. "I'll take the bus, thanks."

"It's too nasty a night," he replied. "I insist."

I looked around for help. Most of the regular riders had already made their way to the bus. The parking lot was nearly empty of cars. I cursed my habit of staying in my seat until the last possible moment, even in a storm.

Chandler drew me deeper into the shadows.

"Let go of me," I said.

The rain plastered his pale brown hair to his skull. His eyes reflected the pinkish glow of the security lights. He ignored my request. Par.

"I'm not in the mood for you tonight," I told him. "Now get your hands off me."

That's when he backhanded me across the face.

Pain exploded in my nose and behind my eyes. Pain so intense it stole my breath and stunned me for a few seconds.

Who suspected Chandler had a temper?

Then I swung my umbrella at him.

He swatted it away like a mosquito.

I inhaled deeply, intending to call for help, but Chandler clamped his hand over my mouth. Biting his palm had no effect.

He flung me into the low shrubbery at the base of the stadium wall. The back of my head hit the rough concrete, and for a minute, tiny points of white light cavorted in my vision, like my own personal mini lightning storm.

I couldn't think. All I could do was react. My fingers found my cell phone in my pocket and fumbled with the keypad.

"I wouldn't scream if I were you," Chandler warned me in a voice I could barely hear over the thunder.

Scream? I was going to kill the son of a bitch.

He removed his hand from my mouth.

"Don't you have more important things to do than attack me in the parking lot of Saltboiler Stadium?" I asked, hoping I'd called 911 and that the operator realized an assault was underway.

The bus rumbled past us. Abandoning me.

I tried to roll away from Chandler, but there was no place to go, even if my body could cooperate. Which didn't seem to be happening. "Why are you doing this?"

"You made a fool of me, and now you're going to pay."

He flung himself on top of me.

I could barely breathe beneath his weight. "No! Get off me!" I squirmed on the wet ground, trying to throw off his body, trying to avoid his groping, hurt-inflicting hands. Cold mud squished through my clothes. He'd trapped my arms under me.

"I heard about that photo of you fucking two men." His breath was rank on my face. Sour scotch. Stale onions. He grabbed my breast and squeezed.

I managed to free one arm as he tore my T-shirt.

"You're a whore," he said. "A whore masquerading as wife material. So I'm going to fuck you like a whore."

I gasped as he twisted my breast. "No! Stop! You're hurting me."

"Shut up." He slapped my face again.

I tasted blood. My ears rang, just like a cliché.

Since he was going to hit me regardless of my level of cooperation, and since he had yet to produce a weapon, why wasn't I screaming my lungs out?

I inhaled as deeply as I could, which wasn't much, and shrieked in his face as I went for his eyes with my free hand.

He swore. Covered his face with his hands.

I used the moment to squirm partially free. I grabbed his ears and pulled on them as hard as I could.

He squealed like a wounded rat. He rolled off me, giving me the opening I wanted. I brought my knee up between his legs as hard and as fast as I could. Soft tissue yielded.

He collapsed to the side, grabbing his crotch.

I scrambled like a crippled crab and had managed to lurch to my knees when a beam of light blinded me.

I screamed again.

"Syracuse City Police!"

Thank God.

A disembodied voice asked me if I was okay.

Okay? Chandler Goodeve, the man my father wanted me to marry, had just assaulted me. Tried to rape me.

Okay? Probably not.

Someone draped a blanket across my shoulders and tried to get me to lie down. No! Not down. Not in the mud. Not again.

I caught a glimpse of Chandler puking as he cradled his private parts.

The heat-filled humidity had fled. The night was now cold enough to freeze living marrow. My teeth chattered. I tried to clutch the wet blanket closer, but my fingers were too numb to hold the rough fabric.

Someone said something about shock. Shock? Yeah. Shock was only part of my roiling emotions.

The rest is a blur of red, blue, and amber lights strobing around me, of being bundled into an ambulance over my protests, and of a female police officer staying with me. "Call my sister," I recall saying. "Lexi. On my cell phone."

I retained an image of Chandler with his hands cuffed behind his back, his head bowed, being herded into the back of a police cruiser.

Mostly I remember a grim satisfaction that I'd finally gotten to kick Chandler in the balls.

Alexandra drove me from the hospital to my apartment. Victoria was with her. I was too weary to open the car door and shove Victoria out, as was my impulse. They followed me into my apartment. I wanted them to leave.

"We promised Win we'd stay until he got here," Alexandra explained.

"Win?" I wasn't sure how he fit into the equation.

"He's on his way."

"Why?" I didn't want him to see me like...

Alexandra pushed me onto the sofa as if I were dandelion fluff. "Because he loves you."

"You had no right to tell him!" Tears were imminent, but I didn't want to cry over Win. I didn't want my sisters believing that I was crying over Win.

Alexandra and Victoria exchanged a glance. "We didn't call him," Alexandra said.

"Then how...?"

"You called him," Victoria said in a small, low voice.

I shook my head, which protested the movement.

"He heard everything," Alexandra said at the same time Victoria explained, "He's the one who called 911 in Syracuse. Then he called Dad."

I closed my eyes and tried to delve past the jumbled images of the evening. Redial. I must have hit Redial when I reached for my cell phone. And Win had been the last person I'd called.

"Call him back," I said. "Tell him not to come."

"Too late. He's already in the air."

I didn't want him in Syracuse. I didn't want to need him. To depend on him. Him.

But I fell asleep before I could convince my sisters to see it my way.

I woke up the next morning in my own bed. Safety and heat surrounded me. I couldn't move without wincing.

"Shhh." Someone's hand skimmed my side. "You're okay."

I tensed, which hurt. "Win?"

"I hope so."

The temptation to melt into him was almost more than I could resist, but I somehow managed.

"You didn't need to come," I whispered.

"My God, Carrie. I had to come. I had to see for myself that you were all right. I heard everything. Everything. Thank God you called me." His voice broke. "Only next time, call 911 first, okay?"

"No next time."

"No, no next time," he agreed. He wrapped an arm around me and pulled me closer, planting my back against his chest. "The only next time is: the next time I see that son of a bitch, he's a dead man."

Worked for me.

"Thank you for calling me," he said a few minutes later.

I almost told him it was an accident, but I was so glad he was there I didn't want to diminish the moment.

"I was terrified," he said. "Thank God Wayne was still in the clubhouse so he could call and convince an operator to patch him through to 911 in Syracuse."

"Wayne?"

"Lammers. Tammy's husband. Why were you at a game with that asshole?"

"I wasn't," I said. "He grabbed me on the way out. Aren't you scheduled to pitch tonight?"

"Damn it, Carrie, you were attacked. Nearly raped. I took an emergency leave."

Like he would have if he'd gotten my message about the baby.

Then the rest of what he'd said hit me. Nearly raped.

I started shaking. Trembling. The bedsprings squeaked, sounding almost as if we were making love.

"You're okay," Win murmured. "I've got you now."

I twisted in his arms until I could bury my face against his chest. The thick hair there tickled my nose. My head throbbed. I wrapped my arms around his waist and clung to him. I felt his breath on the top of my head, heard him murmur soothing nonsense, and I wept.

When I awoke again, I was alone in my bed. I wondered if I'd dreamed Win was there. Then I heard the deep rumble of male tones coming from the living room.

I swung my legs from the bed and cringed at the stiffness in every one of my muscles. The room undulated, and I swallowed a surge of nausea.

I was naked. Win must have undressed me when he put me to bed. It took me several moments to work my way to the closet and my robe and then several more before I made it to the living room.

Win was alone on his cell phone. "I'll call you back," he snapped into the phone when he saw me standing in the door. "What are you doing out of bed?" He came toward me as he spoke.

I shrugged and then winced.

He picked me up and carried me to the sofa.

"Who were you talking to?"

He sat next to me. "Marty. More damage control."

My head seemed to drift toward the ceiling, so I leaned back and let the sofa support me. "Damage control?" My voice sounded weak to me. I wasn't a weak woman, and I didn't want Win seeing me as weak.

"There's a lot of conjecture about why I left the team so suddenly last night."

The sun was bright, as if the rain had washed the sky. "I'm sorry."

"Don't be." He sounded fierce. "Anything either one of us does right now is going to be news."

He sat next to me and took my hands in his. His calloused palms comforted me. Dried blood caked the prongs of my engagement ring. For a moment, I was back in the dark rain with Chandler actively hurting me.

"What happened last night is all over the news."

I started shaking again. My stomach roiled.

"It's okay. Marty's taking care of it." He dropped one of my hands and reached for my face. His finger traced a gentle line along my cheekbone.

We both knew it. If Flash went public, I was in deep doo.

"Hungry?" Win finally asked. "Susie Buddha brought up something she called Healing Soup."

I shook my head and regretted doing so. "Maybe later."

"He hurt you so bad."

He hadn't raped me. That's all that mattered. I wanted to tell Win that but couldn't find the energy to speak the words.

"When I look at your face, when I see what he did to your breast, I want to kill him."

My face? My breast?

Win must have seen my confusion. "You have some nasty bruises."

I opened the front of my robe and tilted my chin. The bruised breast wasn't what made me throw up but rather, the memory of the pain when Chandler had inflicted it.

Win didn't say a word. He simply scooped me up, vomit and all, slid my robe off and then sat me in the shower, stripped off his own clothes and joined me. The hot water felt good. My teeth chattered, and my skin resembled the poultry section of a supermarket meat cooler.

Win lathered me, used his calloused palms to scrub me. As I reclined between his legs, my back resting against his chest, I became aware that he was aroused. I waited to feel repulsed or angry, but neither emotion arrived. Instead, I felt safe. Protected. Warm.

How could I possibly want Win to make love to me after everything that had happened over the past couple of days?

But I did. Badly. I needed him. I wasn't naive enough to mistake sex for love. I tried to ignore my growing need for him to erase what had happened with Chandler. But the slick glide of Win's soapy hands on my nape, shoulders, and collarbone comforted me. The long strokes down my arms with his knuckles brushing the outside slope of my breast puckered my nipples, but not with cold. And Win seemed to know the difference.

I must have sighed or in some other way signaled him, because he knew. He knew exactly how I needed to be touched, where I needed to be touched.

He lifted me from the shower, wrapped me in a fluffy, oversize towel, and carried me to bed. His mouth was as gentle as his hands had been. He took his time kissing every bruise on my face.

I tensed only when my nipple seemed to pop into his mouth. He paused, as if waiting for my permission. When I finally relaxed, he continued. By the time he'd worked his way down to the important stuff, I was a molten puddle of need. And he was so tender, so gentle, as if terrified of hurting me. Yet when the violent strength of my orgasm threatened to annihilate me, I embraced it.

As I lay trembling with a different kind of weakness, Win carefully turned me to my side and entered me from behind. It seemed like it had been so long since we'd made love. I had no doubt about Win's actions. Making love. Even the way he held me when the sex part was finished was another stage of making love.

I knew then that I couldn't let him go.

"Remember when you told me that I was the one good thing about that summer?" he asked.

I nodded.

"Well, so were you. My one good thing. I remember you making grilled cheese sandwiches and tomato soup for me after a game and staying up watching movies with me until I could wind down enough to want to sleep. The day we went looking for daisies and picked a bunch of orange flowers instead. Those are things I remember about you, Carrie."

He wasn't talking about the sex. He was remembering the day-to-day minutiae of those weeks. The little, inconsequential things. The things I remembered.

The things I missed and wanted back.

Chapter Twenty-Three

The intercom woke me. Win eased away from me, leaving me feeling exposed. He'd spent most of the afternoon spooned around me as I curled against his chest.

A moment later, he returned to the bedroom. "It's Victoria."

"No," I said. "I don't want to see her. I will never forgive her."

Win's expression was bleak. "She's not totally to blame here."

I tilted my chin. "I know that. But she had no right—"

"She had no right," he agreed. "But the power of what she did came from you not telling me about the baby. And about keeping Flash a secret. She's on her way up."

I pulled on a clean robe and eased my way to the living room while Win made himself decent. I collapsed on the sofa, still feeling ridiculously depleted. Victoria would have to wait until Win unlocked the door for her.

She looked awful. Dark undereye circles marred her usually perfect complexion. Her hair was pulled back in a loose ponytail, a casual style I hadn't seen on her since childhood. She wore no makeup. Victoria never stirred unless she was perfectly attired and composed. Maybe Brandon's desertion had hit her harder than it should have.

Damn. There was that caring thing again. What was wrong with me?

She stood over me, wincing as she took in the bruises on my face. "Dad's on his way up."

"No!" I didn't want to see him. I'd made Win hang up on him every time he called. "Lock the door."

I was too late. Dad came into my living room. He looked as gray and pasty as he had the night we'd told him about Flash.

"Caroline." He spoke my name in an old man's voice.

I averted my face. If he hadn't made Chandler believe we could be a couple... No. That was wrong. He may have encouraged Chandler to pursue me, but my father never would have condoned Chandler's actions. James Maplethorpe was a bully, but he wasn't a woman beater. He wasn't a violent man.

"I had no idea," Dad said. "I'm initiating a civil suit on your behalf in addition to the criminal charges he's facing."

I guess that was my father's way of apologizing.

"Winston. Thanks for calling me."

I turned in time to see Dad extend his hand to Win.

Win hesitated before taking it. But he shook hands with my dad. I suppose that was the modern equivalent of a peace pipe.

Dad and Victoria finally sat. Win gathered me onto his lap on the sofa. I closed my eyes and rested my head against his shoulder.

Victoria cleared her throat. "This came for you at the office. I didn't open it. It's marked personal and confidential."

My eyelids snapped up in time for me to see her pull a manila envelope from her oxblood leather briefcase. She extended it toward me, but Win intercepted it. That was okay. Better him than me. The *Photos. Do Not Bend* stamp could have been a flashing neon arrow.

If Dad and Victoria expected us to open the envelope while they were in the room, they were disappointed.

They stayed only a few more moments, as if to assure themselves that Chandler hadn't killed me. My father couldn't look me in the eye. If he had tried, he'd see the evidence of his meddling, and I don't think he was quite ready to own up to his part in what had happened.

As soon as they were gone, Win slit open the envelope and pulled out several sheets of paper. "Flash," he said.

The contents of my chest knotted. I caught a glimpse of something. A photo. Just like the envelope promised. "How bad?"

"Pretty graphic." Win handed me the thin sheaf.

Oh boy. How had I even managed *that* position? And Win... Wait a minute. I stopped breathing. Looked past the superficial.

"This isn't us," I said.

"What?" Win snatched the picture from my hand.

"This isn't us," I repeated. "You have chest hair. The alleged you in this photo is bare-chested."

Win swore, then added, "You're right."

We divided the photos. Scrutinized them. Hairless Win, a paunchy Flash—who'd been thin as a whip during his Cortland days—and my head hadn't been inserted at quite the right angle. And I'm certain I don't have sex with my eyes open. And I hadn't worn cosmetics that summer, yet I looked made-up in these photos. As if I were attending...an event. A gala.

"Not your breasts," Win said. "Nipples are too big. Your nipples are much more...dainty."

He'd always loved my breasts the way I was fixated on his beautifully hairy chest.

"That bastard," I said.

"He probably couldn't sell his memoirs without accompanying pictures," Win said.

"So he just made 'em up?" I could only hope. "Where's the first picture?"

"Marty has it," Win said as he pulled his phone from his pocket. He placed the call.

I released a breath I hadn't known I'd held and deflated against the back of the sofa.

Lies. My foundations had all collapsed because of someone else's lies. If I hadn't noticed the lack of chest hair, who knows how long Flash could have injected havoc into my life? Our lives. Without photos, his memoirs were worthless. Anyone could make up lies and publish them. The magazine racks at supermarket checkouts proved it.

"I'll overnight them to you today," Win said, then ended his call. "Marty thought the picture he has looked a little suspect, besides being so grainy, so he turned it over to an expert. He wants the others too."

"He's welcome to them," I said.

"I guess you and I were so intent on general content that we overlooked the specifics."

"Yeah. So maybe Pedro Cruz wasn't in the closet."

"Pedro?" Win thought about it for all of thirty seconds. "If it were anyone, it would be Pedro," he agreed.

Flash had wanted to include him, we said no, and within the week Pedro slammed a line drive into Flash's skull during batting practice. It added up. If anyone had really taken photos, Pedro Cruz would be my candidate.

Win did something on his phone. "Texting Marty about Pedro. Maybe he can track him down."

That made sense.

I glanced at the clock on my desk. It was four in the afternoon, but I wasn't sure which afternoon. "What day is today?"

"Saturday."

It seemed as weeks had passed since my encounter with Chandler. I was sleeping so much that I'd lost track of everything. The only constant had been Win, who shouldn't have been there at all.

"Shouldn't you be back with the team?" I asked.

Win didn't say anything for a long time. "Do you want me to leave?" he finally asked.

I shook my head.

He exhaled as if he'd been holding his breath awaiting my answer.

"But," I said, holding up my hand. "This isn't our life. Our life is when you're with your team during July."

His eyes widened. He nodded.

I hadn't made any promises, made any concessions. We still had a lot of baggage, but I'd just acknowledged he was part of my life. That we had a mutual life.

"I'll let Skip know I'll be back tomorrow," he said. "Right now, I need to overnight some dirty pictures to my agent."

***

Win ended up not leaving until Monday morning. He wouldn't have gotten to DC in time for Sunday's game, and the team was off on Monday. So he spent the time with me.

Not that we did a lot. Iced my face and breast. Fetched food from Susie Buddha. Slept. Made love. But no talking. He must have finally felt as talked out as I did. It was enough that he was there, in my apartment, midyear of his comeback season. It was almost as if he needed to prove to me that I came before baseball with him. Maybe he did.

We went to a Saltboilers game on Sunday night. My idea. I needed to return to my routines as quickly as possible. I couldn't let Chandler ruin what was a big part of my life.

I sat so close to the dugout that most spectators couldn't see my face anyway. Management alerted the ushers to Win's presence and requested privacy for us. I would have been a wreck if Win hadn't been there with me. My father saw me in my seats and called, insisting that I go to the box where I wouldn't be on display. The suite was his baseball experience. First row behind the visitor's dugout was mine. I stayed.

Monday afternoon I met with the district attorney's office. Win wanted to go with me, but I needed to face that demon myself. I told my version of Chandler's attack to the assistant DA as succinctly as possible. I mean, my memories of thunder, rain, a departing bus—what did they have to do with Chandler's actions? The hospital had taken plenty of photos the night of the attack. I saw them for the first time in a little conference room in the civic center.

I looked like a victim.

I looked like someone not me.

I went back to work on Tuesday. Breast Cancer Awareness Month was only two and a half months in the future. The foundation had a lot to do to get ready.

Victoria seemed surprised to see me.

"I still work here," I told her.

"Yes, you do," she replied. "I wondered if you were coming back. I did a pretty rotten thing to you."

Would she think it was rotten if it hadn't backfired so badly? No one ever would have known about the photo if she hadn't opened her foolish, drunken mouth. And it turns out the photo might not be genuine. She'd caused a lot of trouble for nothing.

"Forgive me?" She smiled a pale imitation of her former smile.

"I'm not ready to do that. You should have come to me about the baby instead of blurting out everything, and you didn't. My baby was between Win and me. No one else." My voice didn't tremble at all. "I'm still very upset. Your carelessness caused a lot of residual problems and not just for you."

Her head drooped on her slender neck. "I know."

"Don't you have work to do?" I opened the first file folder I could find.

Win's phone call two hours later was jubilant. "Great news, Carrie. Marty's photography expert came through for us. Those pictures—even the first one—forgeries. Fakes. Not even good ones. And his detective tracked down Gordon. Marty's having an injunction served against the photos."

That was fabulous news. Without photos, Flash's memoirs were just a bunch of unsubstantiated words.

"Any luck finding Pedro?" I asked.

"Not yet. He went back to the Dominican Republic, so it's going to take time. And he may not want to be found."

As far as I knew, Pedro was the only other person who really knew what had happened that summer. Victoria had seen the photo and spread the word, but she didn't *know*. Oh, and Marty. But Marty was like a lawyer. If he didn't keep his clients' secrets, he wouldn't have many clients left.

My summer of indiscretion might not have any more teeth left with which to bite me.

On Friday, I flew to Atlanta, where the Gems were playing that night. My bruises had faded enough for cosmetic concealment. Win was pitching.

I texted him as soon as I arrived at the ballpark. *Good luck. I'll be cheering for you from Friends & Family.*

Tammy Lammers was there. I asked her to thank her husband for me. If he hadn't used his cell phone to call 911 and be patched through to Onondaga County 911, Chandler might have succeeded. She seemed surprised that I would speak to her.

Win won the game. And he hit a grand slam. *How hokey is that?*

"I didn't think you'd come this weekend," he said once we were in the privacy of the hotel elevator. He'd managed to book us a room on the same floor as the team.

"I couldn't stay away."

"Then we're okay?"

I shrugged. "I want us to be okay. I think that's just as important."

"Okay. I guess I can work with that." He cupped my face in his huge, calloused palms and gently kissed the tip of my nose, my cheeks, and my lips.

The elevator doors opened, and we stepped into the hall. A moment later, we were in our room. I hung my bag in the closet and perched on the end of the king-size bed. He sat next to me.

"It really meant a lot to me that you came back last week."

He started to say something, but I laid a finger across his mouth.

"I've done a lot of thinking. Even if we had managed to hook up after Cortland, even if I'd had the baby, we probably wouldn't have made it. We were too young. We'd needed to mature into the adults we were meant to be. The people we are right now."

He didn't say anything for a long time. When he finally did speak, his voice sounded rusty.

"I'm so sorry you had to go through losing the baby and everything yourself. I'm more sorry than I can ever tell you that I lost your phone number and that you didn't try harder to contact me. I get that you thought you were giving me my freedom. I get it, and I forgive you for thinking I was that kind of asshole."

Hot tears rolled from my eyes. My shoulders shook as I tried to swallow my sobs. He was right. I'd treated him as if he were a jerk without giving him a real chance.

"I wanted our baby so much," I whispered.

"Me too," he whispered in return.

We clung to each other, lost in a surreal sort of sorrow.

Seven years is a lot of grief. Especially when it's been buried so deep. Seven years is a lot of resentment, a lot of hurt, and a lot of denial. Seven years was a long time without someone to hold me.

I pressed my face against Win's chest. His wonderful, furry chest. He didn't say anything. He didn't need to. His hand smoothed my hair. I felt his lips on the top of my head.

He grieved for our baby too.

I wasn't the only one allowed to hurt. He'd had his secret sore points too, and I'd been too shallow to allow him his grief. His fresh grief. I'd had years to mourn. He'd had mere seconds when he'd lashed out at me. I needed to keep that in focus.

And respect. His accusation had dissed me, but I'd dissed him by not respecting him enough to question why he'd be so quick to judge me, by not paying enough attention to him to understand that he was reeling with his own pain.

Now that the knee-jerk reactions were over, calmed, examined, and put away, I knew we'd be okay. I was ready to marry him. After the season. When we'd have the luxury of the time we needed to get used to being married before he reported for spring training.

And hadn't I told Alexandra that sometimes love hurt? At least, I'd wanted to tell her that. Another truth I'd never gotten around to stating. This one, however, wasn't going to circle around and bite me on the backside.

I'm as much of an expert on love as anyone. Making a marriage successful involves luck and determination. Marriage is difficult already without adding in something like baseball. But Win and I have baseball, so we'll work around it. The key is to work around it together and to talk to each other. Keep the lines of communication open. Nurture not only the love, but each other.

We'd be okay, Win and me. Somehow. Because being together was what we both wanted. A woman couldn't ask for more than that.

Thank you for reading *Missing the Signs*. I hope you enjoyed it.

Reviews are always welcome.

If you'd like to be kept up-to-date with new releases, please sign-up for my newsletter.

Follow me on Facebook

Toke Lobo & The Pack Series

Moonlight Serenade

Werewolves working for the government?

Reporter Delilah Tenney must choose: the story of a lifetime or a lifetime of love.

And Jericho Burned

Lucy Callahan will do anything to save her sister, even if that means marrying a stranger.

Even if that stranger is an undercover government agent out to destroy the cult holding her sister hostage.

Even if that stranger is a . . . werewolf.

Omega Moon Rising

One desperate woman intent on escape.

One brash werewolf determined to deny his DNA.

Until his destiny becomes her deliverance.

Service for Sanctuary Series

Betrayed by the Moon

Service for sanctuary–that was the werewolves' deal for over 200 years. Now the government is changing the rules, leaving Ethan Calhoun fighting for the only way of life he's ever known—
and Selena Wolfe fighting for her life.

Beware of the Moon

One-night stands don't turn into forever unless you happen to pick-up a werewolf.
She thought the hook-up was just another one-and-done.
He knew she was his one-and-only.
But when his mission unlocks the treacheries of her past, they are forced to put aside their differences as they battle for their lives.

Besieged by the Moon

Fated soul mates.
She's a werewolf assassin in heat on a mission.
He's a werewolf EMT and the father of her future children.
What could possibly go wrong?

MISSING THE SIGNS

Copyright © 2023 by MJ Compton Herwood

All rights reserved.

2nd edition

Originally published in 2015 as SUMMER FLING

This copy is intended for the original purchaser of this book ONLY. No part of this book may be reproduced, scanned, or distributed in any printed or electronic form without prior written permission from Comptonplations Publishing. Please do not participate in or encourage piracy of copyrighted materials in violation of the author's rights. Purchase only authorized editions.

Image/art disclaimer: Licensed material is being used for illustrative purposes only. Any person depicted in the licensed material is a model.

Editor: Heather Sedlak

Cover Art: 100 Covers

Published in the United States of America by

Comptonplations Publishing

EBOOK ISBN: 978-1-959923-00-8

PRINT ISBN: 978-1-959923-01-5

www.comptonplations.com

This book is a work of fiction. While reference might be made to actual historical events or existing locations, the names, characters, places, and incidents are either the product of the author's imagination or are used fictitiously, and any resemblance to actual persons, living or dead, business establishments, events, or locales is entirely coincidental.

The publisher does not have any control over and does not assume any responsibility for author or third-party websites or their content.

Aknowledgements & Dedication

DEDICATION

To Minor League Baseball Players everywhere. I hope your dreams come true.

ACKNOWLEDGMENTS

The Purple Hazers: Carol Lombardo, Christine Wenger, Kris Fletcher, and Gayle Callen. Your friendship and support mean more than you will ever know.

The Gang in Section 207, Row 1 at the local Triple A stadium: Sandee and Anthony Dain; Russ and Linda Andrews; and Dave "The Maven" Okun. We saw some amazing games and incredible players.

Former Syracuse Chief players Matt Antonelli and Ryan Tatusko for answering my sometimes crazy questions.

My husband Steve, who left work early so we could go to baseball games together. Love you!

MJ Compton

M J Compton grew up near Cardiff, New York, a place best known for its giant—a hoax so successful, P.T. Barnum duplicated it. The tale of the "petrified man" convinced MJ that inventing stories could be a career.

Although her 30 years working in local television included such highlights as

- being bitten by a lion

- preempting a US president for a college basketball game

- giving a three-time world champion boxer a few black eyes

- meeting her husband

MJ never lost her dream of creating her own stories.

MJ still lives in upstate New York with her husband. Music and food are two of her passions. She also enjoys baseball, college basketball, and sitting on her patio on summer mights to count lightning bugs, but she's primarily focused on reading and writing.

www.ingramcontent.com/pod-product-compliance
Lightning Source LLC
Chambersburg PA
CBHW030926210726
48290CB00007B/2088